Ovidia Yu is one of Sing...... best-know.. and most a.....
writers. She has had over thirty plays produced and is the author
of a number of comic mysteries published in Singapore, India,
Japan and America.

She received a Fulbright Scholarship to the University of Iowa's
International Writers Program and has been a writing fellow at the
National University of Singapore.

Also by Ovidia Yu

The Frangipani Tree Mystery
The Betel Nut Tree Mystery

The Paper Bark Tree Mystery

Ovidia Yu

CONSTABLE

CONSTABLE

First published in Great Britain in 2019 by Constable

1 3 5 7 9 10 8 6 4 2

Copyright © Ovidia Yu, 2019

The moral right of the author has been asserted.

A CIP catalogue record for this book
is available from the British Library.

ISBN: 978-1-47212-524-8

Typeset in Contenu by SX Composing DTP, Rayleigh, Essex
Printed and bound in Great Britain by Clays Ltd, Elcograf S.p.A.

Papers used by Constable are from well-managed forests
and other responsible sources.

Constable
An imprint of
Little, Brown Book Group
Carmelite House
50 Victoria Embankment
London EC4Y 0DZ

An Hachette UK Company
www.hachette.co.uk

www.littlebrown.co.uk

This is for Richard, Peach and Hermione

Prologue: Early Morning

'There's just so much stuff. The men keep dumping papers on the desk and rushing away without telling me what I'm supposed to do with them,' Dolly Darling wailed. 'And then they ask for reports and itemised records, and they look at me like I'm an idiot when I don't know what they're talking about – and the filing system is such a mess. It's not even alphabetical!'

It was a good thing she wasn't watching me because I probably had the exact same expression on my face.

It was I, Chen Su Lin, who had set up the Detective Unit's exhaustive cross-reference card filing system, and even my Chinese never-tempt-fate-with-self-praise self was damned proud of it.

Starting with any suspect or piece of information, you could trace connections through all the data the local police force had on family background, associates and previous convictions of a suspect. But, apparently, it was beyond Miss Dolly Darling, who had replaced me because she was 'more suitable for the job' (in other words, white).

I wondered if my former colleagues at the Detective Shack were deliberately giving Dolly Darling a hard time. I couldn't believe that of huge, good-natured Sergeant Ferdinand de Souza, though, and Constable Kwok Kan Seng was too new and shy. Sergeant Prakesh Pillay? Possibly. But Prakesh was more likely to flirt with Dolly than make life hard for her. He had even flirted with small skinny me at first, despite my polio limp. Why not pretty, buxom Dolly, with her pale freckled skin, curly ginger hair and ready smiles?

Thinking of my early days at the Detective Shack was depressing. Working with Chief Inspector Le Froy – unofficially at first, then officially – had been the best eighteen months in my life, but it seemed our collaboration was over now for ever, thanks to newly arrived operations adviser Bernard 'Bald Bernie' Hemsworth, who had declared it unfitting to have a local girl in the post and replaced me with Dolly. Of course the man was always 'Mr Hemsworth' or 'sir' to us. Even calling him 'Bernard' would have got me into serious trouble for disrespect. Still, we referred to our supposed superior as 'Bald Bernie' among ourselves: he was like a spoiled brat of a child who thinks he's king of the world.

In her way, Dolly was smart enough. She was girlishly sly, and good at getting people to do what she wanted, which was one of the reasons I was there with her that Friday morning, long before the work day started, to sort out the accounts and filing system. The main reason I had agreed to help was that I wanted to find out the truth about Amelia Earhart's missing plane. The aviatrix had disappeared almost a month ago and officially there was still no news, not even of wreckage from her plane.

There had been rumours of wires from India and Japan about searches for and sightings of the missing plane but, so far, nothing had been officially confirmed. But even if the authorities ordered information withheld from the press, details would be in the Detective Shack. More precisely, on Sergeant de Souza's desk. As Le Froy's second in command, de Souza had carbons of all official communications. They piled up on his desk, towering dangerously till he passed them to me for filing. All I wanted now was a quick look through before I put them away.

'You brought the key?' I made for the front door of the Detective Shack.

'Oh, we're not going in there,' Dolly said. 'I brought the accounts books over to the Dungeon since that's where the cross-reference card files are. I thought it would be much easier to have everything in one place.'

That was true. It also meant I wouldn't get a chance to look through the papers on de Souza's desk.

'And I thought you'd have more privacy there,' Dolly added.

'Privacy from whom?' The Detective Shack wasn't manned at night, unlike the Police Headquarters across the road. 'The men won't be here till the first tram arrives at eight thirty and we'll be gone by then.'

'In case it takes you longer than you expect to get through all the filing. There's a lot, you know. It's been piling up since you left.'

She made it sound as though I had irresponsibly walked out on the job and she was giving me a chance to make amends. I almost turned around and went home to bed right then. Instead I stopped walking and stood still until Dolly looked back at me.

'I'm only going to show you how the system works,' I said. 'I'm not doing your work for you.'

'Come on, you know it doesn't really matter who does it. We're just there for show. Don't you want to make it easier for the poor chaps? They get so cross when I can't dig up their old reports. You'd think if they *wrote* 'em they'd know what's *in* 'em, wouldn't you?'

'What do you mean we're there for show?'

'They need a female employee on the staff to keep the Royal Commission happy.'

I knew about the Royal Commission's recommended 'it's a fair field and no favour' policy towards women employees because Le Froy had used it to take me on. 'That just means we have to do the job *better* than a male employee could.'

'Oh, come on now. You sound just like one of those suffragists!'

'Mr Hemsworth said a local girl couldn't be trusted to work in the Detective Unit because it was too important.'

'Well, there's that. He did tell me to watch out for any news about that missing plane.' Dolly frowned. 'I'd forgotten all about it. He said it was very important. I supposed he needed someone who could understand English.'

'I understand English.'

'Oh, yes. You've learned it very well, Su Lin, but it's not the same thing.'

I knew that only too well. But going into native and non-native language skills with Dolly wouldn't have done any good. Besides, I wanted to find out more about the plane. 'Is it news of Miss Earhart's plane he's looking out for?' I asked.

'Oh, no!' Dolly laughed at the idea. 'He says her disappearing just proves women shouldn't be allowed to pilot planes. He thinks women shouldn't drive cars either – machines cause too much stress on the female brain and system. But it's really her husband's fault for not keeping her safe at home. It's the other plane that disappeared. The one from India. He wants them to put out warnings that any surviving passengers are dangerous and should be shot on sight, but the local authorities aren't passing the word on.'

'That's terrible!' I said.

'Yes. He says it's a job making people understand anything here.'

The high melodious notes of the morning call to prayer floated over us. That meant it was almost six a.m. The sky was still dark and the streetlamps would be on for another hour, but a lighter grey at the horizon promised dawn was almost with us. This was the only time the air was chilly in Singapore and I shivered, enjoying the sensation. Sparkling dewdrops highlighted beautiful cobweb patterns on the roadside grass and the smell of night jasmine was sweet in the air. I breathed in the promise of a new day.

It felt good to be alive. Better to be living with fools than dead in the company of sages, as my grandmother always said.

'We'll work out a way to simplify the filing system,' I said.

It wasn't Dolly's fault she had replaced me at the Detective Shack. That was all Bernard Hemsworth's doing. 'We'll set up a new central index and connect everything else back to it alphabetically. Then, when they ask you for something, you just find the card in the central file and that will show you where to find everything else.'

It would be fun. There was nothing I liked more than analysing, classifying and organising things.

Dolly looked miserable. 'Mr Hemsworth told me all I'd have to do was make coffee and post letters. He never mentioned filing and typewriting. Oh, sometimes I just hate that man!'

So did I. In fact, if I'd known how to put a *gong tau* on him, I might have done it. Black magic curses are risky because they release dark energy, which always has consequences. But if it got rid of Bald Bernie Hemsworth it would be worth it.

It was as though I unleashed the curse on the man just by thinking about it. And of course there were consequences.

Part One

Investigative Reporter

———◆———

'I took the office keys and unlocked the door yesterday before I left,' Dolly said, as we walked around the Detective Shack to the Dungeon, as the building that stood behind it was known. She looked pleased with her cleverness.

'You shouldn't have! It's dangerous. Anyone could have come in.' I couldn't believe this walking security risk now had my job.

'Who on earth would want to? There's nothing in here except papers. I didn't want anyone to see the key wasn't on the hook if they came in while we were still here.'

Before it had been turned into a storeroom for files, the Dungeon had housed the police holding cells. From the doorway there were three cells on the ground floor with three more stacked on top, reached by the narrow metal staircase that led up to a narrow railed walkway. One guard stationed at the desk by the door could keep an eye on all six cells. In the old days, especially after racial riots or football matches, they overflowed and drunks had been chained outside until they sobered up. Now the cells were crammed with metal shelves holding box files. But years of piss and vomit had left an odour overlaid by the stink of rat powder. As Dolly turned the handle and pulled open the heavy door, though, I smelt a new stench over the old familiar odours.

'Wait, Dolly!' It was the smell of recent death. A rat, I thought. A rat must have come in through the drains after cockroaches and eaten one of the poison pellets left along the walls. Or a crow had got in through the roof and died.

Dolly stood in the open doorway, blocking my view. 'I hate coming in here. It's so stuffy and dusty,' she said, over her shoulder, as she groped for the electric light pull by the door. 'And Sergeant Pillay keeps telling me there are ghosts of prisoners here. I don't believe him, but when I'm inside here alone, I keep hearing things—'

Then she started screaming.

'Oh, my God, there's someone here! And I think he's dead!' Dolly flapped her hands, like a child in a panic. 'Let's go! Let's go! Let's go! Su Lin, what are you doing? Don't touch him!'

Despite the smell, I knew we should confirm he was dead.

'It's Bald Bernie. He's dead, isn't he?' Dolly squealed.

Bernard Hemsworth was slumped on the narrow wooden table to the left of the door with something tied tightly around his neck. He was facing us, and the tuft of hair normally pomaded to the bald patch on top of his head had fallen forward, covering his nose and one eye. The other eye bulged horribly out of a face that looked like a huge swelling bruise. A small patch on the back of his shirt suggested he had also been stabbed. There was not much blood.

Feeling light-headed, I put a hand on the wooden table for balance, felt a damp patch and jerked away. It was not blood, just the damp from a ring of condensation where a glass of something cold had stood for a while. There were two rings, so there had been two glasses, but they had gone.

'Let's just go! Nobody knows we're here! We shouldn't be here! Oh, the Indians are here! They've come here and killed him too!'

I must admit I was tempted to turn and leave. But there's no point in running unless you have a chance of getting away. And I knew there was no way Dolly could keep quiet about finding Bernie Hemsworth's body. Things would be much worse if it came out later that we had found the wretched man and done nothing.

I grabbed Dolly and pulled her out of the building, pushing the door shut behind us. 'What Indians are you talking about? Who killed him? Who else did they kill?'

'I don't know! I don't know! I don't know!' Her voice grew louder and shriller with each repetition.

'Dolly, calm down. Go over to the HQ building. There'll be a corporal on duty. Tell him what happened and to send someone over. I'll wait here.'

There was always a corporal on duty at the twenty-four-hour desk in the Robinson Road Police Headquarters across the street.

'I can't! I can't! I won't know what to say! What if the Indians are hiding in there? This is so awful, Su Lin. How can Mr Hemsworth be dead?'

'Then you stay here with the body while I go and report it.'

'No! Don't make me stop here with him! I can't!'

Dolly was frighteningly easy to manipulate.

'Just tell whoever is at the desk that you found a dead man. They'll know what to do.'

'Can't you come with me, Su? I'm scared. What if they don't speak English?'

11

'It's quite safe. It won't take you five minutes. And they'll speak English.'

I watched her cross the street. Sometimes I wondered if Dolly was smarter than all of us and laughing inside at how well she was fooling us. She always seemed to be hugging a secret to herself, and I knew she had managed to convince the late Bernie Hemsworth she had feelings for him, even as she laughed at him behind his back. It had been Sergeant Prakesh Pillay, with his sharp sense for people's weaknesses, who had nicknamed him 'Bald Bernie'. And Dolly had used it in her first panic.

My stomach heaved – I tasted bile – but luckily it was empty. I shut my eyes. I could still see the horror of that swollen dark red face. But my dislike of the man remained undiminished by his death. Bald Bernie had cost me my job at the Detective Shack.

Bernard Hemsworth had come to Singapore's Detective and Intelligence Unit as an adviser from the Home Office, appointed by Colonel Mosley-Partington. I was introduced as Chief Inspector Le Froy's secretarial assistant and cultural liaison, and he questioned me extensively on what I did. He would have made a good administrator. He was almost as particular about details and precision as I was, and I was impressed by what he knew of filing and cross-referencing systems. At first, I actually liked him. Then he'd said that an unqualified local girl should not have access to sensitive police documents, and I'd suspected he wanted my job for himself.

At first Bernie announced a Miss Radley would take over my post, but Dolly Darling had turned up instead. According to Sergeant Pillay, Bald Bernie hung around in the Detective Shack with Dolly all day, the two of them chatting as the work piled up.

I had stayed close by, asking Prakesh for updates, because back then I naively thought Bernie was trying to show Dolly how the work should be done. And that, once he realised no one (certainly not Dolly Darling!) could manage the accounts and filing as well as I could, he would apologise to me and give me my job back. Yes, I am incredibly stupid at times.

Dolly being stupid didn't really matter. She was a pretty girl with reddish hair and brown eyes, who frankly admitted, 'I'm thick!' Her gaiety and high spirits made her an agreeable office decoration because, of course, she was white.

But I liked Dolly. She had come to suggest that, since she now had my job, I might be interested in taking over the freelance typing and shorthand she had been doing for Mrs Lexington, with whom she boarded. Catherine Lexington ran a freelance secretarial service for offices and businessmen who didn't have their own assistants in Singapore.

When we'd first met, Mrs Lexington was so agreeable that I guessed the suggestion had originated with her. If so, she definitely got the better deal when she exchanged Dolly for me. I was probably the fastest, most accurate typist and shorthand stenographer in Singapore and Johor. Dolly might be earnest and willing to please but, try as she might, she was never competent at anything she undertook, probably because she was so easily distracted.

It benefited me, too, because Mrs Lexington was soon paying me double what I had earned at the Detective Shack.

But if all I'd wanted to do was make money, I would have asked my grandmother, Chen Tai, to arrange for me to marry into a business I could expand. With her backing, Uncle Chen's black-market connections and the ability they had cultivated in me to assess people and investments, I could have made a success of any husband or business. Or I could have gone back to Chen Mansion and helped Chen Tai run her own businesses. After all, that was why she had sent me to English school.

And my newly launched writing career was taking off.

During the Great Depression, advertising revenue had decreased and many newspapers and magazines survived only by firing reporters. So hiring freelancers, especially out east, made sense. Recently I had been a regular contributor to several syndicated columns, writing as 'Ascanio in Alba', after the Mozart opera on scratchy vinyl records in the Mission Centre. As Ascanio, I had developed a small but faithful following. Being based in the Far East, I could express myself more freely than British writers on politics and such sensitive topics as government relief efforts and unemployment, provided I made clear I was talking about the situation in Singapore. Of course, what happened in the far reaches of the British Empire reflected what was happening in Britain.

To make things even more promising, Henry R. Luce, founder of the American news magazine *Time*, had just founded *Life*, a magazine devoted to photojournalism. And I could use a camera.

But working for Chief Inspector Le Froy had felt a step closer to my dream of becoming an investigative reporter, like Henrietta Stackpole, the American journalist in Henry James's novel, *The Portrait of a Lady*. It wasn't the same, writing political and sociological pieces. And there was no guarantee the work would last. Pip's Squeaks, the previous column I'd submitted pieces to, had been cancelled after one of the other 'Pips' was arrested in Germany for spreading false propaganda.

'But Daniel Eisen is an Englishman writing for an American paper!' I had protested in disbelief.

'He is an Englishman with a Jewish surname,' Le Froy pointed out, 'These days, that's as dangerous as attending the secret meeting of the wrong clan association.'

I knew Le Froy had gatecrashed more than one clan association and survived, though he never spoke of it. He was the reason why the underground triads in Singapore coexisted relatively peacefully. But it was true things were getting worse in the world beyond us.

It shouldn't have been surprising. Never believe things are getting better, my grandmother always said. Modern innovations only make industrialists and bankers rich. Poor people traded the land that supported them for money and promises, but no guarantees, of paid employment. An old farmer can still rear freshwater prawns and catfish, and grow enough vegetables to eat and exchange for charcoal, cigarettes and rice wine. Trees on his land will produce even more bananas, mangoes and rambutans for his grandchildren than they did for his children. But the old factory worker? She is kicked out of the door once she can no longer keep up with the assembly line.

It was these things I wrote about, as well as Amelia Earhart trying to fly around the world, and the Japanese Army marching into China. And, yes, now I wanted to write about what had happened to Bernard Hemsworth.

I took out my notebook and sat on the stone step. I didn't lean against the door because the knowledge of what was on the other side twisted my guts. My back and hip hurt – childhood polio had left me with one leg shorter than the other so walking or standing for any length of time hurts.

I took out the little glass bottle of Tiger Balm lotion I always carried and rubbed it on my aching muscles, reaching under the thin cotton of my *samfoo*. The soothing heat brought relief and I took out my notebook to record what I had seen in the Dungeon.

It's no use seeing without taking notes, or your brain adjusts your memories to match your beliefs, and you may as well be a bug on a tree shifting around to follow your shadow. Once I observe my movement and the passage of sunlight, though, I'm an observer and a scientist: a human being reporting, if only to myself, my observations and deductions. Even if, despite the appreciation of Mrs Lexington and her clients, they saw me as no more than a crippled native who could type.

I looked across the street to the police building. Dolly had disappeared inside. Surely someone would be over soon. The sky was lightening to grey and I could see people walking and cycling to work between the cars, trishaws and road-sweepers.

Why was it taking so long? What was Dolly doing?

'Miss Chen?'

A voice cut into my thoughts. I yelped, startled, and tried to struggle to my feet, scattering my notebook and pencil.

I hadn't seen Constable Kwok Kan Seng coming across the street. He must have circled around from the side door of the main police building and crossed further up to come around the back of the Dungeon in case anyone was lurking there.

That was smart of him. I was annoyed that the thought hadn't occurred to me. If someone had been hiding behind the Dungeon watching us, I could have been dead now.

'Bald Bernie's dead? You must be joking. Don't raise my hopes!' Constable Kwok said lightly, as he helped me up and handed me my things. I saw his eyes darting around, taking in the shadows surrounding us. And his right hand remained on the hilt of his revolver.

'Inside there,' I said. 'He is.'

I didn't follow him in.

The sole pride and joy of a widowed mother and grandmother, Constable Kwok was the sweetest-natured and sweetest-looking young man you can imagine. Even hardened gangsters teasingly addressed him as *leng zai* or 'pretty boy' and told him to marry their daughters so they would have grandchildren as cute as he was.

It said something for Bald Bernie that he had managed to antagonise even Constable Kwok.

Questioning

◆

'The address on my registration papers is my grandmother's house in East Coast Road, but right now I'm staying at my uncle's shop in town,' I explained. 'Eighty-one South Canal Road.'

I didn't add that until three months ago I had been living in the little attic-storeroom above Le Froy's office, where Dolly and I were now being interviewed.

Le Froy knew, of course, but said nothing. It was Colonel Mosley-Partington who was questioning Dolly and me over the discovery of Bernie Hemsworth's body that morning.

All of us locals knew that Chief Inspector Le Froy and Colonel Mosley-Partington were old acquaintances, not friends. When the colonel's name appeared on the list of high-level transfers from India, the gossipmongers on the island, including my grandmother and Sergeant Pillay, had related with relish stories of how the two men had fought over the beautiful woman who had become Le Froy's wife, then died within a year of their marriage.

Over mah-jong, *tai-tai*s debated whether Le Froy's grief had driven him out of England, or if Mosley-Partington had had him exiled for driving the woman they both loved to her death. When the chief inspector didn't attend the official Government House welcome reception the month the colonel arrived, it was speculated the men had sworn never to be in the same building. This, although another favourite gossip topic concerned how Le Froy avoided all official and ceremonial functions. Even Governor McPherson once joked that the only invitation that guaranteed Chief Inspector Le Froy's presence was a bomb threat.

Well, they were both in Le Froy's office in the Detective Shack now, with Colonel Mosley-Partington behind Le Froy's desk and Le Froy to his right, by the wireless machine. The colonel had asked to be part of the investigation when he came to view Bernie Hemsworth's body.

'The system doesn't spell out who has seniority in this investigation. This is your territory, Le Froy. But Hemsworth was my man. I brought him over from India with me and I feel responsible for him. I suggest we work together on this.'

Le Froy could hardly say no. As a representative of the Home Office, Mosley-Partington overruled all local administrators.

'Why did you leave home, Miss Chen? I know girls like you. You stay with your family till you move in with your husband's. Was it a fight with your family? Over what? A lover? Who is it, girl? Did you come here to meet him? Were you carrying on with Hemsworth? Leading him on? Speak up, girl!'

I only shook my head. I had tried to answer his questions at first. But every time I started to speak, he launched a new barrage. Colonel Mosley-Partington was trying to intimidate us. He wouldn't believe anything we told him until he thought he had broken us down.

But it was as though the shock of finding Bernie Hemsworth's body in the Dungeon had insulated me against further shocks that day. What had the wretched man been doing there? That seemed as great a question as who had killed him. I was too distracted to feel frightened of the blustering colonel who could have me locked up indefinitely or shot without trial.

Besides, Colonel Mosley-Partington's questioning showed how little he knew. I couldn't help comparing his manner to Le Froy's ('Always study a situation before you speak').

It was the first time I had seen Oswald Mosley-Partington close up and he didn't look like the monster I had expected. He was about the same age as Le Froy, but appeared far more distinguished. The material and make of his clothes must have cost at least three times what Le Froy had paid for his khakis (growing up in a market economy makes you notice such things).

'Are your uncle and his wife staying at the shophouse too?' Le Froy asked me a question I could answer. One that he could have answered himself.

'My uncle and his wife usually live above their shop. But they moved back to the family house in Katong because my aunt is having a baby, her first, so she is being careful and resting. That's why I am staying there now.'

That was the official story, at least. Uncle Chen's wife Shen Shen had already lost two babies. Since both stillborns had been female, they were never mentioned in case they brought bad luck to the family. My own dead brother had his own shrine next to that of my parents, who had died in a cholera epidemic soon after I was born. That, along with my bout of childhood polio, had marked me in the eyes of the superstitious as a carrier of bad luck.

It was against the advice of all the best fortune-tellers that my grandmother had kept me in the family. After her second pregnancy had failed, Shen Shen had made Uncle Chen move them out of the family home in Katong to the relative austerity of their shophouse in town. Like everyone else, she was afraid of my grandmother, but she believed that my bad-luck presence had caused her miscarriages. She had only agreed to move back to Chen Mansion because I was staying in the Detective Shack.

I didn't want to upset her close to her time, so even after losing my job and my room, I didn't return to the house in Katong. I would stay away till her baby was safely born. I knew my grandmother understood. There had been no irate summons when I missed my weekly visit to pay my respects to her and my parents' altar. Instead she sent me gifts of smoked duck and waxed sausage through Uncle Chen, who came to the shop every day.

'How is your aunt?' Le Froy asked.

In contrast to the colonel's fashionably brushed and Brylcreemed (or could that be expensive scented Vaseline?) light-brown hair and moustache, Le Froy was clean-shaven and had just had his weekly crew cut. He always went to roadside barbers, as much for their vigorous scalp and shoulder massages as for the ground-level information he got from them. With his skin tanned dark as a coolie's, Le Froy looked like he had 'gone native', especially when seen next to the likes of Colonel Mosley-Partington. The locals liked him for it.

In fact, my best friend Parshanti thought the chief inspector looked like Errol Flynn as Captain Blood (then showing at the State Theatre at New World Amusement Park) and I agreed with her.

'Miss Chen?' Le Froy prompted. 'Your aunt?'

21

My thoughts had wandered off again. I sat up straighter on my wooden stool and took a deep breath. 'She is well. Thank you, sir.'

I had to deal with the problems of my present before I could dig into Bernie Hemsworth's recent past. I took a deep, steadying breath and looked around me.

I knew Le Froy's office, of course. I had been in there a hundred times before. But today felt different. It was not only because of the air of disarray that now penetrated the whole office. No one had noticed my daily ministrations, but since I had left, the floor had grown grimy with mud, the desk and shelves were dusty, and there was a stack of plates and chopsticks in a corner that had not been returned to the street hawkers.

But that was not why the once familiar room felt like a strange and dangerous place.

Today I was the one being studied on a wooden stool, instead of tucked into a corner translating or taking notes. If only I were an employee instead of a witness, I would have got us all cups of tea. I was so thirsty by now and Dolly must have been feeling worse, given how much she had been crying. She was still sniffing into a dirty handkerchief.

Behind Dolly and me, Sergeants de Souza and Pillay stood on either side of the door, as though afraid we might make a bolt for it.

'So tell me again, why did you girls arrange to meet Mr Hemsworth in the records room this morning?' Colonel Mosley-Partington sounded bored.

'We didn't, sir,' I said, as I had said before. 'We didn't know anyone would be there. We had no reason to arrange to meet Mr Hemsworth anywhere.'

'Nor did you have any reason to be in the records room. Tell me, Miss Chen, did you have any particular reason to dislike the late Mr Hemsworth?'

Oh, I had a hundred thousand reasons to loathe, hate and detest Bald Bernie! Bald Bernie, with his round fleshy face, always fussing with the long lock of hair he combed across his bare scalp that was always falling into his face.

But before I could answer Dolly burst out tearfully, 'He was pushy and creepy! No one liked him. He was always following and pestering me and refusing to take no for an answer. He would sit at my desk and go through my things. My private and personal things!'

They really should have separated Dolly and me for questioning. They had tried, but she'd got so upset that they'd let us stay together. I must admit I found her presence comforting too. And the men's helplessness in the face of Dolly's hysterics made me feel a little smug. She would have fallen apart completely, and they wouldn't have been able to handle her, if I hadn't been around. Chaperoning and searching female witnesses and suspects had been another of my duties at the Detective Shack that Dolly couldn't take over.

On my part, I noted it might be useful to learn a little female helplessness.

'A pretty girl like you, I'm sure you're used to men paying you . . . attention.'

The words sounded like a compliment, but they were delivered in a cold, measured tone that felt like a threat. Dolly's face went back into her handkerchief and she fell silent.

I knew this was routine. Of course they had to find out all we knew, all we had seen. But by then I was so thirsty that any common sense I had was all dried up. We had been there for hours and, in addition to being thirsty, I was desperate to use the toilet. I was beginning to understand suspects who confessed to things they hadn't done, just to stop the questions coming.

Having silenced Dolly, Colonel Mosley-Partington turned back to me. 'Miss Chen, you must have resented Mr Hemsworth for removing you from your comfortable job in this office.'

The colonel had strange light blue eyes, with dark rims and pupils. He turned them on Le Froy now. 'Chief Inspector, you resented Hemsworth yourself. I saw your letters to the Home Office, to the governor. You seem to think Hemsworth charged in and disrupted the order of the little kingdom you had set up so beautifully here for yourself.'

Le Froy raised his eyebrows and said nothing. I was touched to learn he had written to the Home Office to try to save my job.

I hadn't known this. In fact, I had resented him for not kicking Bernie Hemsworth out. Now I hoped it had not put his own position at risk.

Le Froy was my *sifu*, my instructor, but in Oriental tradition the relationship was far closer to 'master-father' than teacher. He had taken on the role when he promised my grandmother he would protect and prepare me to enter the working world instead of accepting the arranged marriage or spinster-aunt role expected for me. He seemed surprised and pleased by how fast I learned, and all the men appreciated the order I brought to the Detective Shack.

Was his standing aside to let Mosley-Partington question us a sign that he had washed his hands of me? I knew the bored look on his face was a mask, but I couldn't tell what he was thinking. Chief Inspector Le Froy might represent British colonial law at the office, but in person he was as impassive as an ancient stone Buddha.

'I was doing a good job here,' I said. 'Mr Hemsworth said so himself, when he went over the accounts and filing system I set up. I don't know why he saw me as a security risk. But he should have made sure my replacement understood how to do the job. I was only trying to help Dolly.'

'It was supposed to be Rose!' Dolly burst out, sobbing again. 'Rose understands accounts and figures, but she said she was afraid to work among natives, so Bernie said I should do it instead. And I thought I could. He said if an ignorant native girl could do the job, I could handle it with one arm tied behind my back!'

'But you couldn't?'

'It's all the columns. All different columns, and cards in all different drawers. It's so complicated. That's why I needed Su Lin to come and help me sort it out. She knows how it works.'

Dolly's eyes were red, her face dirty and her nose was running, but she was still pretty. Like a baby pig smeared with mud but still fat and healthy. I realised it wasn't just 'her bones', as the recently departed Bernie Hemsworth had been so fond of saying. A skull has bones but no charm. Prettiness is at most skin-deep and maybe even shallower than that. Beauty is in the breath and movement, and the moment that the eyes catch the light. Even now, in her shock and grief, Dolly was pretty.

'Miss Darling, let me get this straight,' Colonel Mosley-Partington said. 'You approached Miss Chen for help. It was your idea to come here this morning, not hers.'

I knew I had planted the idea in Dolly's head, but without her knowing it. She wailed again, instead of answering. I reached sideways and touched her hand. She grabbed my fingers and squeezed them tightly. 'I wish we'd never come here – I hate this place! I wish I'd never come out east at all!'

'Miss Darling.' Le Froy spoke up now. 'You remember signing a work contract stating that everything in the detective headquarters is confidential? That no papers can be taken out, no outsiders allowed in?'

'You know I did. You were there when Bernie gave me those papers to sign. I don't know exactly what they were about but I signed them all. That's why I didn't bring Su Lin in here. And why I didn't ask her to come during office hours. That means I wasn't at work. Besides, Su Lin used to work here so she already knows all your confidential things. I wish to God she was still working here instead of me.'

Le Froy's mouth twitched, but he nodded. 'This was the first time you asked Miss Chen or anyone else to come here with you to help you with your work?'

'And the last time ever! I swear! I never want to come back here!'

'Well, then. That—'

'You're certain Mr Hemsworth was dead when you found him?' Colonel Mosley-Partington reclaimed the reins of interrogation.

'I – he—' Dolly's tears returned. 'I don't know! I didn't go in! I don't know anything!'

'I'm certain he was dead,' I said. 'His face was blue and bloated. He was cold, but not yet stiff. I believe he was stabbed after he was strangled.'

'You do, do you?' Colonel Mosley-Partington sounded contemptuous, but I saw he was studying me with interest. 'And you're now an expert in criminal investigation as well?'

'I saw a stab wound and a little blood, but not much. And the cord was still around his neck,' I explained. 'His hands were undamaged. He hadn't been fighting.'

'Do you think a woman could have killed him?'

'Miss Chen is crippled.' Sergeant de Souza spoke up from where he was standing at attention by the door. We all turned to him and his eyes met mine briefly. 'Miss Chen is a polio victim. She couldn't kill a man.'

'And who are you?'

'Sergeant de Souza, sir.'

'And how do you know so much about Miss Chen's killing abilities?'

The way the colonel said that suggested he knew more about my recent past than he had revealed up till now. De Souza was risking his position to defend me. I didn't want him to get into trouble as well. Tears stung my eyes and I clasped my hands tight, digging my fingernails into my palms for self-control and telling myself not to cry.

Colonel Mosley-Partington might go easier on me if I cried like Dolly, but I hadn't had as much practice.

'Miss Chen didn't kill Mr Hemsworth. I will vouch for her.'

'Don't, Ferdie,' I hissed. But I understood he was speaking up for me because I wasn't speaking up for myself. I turned back to my interrogator. 'I didn't kill Mr Hemsworth. If I had, I wouldn't have been anywhere near the place he was found.'

———◆———

We all jumped when Colonel Mosley-Partington crashed his

notepad loudly onto the table, then leaned back in his – in fact Le Froy's – chair. To my amazement, he was laughing.

'Bravo!' he said. 'Well done, Le Froy. Whatever else you're up to here, you've built a tight ship. Your little team is as loyal as a gang of thieves!'

I was confused by the change in his tone. Dolly, startled out of her tears, stared at him with her mouth open.

'We have to follow procedure here, Miss Chen, Miss Darling. There are certain rules in such cases. You wouldn't want people to think your relationship with Tommy Le Froy here gives you special privileges, would you, Miss Chen? You know how people talk.' The colonel's tone was easy and relaxed.

'There's nothing for them to talk about, sir,' I said.

'That's never stopped anyone. You girls were trespassing. You could still be charged with breaking and entering government property. But . . .' he held up a hand to silence Dolly's protest that she had used the key and not broken anything '. . . I know you are not guilty of murder. Do you want to know why?'

Just then there were noises in the main office. A woman's voice shrilled with insistence and increasing volume as Constable Kwok, his voice trembling only slightly, repeated that she should take a seat and wait.

Mrs Catherine Lexington had arrived.

Mrs Lexington

◆

Despite Constable Kwok's efforts, it was mere seconds before the office door was pushed open. Catherine Lexington was a dignified blonde woman, who looked somewhere between forty and fifty and was probably upwards of sixty. Although her hair was greying – but age shows less on blonde hair than black – and her figure a little chunky, she was still good-looking.

That day she was wearing a calf-length grey dress with black lace trimmings. But standing there, formidable in her rage and indignation, she might have been a vengeful temple deity come to life to wreak vengeance.

Constable Kwok followed close behind, sounding desperate, 'Madam, please! Sir, I'm sorry—'

Mrs Lexington had no right to be there, but a local, even an officer in the course of duty, could get into serious trouble for laying hands on a white woman. Last year, two cadets in training had been arrested for outraging the modesty of the British woman they had rescued from the sea after she and her husband had fallen off the

29

pier upon which they had been quarrelling violently. There had been no charge for rescuing the husband.

A small shake of Le Froy's head absolved Constable Kwok of responsibility. I sensed his relief as he shut the door behind him.

Mrs Lexington was a widow. I had met her when she came to the Detective Shack on her arrival from India to ask about curfews and safety patrols. 'Everyone tells me there aren't any, that it's safe. Is that true or is it propaganda? I've been based in Calcutta for some years, so nothing you've got in Singapore will frighten me.'

Mrs Lexington was bright and friendly . . . almost too friendly. She reminded me of my grandmother, who was always much nicer to people she didn't trust. Or Mrs McPherson, the governor's wife, who confessed to having a cache of stock compliments she applied when official conversations were boring her to sleep.

'You speak English so well,' Mrs Lexington had told me. And she'd scolded Prakesh: 'You're Indian! What do you mean you can't understand me?' He hadn't known the Bengali words she had picked up in Calcutta. She couldn't see that it was like expecting a Frenchman to understand Dutch because both countries were in Europe. Prakesh didn't mind and even said she was a good sport. I liked her, too.

She had also tried to flirt with Le Froy. I doubt he noticed but I did. She was subtle enough to do this by asking him about books and the history of Singapore. Men who are smart in every other way can be blind in this. Maybe it's to do with Darwin's natural selection. If only the men who fall for women's wiles get to reproduce, it stands to reason that the men alive now are all descended from them.

'You poor dear girls, I've just heard. How terrible for you both. Poor Mr Hemsworth!'

Dolly rose and flung her sobbing self into Mrs Lexington's arms. The older woman reached out and pulled me towards her too. I was not used to being hugged. Asian families prefer to demonstrate affection through food and criticism. But I knew she meant to comfort me and I was touched.

Mrs Lexington whispered in my ear, 'Are you all right, child? Have they done anything to you?'

'We're all right,' I said. 'Actually, we're both fine.'

I don't know what Mrs Lexington thought the police might do to us, but I liked being included in her worry over Dolly.

Dolly was clinging to her now, and babbling disjointedly, 'It's really Mr Hemsworth! He's well and truly dead! I know they think we did it! It's happening here too! It's followed us!' as Mrs Lexington tried to hush her.

'What a surprise,' Colonel Mosley-Partington said. 'Madam, this is a murder investigation.'

From the way they looked at each other I saw at once they weren't strangers. From the colonel's tone and Mrs Lexington's next words it was clear they weren't friends either.

'Can't be much of a surprise to you.' Mrs Lexington gave him a formal nod. 'Of course you knew the girls and I were in Singapore. That was why you got that man of yours to spy on us. Led the assassins right to our door, didn't he?'

'That is not true. And you can hardly blame Hemsworth for leading anyone to you, given what happened to him. Though you must be getting used to men dropping dead around your girls by now.'

This was so intriguing I almost forgot my thirst.

'Nonsense. And thanks to you tailing us, the assassin has found us again, hasn't he?'

'Is that your excuse for leaving Calcutta in such a hurry?'

'Given how things were going there, could you blame *anyone* for leaving in a hurry? How long are you keeping them here? Can't you see the poor girls are upset? They've just had the shock of their lives. Why, I would have fainted dead away if I'd found poor Mr Hemsworth dead. What happened to him?'

That made Dolly wail again: 'It's happening here too! Just like in Calcutta. I thought we'd got well away from it.'

Mrs Lexington clucked and made soothing sounds, but I saw she was waiting for Colonel Mosley-Partington's answer.

'What exactly were you were running away from in Calcutta?' Le Froy asked.

The colonel snorted but said nothing. He glared at Mrs Lexington, somehow managing to look down his nose at her, though he was seated and she standing.

'You know why we left,' Mrs Lexington said. 'I'm surprised anyone stayed in that city. Indian Nationalists think they can overthrow the British with riots and uprisings. They say they want self-rule. How do they think they can run a country when they can't even run a reliable bus service?'

'And poor Alan Weston was killed,' Dolly said, 'practically on our doorstep!'

There was a silence. Dolly buried her face in Mrs Lexington's shoulder, like a dog trying to hide when it knows it has made a mess where it shouldn't.

'Poor Mr Weston was coming to say goodbye to us,' Mrs

Lexington said. 'But he never made it to the house. Surely you can see it was impossible for us to stay after that.'

We had all heard about the troubles in India. I understood better now why Mrs Lexington had come to ask about safety and security when she had first arrived. And why she had been so taken aback to find locals, like Prakesh and me, working in Singapore's Detective and Intelligence Unit.

'You left word that you were making for Australia. Or New Zealand. Without giving notice to your landlord.' The colonel's voice and manner were cold, though he could hardly have been concerned about her rental arrangements.

I saw Le Froy, too, was following the exchange with interest.

'We booked passage on the first steamer we could find with berths to spare,' Mrs Lexington said. 'It was going through Singapore. This island is supposed to be the safest of the British colonies, isn't it? We just had to get away from all the madness. We hadn't really thought about where we would end up. But once we came ashore here, despite the hot, humid climate, with the nasty vapours around the canals, the bugs and bird dirt everywhere, well, it was nice to be back on solid ground. The locals here understand English and know their place.'

'Tamed, trained and kept in order,' Le Froy murmured.

'Exactly,' Mrs Lexington said, with no trace of irony. 'So when I had an opportunity to take a house for six months, I jumped at it. I thought it would give us time to think about what we were going to do next. Rose wasn't keen on going back onboard. After the incident, she doesn't like being near natives, and the passenger steamers are full of native sailors and cleaners. In any case, it's only until they settle the revolts in India. Singapore seemed like the best place to wait.'

Like all the other expatriate Anglo-Indians who had arrived in Singapore in recent years, Mrs Lexington didn't doubt that their exile would be temporary. It was only a matter of time before the world returned to the way it should be.

'I can't imagine you ending up in Singapore of all places,' Colonel Mosley-Partington said. 'A small, closely governed island, full of churches and missions.'

'Well, why not Singapore?'

Why not, indeed? In Singapore we had a new railway station, motor-cars, buildings up to five storeys high and an airport under construction in Kallang. But what must have appealed to her most of all was that Singapore was firmly under British control, unlike India just then. Singapore was safe.

Since I had taken over the work Dolly had been doing at Mrs Lexington's Secretarial Services, I had suspected I was doing far more than she had done. I used the typewriter in the office Mrs Lexington had set up in the ground floor of her rented house, where she had ample supplies of paper and carbons. When she found I could do accounts swiftly and accurately, she asked me to help with some of her accounting work too.

Mrs Lexington's secretarial work was mindless, routine work, mostly assessments and reports. The main reason I appreciated it was because Mrs Lexington enjoyed singing my praises, to get back at Bernie Hemsworth for his high-handedness and Dolly for abandoning her. And it was Mrs Lexington who had arranged for me to help Mrs Maki with translation at the Japanese Commission house. Mrs Maki was the wife of Consul General Yasujirō 'Jimmy' Maki, the unofficial Japanese ambassador, who oversaw trade and the welfare of Japanese citizens in Singapore.

Mrs Maki did for her husband what I had been doing for Le Froy. I helped her translate Malay and Chinese into English, teaching her English geographical and political terms, and she taught me basic Japanese.

Of course, Mrs Lexington always asked about who and what I saw at the Maki house, just as Mrs Maki always asked what was happening at Police Headquarters or in my grandmother's business. But I was familiar with that. After all, I had grown up balancing a traditional family, who suspected the Mission Centre school of trying to brainwash me into forgetting my ancestors, with the Mission ladies, who worried about me living surrounded by joss sticks and false gods.

I had learned to answer questions with limited information that didn't trigger alarms in different worlds that didn't trust each other. I thought Mrs Lexington was good at that too. She wasn't going to let Colonel Mosley-Partington intimidate her.

'How did you hear that Miss Chen and Miss Darling were being questioned here?' Le Froy asked.

'Everybody knows,' Mrs Lexington said. 'The newspaper told us.'

'Bosh. Rubbish. It can't have been in the newspaper,' Colonel Mosley-Partington jumped in. 'The man wasn't found till long after press time!'

'The newspaper *boy* told us,' Mrs Lexington said, with the exaggerated patience of a long-suffering teacher dealing with a cheeky student. 'That's why the papers were so late this morning. The boy had to tell the news to all the houses he went to. Of course we didn't believe it so he had to tell us twice, making him even later. But I'm sure people didn't mind. News like that is worth waiting for, if you can get the details.'

She put an arm around Dolly's shoulders. 'Come, Dolly. Let me take you home. And, Su Lin, you must have a good rest and decide whether you're up to typing up the Listerine cigarettes advertisement copy you corrected yesterday.'

'Of course I'll do it.' I didn't normally enjoy working on what my grandmother called 'Come and waste your money' advertisements, but getting back to work would be a relief.

'They accepted all your comments, by the way. Even said I must thank you. Good girl.'

She started to bustle us towards the door, but Le Froy shook his head slightly and de Souza took a sideways step to stand squarely in front of it.

'They haven't finished giving their statements to us.' The colonel turned to Le Froy. 'Do you always have civilians barging in on interviews? Doesn't say much for your security set-up.'

'These boys have excellent security arrangements,' Mrs Lexington snapped. 'Not like in Calcutta, where your men shut themselves up playing cards, with people shouting and lighting fires on the streets. If you want to ask the girls questions, you can come and ask all the questions you want at the house. Su Lin, come along now.'

I started to follow.

'Not you,' Colonel Mosley-Partington said. 'Miss Chen, you will stay.'

I looked at Le Froy. He was impassive.

I was horror-struck. If he was letting Dolly go but not me, was I going to be accused of murdering Bald Bernie? I had certainly wished him gone, and three of the four men in the room knew it. But it was the fourth man, the colonel, who mattered now.

All locals know that once an *ang moh* accuses you of something, the easiest thing to do is to confess, whether you're guilty or not. That's true, especially if arguing makes it obvious they're wrong. In that case, your punishment is likely to be even worse, because making a colonial administrator look foolish upsets the system, which is a far more serious crime than stealing, vandalism or assault.

'Miss Chen has to give an English lesson to the wife of the Japanese consul general this morning. Should I let Mrs Maki know that her English teacher has been arrested?' Mrs Lexington said, with exaggerated politeness. 'On suspicion of murder, shall I say?'

'Thank you, Mrs Lexington, but I'm sure I'll have finished by then,' I said. 'Just before you came in, Colonel Mosley-Partington was about to tell us why he doesn't believe we murdered Bernard Hemsworth.'

I hoped that was still the case.

The Assassin

───◆───

'Miss Chen, what exactly do you do for the Japanese?'

'I help Mrs Maki, the deputy's wife, translate articles he marks out in the Chinese and Malay newspapers.'

'You really get about, don't you, Miss Chen? I suppose that's hardly surprising, given your family background. I've found out some very interesting things about you, young lady.'

The colonel looked smug, expecting me to show embarrassment, but I looked back at him steadily. 'You asked if we wanted to know why you don't believe us guilty of murder. Yes, sir, I do.'

Colonel Mosley-Partington studied me for a long moment. I risked a quick glance at Le Froy and sensed amusement coming out of him.

Finally the colonel laughed. 'I'm impressed,' he said. 'You really know how to pick them, Le Froy. Mrs Lexington, Miss Darling, close the door behind you.'

'Now, look, we have as much right to be here as anyone – as Miss Chen over there. What do you intend to do with her?'

Now it seemed Mrs Lexington didn't want to leave without hearing what Colonel Mosley-Partington had to say, and Dolly didn't want to leave without me.

'You mustn't let them walk all over you, Su Lin,' Mrs Lexington went on. 'Why are you holding her if you're letting Dolly go?' she asked the colonel.

'Please! Let's go! Now!' Dolly wailed, suddenly afraid she would be made to stay too. 'Come on, Su Lin. Just come with us now. They can't stop you. Isn't that right, Mrs L?'

'I will be all right, Mrs Lexington.'

'Come to see us as soon as you can, Su Lin,' Mrs Lexington called, as Dolly pulled her out of the room.

As the door closed behind them, I felt the tension ease.

'You know that woman from Calcutta, sir,' Le Froy said, stating the obvious.

'She ran a secretarial and typing bureau. Supposedly. Left India in a hurry after Alan Weston was killed practically on her doorstep.'

'So you're looking into her for that, too.'

'I'm looking into everyone who had anything to do with the Indian assassin Chirag Bose.' The colonel jerked his chin in my direction. 'So, Le Froy, you trust this girl?'

'With your secrets? Of course,' Le Froy said. 'Until your man's interference, Miss Chen was responsible for processing confidential information for the region.'

'What happened to Hemsworth was clearly premeditated murder. It's a dirty business, and it started in India.'

He wasn't accusing me of Bernie's murder. Shock and relief flooded through me. I was so grateful for the reprieve I almost forgot how dry my throat was. Though my eager 'Why?' came out in a croak, I pressed on: 'It must have been someone Mr Hemsworth knew. He must have arranged to meet someone there.'

'You need water. You, boy, go and get her some water.'

Prakesh couldn't have been happy to be addressed in that way, but he went. As soon as he was out of the room, the colonel's tone changed again. He leaned forward and spoke swiftly to de Souza: 'You. Lock the door.'

I never did get my water.

'Damned Indians everywhere. Alan Weston, one of my best men, was murdered in Calcutta. He was a special friend of Miss Darling. In fact, he was leaving on a courier mission when the young fool stopped to say goodbye to her. She was then living in Mrs Lexington's Calcutta establishment. Weston didn't make it as far as the house. He was ambushed, killed, and the package in his care was stolen. Weston was strangled and stabbed. Bernard Hemsworth was killed in the same way and, I believe, by the same hands. Do you know whose?'

'No,' I said automatically.

Le Froy's eyes had dropped to some notes in a file but his lips were in a straight line and I knew he was listening.

'A man named Chirag Bose. He is a dangerous villain and assassin, no respecter of ladies. Been giving us trouble for years. He must have learned of Weston's mission and was lying in wait outside Mrs Lexington's residence. He murdered Alan Weston and stole the package. One of Mrs Lexington's girls came upon him as he was getting away, and he beat her quite savagely to prevent her from raising the alarm.'

'Rose!' I realised.

'Yes. Rose Radley was the witness who identified the bounder.

He beat her pretty badly and broke her nose. But she pulled through and was able to identify him. No doubt about it – knife scar on his arm, birthmark on the right temple. We suspect that's why he followed her to Singapore.'

Rose Radley was the other young woman lodging with Mrs Lexington. She had arrived in Singapore with her face bruised. Till now I had believed it the result of a motor-car accident. Now I understood why Mrs Lexington allowed Rose to board at her house without seeming to do any work. Rose hardly ever stepped out alone.

Rose, who had been Bernie Hemsworth's first choice to replace me.

'Miss Radley is the only witness to the attack on Weston, which may be why Bose followed them out here. To silence her.'

'Does the man kill all the witnesses to all his crimes? Why didn't he kill her when he had the chance? If somebody stopped him in the act, that person would be a witness too.'

Colonel Mosley-Partington ignored Le Froy's question.

As I was to learn, he simply ignored anything not in his script. Instead, he changed the subject. 'What do you know about Mrs Lexington, girl?'

'Mrs Lexington is strict, but she pays her cleaners and washerwoman regularly and she cleans her own room and WC.'

In recent years, because of the troubles in Europe, there had been a great influx of Europeans running away to Australia and New Zealand via Singapore. Many of these people seemed to feel entitled to the best of everything, for free, just because they were white Caucasians on an island of brown people. They would get angry and sometimes violent when locals didn't understand instructions in English, Dutch, Russian or whatever language they happened to speak. At least Mrs Lexington tried.

This seemed to please the colonel. 'That's the kind of detail you need a local for. Le Froy fought very hard to keep you here, you know. Made me wonder what he found so interesting about you.'

'Have you noticed how some children only want to play with toys belonging to other children?' Le Froy wondered aloud.

'What else do you know about that woman? What's she been telling people about herself here?'

'She's very respectable.' I knew Mrs Lexington was respectable by British standards because she never wore trousers or played tennis with young men. 'She is an independent businesswoman. She works with travelling businessmen and with foreign companies based here. She provides all the services of an office secretary and assistant. People come to have letters written and reports typed. You can send in your notes, or if you make an appointment, someone will take dictation and have it typed while you wait.'

Recently, that someone had been me.

'It's very important for a woman to work and have her independence,' she once told me. 'Men are never more than a temporary answer. Even if they don't throw you over for a younger girl, they die or turn to drink and leave you holding the baby.'

I already knew Mrs Lexington had lost a husband, and her saying that made me think she had a child she never spoke of. Perhaps it had died, like my brother. But that wouldn't be what Colonel Mosley-Partington was interested in.

I liked Catherine Lexington not least because she had offered me work when Bernie Hemsworth had had me dismissed.

'All that belongs on an advertisement poster. What about *her*, girl? What do you know about her?'

'She was married to a government administrator who was

posted out east after his family got into financial difficulties. He died of fever soon after arriving in India and she decided to stay on. She had no close relatives or friends in England and saw it as a chance to make a fresh start.'

'That was what she told you?'

It was what I had heard on the grapevine long before I met her, but I nodded. Local gossip is usually more accurate than what someone tells you of themselves. Not because they're lying, but in the same way as a stranger, looking at you from behind, can tell your petticoat is showing better than a vanity mirror that shows only your face.

'Her husband probably died from drink and women. And she probably drove him to it - she's the type. If she's so respectable, why didn't she go back to do her typing in England when her husband died?'

'England during the Depression was not the best place to be for a woman without connections,' Le Froy observed. It sounded to me as if he, too, had looked into Mrs Lexington.

Colonel Mosley-Partington shook his head. 'She stayed because at home being a white sahib is not an instant pass to respectability. The woman knew she couldn't fool them there. When she arrived in Calcutta, your Mrs Lexington claimed to be the daughter of a country squire. Poor but respectable, she said. Said she followed her husband out to Bombay where he died of fever. You know why it didn't ring true? She hadn't heard of my wife's family. Daphne was furious. The daughter of any kind of country squire would have heard of her and her sister.'

I knew deep down that Mrs Lexington had made up some of her past. You could tell - from the way she spoke and sat, the way she gulped her tea instead of sipping it - that her origins were different from those of someone like Miss Shelford, the Mission Centre librarian. Miss Shelford came from an old, once wealthy Dorset family. After her father died and what was left of his estate was lost to taxes, Miss Shelford had come east meaning to do Good Works by reading to people who couldn't read English. As a girl, she had greatly enjoyed reading to the elderly, but with the advent of wireless programmes, English people weren't as keen to be read to. Miss Shelford had hoped there would be fewer wirelesses out east. On her arrival in Singapore, she had been dismayed to discover that people who could not read English for themselves could not understand it when it was read to them. Not even if it was read very slowly and loudly, and clearly enunciated. But her story had a happy ending. She had started the library at the Mission Centre, finally realising it was the books, not the elderly, that had brought her fulfilment in her youth. But Bess Shelford's main claim to fame, where we girls at the Mission Centre school were concerned, was a letter she had once left tucked into a library volume of Gibbon: 'Dearest Bessie, I am to be married!' from 'your ever-loving Alice', who turned out to be Lady Alice Montagu-Douglas-Scott, now Duchess of Gloucester and sister-in-law to the King of England.

No, it was clear even to me that Mrs Lexington came from a very different background.

Still, it didn't matter. The advantage of a young colony like Singapore is that you can choose who you want to be, rather than be pushed into a slot by generations of custom. Here, rules and taxes changed according to British whim and everyone got on, as long as locals remembered their place and didn't try to get whites-only jobs or join their clubs).

The fact is, we were on the trail of this Chirag Bose in Calcutta.

Had him pinned down and cut off. Locked up every member of his family we could find and made sure no one could leave the area. But he got out somehow and headed for the Ajodhya Hills. I sent men after him, but he gave them the slip. We found out too late he'd made it to an airfield and boarded a plane.'

'There must have been flight communications to track him.' I had been reading about the efforts to track Amelia Earhart's missing plane.

'There were. Then they stopped and the plane disappeared.'

'Just like Amelia Earhart's,' I said.

Colonel Mosley-Partington nodded. 'Hemsworth and I came over to see if we could pick up his trail. Your authorities don't know what the man's capable of. I swore I wouldn't stop till Bose is dead or in custody. The terrorist assassin killed Alan Weston and now Bernie Hemsworth.'

'You're certain he's here?' I asked. 'Why Singapore?'

'Chirag Bose is a cousin of Subhas Chandra Bose, a villain reputed to have a network of assassins across South Asia, with a base here in Singapore—'

'Subhas Chandra Bose was a respected Indian politician,' Le Froy said, 'who, despite being gaoled repeatedly, fought through legal channels for India's independence from British rule until he was killed under suspicious circumstances. More victim than villain, I would say.'

'Sometimes I can't tell which side you're on, old man,' the colonel said to Le Froy. 'Anyway, we suspect Chirag Bose brought the package stolen from Weston to Singapore, hoping to use it to bargain with Japanese spies for arms and explosives to employ against the British.'

'His plane was reported lost over the sea,' Le Froy said. 'Even if the plane made it to these parts, it could have landed anywhere in Burma, Siam or Malaya. What makes you think he's in Singapore?'

'What makes you think he isn't?'

Le Froy had no answer to this.

'We have information that Chirag Bose, popularly known as "Handsome" Bose, has an extensive network and connections in Singapore liaising with the Japanese agents. We also know that Indians in Malaya have been told that, if they help the Japanese take over from the British and Chinese, they will be put in charge here and the Japanese will help them win independence in India. The matter is being handled directly by the Home Office.'

Now I understood why he had sent Prakesh out of the room.

'We need all the resources we can muster to find him. It's easier for someone like Miss Chen to move around the local people, the women, and find out what they know. Le Froy, I know we haven't always got along, but this is bigger than both of us.'

I had been fiercely prejudiced against Colonel Mosley-Partington even before he arrived in Singapore, but now I found myself almost liking him.

'Why weren't we informed,' Le Froy asked quietly, 'through official channels?'

'If your intelligence was any good, you would have known.' The colonel's laugh was almost a giggle. 'You're not on the inside of things any more, old man. I'm not saying the boys upstairs don't trust you . . . but they don't.' But I could tell he was genuinely upset over Alan Weston's death. And genuinely indignant that his man Hemsworth had been killed.

'You think Bose will try to attack Rose again? Was that why Mr

Hemsworth wanted her to take my job here, surrounded by detectives?' I asked. 'To protect her?'

'He believed those women might have information. Whether or not they were aware of it.'

'Singapore is full of places where you can kill and dispose of a white man with far less risk. Why do the deed in here, opposite Police Headquarters? It's a statement. A challenge. A threat,' Le Froy said.

'I repeat, it's the Indian Nationalists. They are full of statements, threats and lawyers. We have reports that they're becoming more active in Singapore. They must be rooted out before they incite local Indians to violence. In fact, I recommend all local Indians be screened very thoroughly. If there is the least doubt—'

The (locked) door opened. The key being on its hook as usual, Prakesh Pillay couldn't have known he was meant to stay out. He came in with a jug and a tray of cups. 'I thought you might all like some water.'

Colonel Mosley-Partington stopped talking abruptly and glared at him.

'Sergeant Pillay,' Le Froy said.

'Yes, sir?'

'Have Indian Nationalists hiding on the island been trying to incite you to violence?'

'No, sir.'

'There you have it,' Le Froy said, as though that settled everything.

'You haven't changed,' Colonel Mosley-Partington said. In a strange way, he seemed pleased. 'You still haven't learned anything. Maybe you never will.'

Prakesh

———◆———

'There's something wrong with how Bernie was killed.'

'Murder is always wrong. Only this time they picked the right man,' Prakesh said flatly.

After my interview, Prakesh had insisted on walking me back to Uncle Chen's shophouse, though it was such a short distance, a little over a mile and most of it along modern macadam-surfaced roads without mud and stones. Usually it took me just over half an hour, even with my polio limp.

It was nice of Prakesh. I hadn't realised how shaken I was till they said I could go and I found my legs were wobbly. Then I couldn't open the door. It was almost as though my hand was afraid of what might be on the other side. What if the murderer was still around? What if he had seen me finding the body and was waiting for me? I knew I was being silly, but I couldn't reach out to turn the handle.

'Off we go,' Prakesh said, then announced he was going out to check something and held open the door for me.

He followed me out and fell into step beside me. After the

dreary grey interior of Le Froy's office, the noisy, colourful vibrancy of the street was a shock. And a relief.

Out there, Prakesh and I were the only people speaking English over car horns, marketing cries and conversations shouted in a variety of dialects. Of course I told him everything Colonel Mosley-Partington had said while he was out of the room. Everything except the warnings about not trusting local Indians because of Nationalists. Prakesh could see that all too clearly for himself.

'So that's what drove Mrs Lexington out of India,' I said. 'I know they were having riots and demonstrations in Calcutta, but she doesn't strike me as the kind of woman to run away.'

'Not if her business is doing well.' Prakesh didn't approve of women running businesses. 'Maybe it was having problems and she used the trouble as an excuse to leave without paying her creditors. The colonel says she ran away from Calcutta.'

'They left because Rose Radley saw and identified the man who killed Alan Weston on his way to her house. Poor Rose. It must have been terrible!' I felt guilty for not liking Rose. Of course she was suspicious and withdrawn after such an experience.

I decided I would stew some ginseng black chicken soup for her. Out of goodwill, of course. And maybe I could coax her into letting me interview her for a piece. Surviving an attack by a murderer who had just killed a government agent? That would be a great story! No news magazine would be able to resist a murder story related by an assault victim.

And talking through what had happened might help Rose.

'If a man attacks you, you run away. That is common sense. But if this man attacked her, she survived and he had already left the area, why did she run away? And why not run away to England? Why come here where that man is supposed to be?'

I had wondered that, too, and had come up with my own answers. 'Maybe they didn't have enough money for tickets back to England. And maybe they came here first, and that man Bose followed them.'

Which would mean Colonel Mosley-Partington was right. Bose was after Rose because she could identify him.

'If Rose is the one Bose is after, what was the point in protecting Dolly from him?'

'Love,' Prakesh said. 'That *goondu* was in love with her. Should have called him Blind Bernie. Worse, he was trying to impress her by pointing out all the things she was doing wrong. Women hate that.'

'Maybe she *was* doing everything wrong.'

'Anyway, they should have let the local police know what was happening before barging in like that.'

'I think Colonel Mosley-Partington doesn't trust the local police. He said it was their own locals who betrayed them in India.'

Prakesh snorted.

'Even if Bernie Hemsworth was sweet on Dolly, why didn't Colonel Mosley-Partington stop him and remind him his instructions were to protect Rose?'

Another snort, this time directed at me. 'You think Bernie told him? You think Le Froy knows everything I'm doing?'

'But Bernie must have come across something important. Or else why did he get killed?'

'I wanted to kill him plenty of times.'

'But you didn't. And why in the Dungeon? Did Bald Bernie arrange to meet his killer or follow someone there? And why this morning?' I couldn't help wondering if Dolly knew something about the terrorist Bose. Had she somehow arranged to meet Bernie to pass him information that morning?

I found that hard to believe. But then I also found it hard to believe someone could be as hopeless as Dolly without forgetting to breathe.

'Oh! I wish I was still working at the Detective Shack!' I said. 'Could Bose have tried to get to Rose through Dolly? What if Bernie found out and that was why he was sticking to Dolly – and why he was killed?'

'You think both Dolly and Bald Bernie are smart people pretending to be stupid?' Prakesh asked.

'Keep an eye on Dolly. Let me know if the man Bose shows up or tries to contact her, now that Bernie's gone. He'll have to contact her at work. Mrs Lexington and Rose are already so jumpy about strangers, they'll sound the alarm if a shadow comes near the house.'

'You know something? I'm sure Chirag Bose didn't kill Bald Bernie. Or that man in Calcutta. But they will pin it on him nonetheless,' Prakesh said. 'The colonel wants him to be guilty, you can see it.'

I had sensed that from Colonel Mosley-Partington too. 'The chief will investigate. But he was identified, remember? The witness – Rose – recognised him. Though, of course, Bose couldn't be the only man in India with a scar on his arm and a mole on his temple.'

'Le Froy will have to follow the official line. Now the colonel is here and is the big shot ruling over all the small shots, we can't trust Le Froy. What if Colonel Mosley-Partington killed Bernie himself? Maybe he was getting just as fed up with Bernie as everybody else was. And he knows exactly how the other man was killed so he repeats the pattern and blames it on Bose. You think Le Froy will turn him in? If he tries, they'll just get rid of him too!'

I laughed. I really thought Prakesh was joking.

'There are stories about Colonel Mosley-Partington's illegal activities in India.' Prakesh walked on grimly. 'But you know what the British are like. As long as they get their money and their whisky they don't care what their men do. Now he comes here and we also have to swallow whatever he does. Le Froy is supporting him because he was ordered to. And because, at the end of it, he is a white man. He will always side with the other white men.'

I had to stop walking. I tugged Prakesh to a stop. He had always been quick to shoot off his mouth, but until now he had always spoken of Chief Inspector Le Froy with respect. 'Prakesh, what's wrong?'

Of course I wanted to hear more about the colonel's illegal activities in India, but that would have to wait.

Prakesh looked at me, glanced around us, then tugged me back into motion before answering. I had never known him so paranoid before. 'I'm thinking of quitting the police. I thought we could make a difference, but nothing's going to change. We can't trust any of those people. Do you even know what's happening in India right now? After all their big talk about education and clean water, when it comes down to it, they are the white bosses making money off us. They pretend to be friends but they see us as pigs.'

I hadn't seen Prakesh Pillay and the other men in the two weeks since I'd left, but I couldn't believe how much he had changed. 'Did something happen that you're not telling me about? Was it something Bernie Hemsworth said or did, or something else?' Bald Bernie's appearance in the Detective Shack had marked the start of everything going downhill.

A small unworthy part of me wondered whether things could go back to the way they had been now the man was dead. I would (almost) have killed him myself, if I'd thought so.

Prakesh shook his head, but the impression I got was 'I'm not telling' rather than 'No'.

'Look. Bald Bernie went to the Dungeon to meet somebody he knew,' I said, 'and he did meet someone. They were there long enough to have cold drinks in glasses that left condensation circles in the wooden table top. And there was no sign of the glasses when we found him, meaning whoever was there took them away after he died. So at least one other person was there before us. And someone may have seen them going in. The road sweepers?' I couldn't question them but Prakesh could.

'Obviously Bernie was there with someone. The someone who killed him. If you play detective and track him down, tell him I said, "Thanks." Why do you care, anyway?'

I wanted to find out who killed Bernie Hemsworth because I had hated him enough to want him dead. Now that he was dead, I felt guilty. To exonerate myself, and prevent his possibly vengeful spirit from visiting me during the seventh-month ghost festival, I had to find out what had really happened.

'They shouldn't have killed him in my file room,' I said. This finally got a laugh out of Prakesh. He knew how particular I was about my file cards.

'If we can clear this up, maybe they will leave and you can come back.' Prakesh sounded almost wistful. But his eyes were still hard and I knew things would never go back to the way they had been before Bernie Hemsworth's appearance in the Detective Shack as 'advisory officer'.

'Just tell me if you find out anything, okay?' It was no use arguing with Prakesh, but he was never stingy about doing favours. 'Talk to Dr Leask. He will be examining the body. When he does, can you ask him if he can find out exactly how Bernie was killed? Whether he could have been drugged by something in a cold drink first? Dr Shankar will know how to test for that.'

Dr Shankar, my best friend Parshanti's father, often helped the overworked Dr Leask, the official police surgeon and pathologist.

'Fair exchange. I need you to help me with something. Secretarial stuff, but confidential. No point asking that useless one in the office now.'

'Of course I will,' I promised. 'If I can. What kind of work?'

'I'll show you,' he said. 'I'll bring the books over.'

Current Living Quarters

Prakesh left me at the corner. I went down the steps to the canal path that ran behind the buildings. Uncle Chen would be in the shop by now and I wasn't ready to answer his questions.

What could he say?

In the old days, whenever something had gone wrong in my life, Uncle Chen would tell me I should move back to Chen Mansion, behave as a respectable girl should and let the family take care of me. Uncle Chen, generally known as Small Boss Chen, despite his enormous size, was my grandmother's second and only surviving son. He had become the official head of the Chen clan after the death of my father, Big Boss Chen. Uncle Chen's aggressive exterior hid a shy younger son who had grown up in the shadow of the smarter, stronger elder brother. He had always slipped me iced biscuits and coconut candies, and used to tease me that I could have been as clever as my father and as pretty as my mother, but instead I came out the reverse.

Some people believed Uncle Chen ran Singapore's largest black-market and loan-shark business, but that wasn't true. Uncle Chen answered to Chen Tai, my *ah poh*. She was the one who managed the Chen family businesses from Chen Mansion in Katong.

But Uncle Chen couldn't tell me to move back to Chen Mansion now.

'Do me a favour and help out,' Uncle Chen had said, the evening I'd lost my room above the Detective Shack along with my job. 'Move into my shop. If people know someone is staying here at night, nobody will try any funny business.'

Uncle Chen and his wife Shen Shen had moved back to Chen Mansion two months ago. If Shen Shen had a boy child and it lived, it would be Ah Ma's first surviving grandson born to a son. Her daughters' sons didn't count, of course. And I was only a granddaughter.

I knew Uncle Chen didn't need my help. It was his way of offering me a way to stay in town without making me lose face. After all, the Chen family owned that whole row of shophouses as well as those on either side and across the road. All the shopkeepers and residents paid rent to Chen Tai, though the title deeds were made out to a variety of names. Chen Tai preferred to let the British believe she was a frail old widow who had nothing to do with the black-market empire her late husband and eldest son had run. It was easy for the colonial administration to accept because there were fewer complaints of intimidation and gang violence, these days, compared to when my grandfather and father ran things.

'That's because your grandmother manages the business better.' Le Froy was not deceived. 'And because even the worst thugs are afraid of their wives and mothers and those women trust Chen Tai to keep their men working and their children fed.'

Le Froy believed that. He also believed a peaceful surface was better than no peace at all.

Most of the people who lived and worked on these streets answered to Small Boss Chen. I don't know what business was carried on in all the properties, but I'm sure there would be bonuses for extra duties – keeping an eye on his niece, for instance. I would be as safe there as in Chen Mansion. And a lot more comfortable, with electric fans on the walls. Chen Mansion might be grand, but my grandmother was mean when it came to home comforts.

And here I had a lot more space and privacy than I had had back at the Detective Shack. So why did I hate my current living quarters in the back courtyard of Uncle Chen's shophouse almost as much as I was grateful to him for providing them? Because, after all my contributions, after solving murders and saving the reputation of the local administration, I had been kicked out of the job I had worked so hard to prove myself good at.

And even though it was my own decision to stay away from Chen Mansion during the last months of Shen Shen's pregnancy, it felt like one more rejection.

Shen Shen was the daughter of wealthy and superstitious Johor pig farmers. Her people's voices had been among the loudest demanding I be removed from the family after my parents' deaths marked me as 'bad luck'. I didn't hold it against Shen Shen, then just thirteen years old and newly married to Uncle Chen. After all, her family hadn't changed my grandmother's mind about keeping me. But ever since, they had forwarded predictions from their fortune-tellers blaming my presence at Chen Mansion for Shen Shen's lack of sons.

My grandmother claimed she had counteracted any bad luck by educating me like a grandson.

It might have been Shen Shen's relatives who insisted they move out to his shophouse in town but I suspect Uncle Chen didn't mind the increased independence that came from living away from his powerful mother.

I appreciated my uncle's attempts to help. Especially when it felt like my grandmother and the chief inspector had both abandoned me.

When I first moved in I was surprised to find two pots on the drain steps. The plants in them were dead in the cracked soil, but I recognised the wilted black stalks as *chow choe*, or smelly grass – Mrs Shankar called it 'rue'. I never understood why it was called 'smelly'. When you crush *chow choe* it has a pleasant fragrance. Even people who don't cook often have pots in their homes because it is supposed to act as a mosquito repellent.

I knew Shen Shen used young *chow choe* leaves as a cooling ingredient in her sweet mung-bean soup. Then I remembered pregnant women were supposed to avoid eating *chow choe* because it could trigger miscarriage. Shen Shen loved plants. Pots crowded the walls of the tiny backyard washing and cooking area, lush with greenery and sweet-smelling blossoms. They all flourished except those two dead ones.

Looking at them, I had seen how worried Shen Shen was about the baby she was carrying. No matter what I thought of her superstitions, if she believed I was a danger to her and her child, I would stay away. This was not the time to upset her.

So I had stayed away from the family home since she and Uncle Chen had moved back. It was a small sacrifice, but I didn't know how things would change for me if Shen Shen had a son. Of course my grandmother would want her grandson to grow up at Chen Mansion. I knew the facts of life, of course. You don't grow up around dogs, cats, geese, chickens and ducks without learning them, the most important being that if you don't produce eggs you end up as meat. Did that mean I would never go back to live there? I had wanted to leave and be independent but now I would have liked somewhere to go home to.

And I desperately missed my little upstairs room in the Detective Shack, with its shaky walls and leaky roof. I had felt I was doing some good there. Not only for myself, but for all the local girls who aspired to support themselves in ways that didn't involve serving food or sex.

I drank two big mugs of water, used the toilet and washed my face. There were customers in the shop and I could hear Uncle Chen talking and laughing with them in a way that suggested they were children. Uncle Chen loved children.

I didn't have to leave for Mrs Maki's session for another two hours, but I didn't want to help in the shop and I was not ready to write about Bernie Hemsworth's death.

As I usually do when I'm feeling at a loss, I got out rags and the scrubbing brush and put a big pot of water on to boil. Cleaning always clears my mind.

The tiny back courtyard was open to the sky, but smelt of all the food that Shen Shen prepared. She sold coconut-rice meals wrapped in banana leaves out of the back door. And workers could pay five cents to wash in the zinc-sheeted cubicle, where soap was provided with a dragon pot of clean water and a scoop, while Shen Shen washed their clothes. My room was close to the makeshift bathing area and I could tell that some men pissed against the drain outside or the back wall.

I gave that a good scrubbing down too.

Soon I was sweating and feeling better. I might have lost my job at the Detective Shack, but my articles and Mrs Lexington's freelance jobs paid well, not to mention Mrs Maki's English sessions. Things could have been worse. And with Bernie Hemsworth dead, I might get back my job at the Detective Shack. Especially if I helped find out what had happened to him.

'*Alamak*. My house so dirty you must clean, ah?' Uncle Chen grinned when he saw he had startled me. I had been squatting at the drain grating. He was shaking his head but he looked pleased to see me. It's always easier to feel positive when your floors are clean.

'Oh, no. Of course not. I just wanted to do something. To help Shen Shen. How is she?'

'Bad-tempered,' Uncle Chen mumbled. Then, 'If you want to help, you know how to make *fah sung tong* or not? In front no more already.' In other words, an old friend had come in with children or grandchildren and Uncle Chen had given away the stock. Again. Despite his show of grumpiness, he was far more generous with money than his wife or mother.

'Of course. I'll roast the peanuts now and make it when I get back.'

'Your grandmother wants to know why you so busy never go to see her.'

In other words, I should go on using the 'too busy' excuse to stay away.

I was surprised Ah Ma had not objected to my working for Mrs Lexington. Usually she objected to any change she had not initiated. I wondered if she trusted me more or worried about me less. I would have started scrubbing again but Uncle Chen's next words diverted me.

'Your Ah Ma wants to know, has your police demon found out who killed the foreign devil yet?'

'Only happened this morning, Uncle!'

'Tell him better find out fast-fast what happened to that man. *Sekali* next time the gates of hell open, his angry ghost will come and look for him. Or for you. You found him, right?' He knew I had.

'When are the gates of hell opening this year?'

'Your Western calendar, August the twentieth.'

In two months. Le Froy, with his intensive knowledge of local lore, wouldn't have had to ask. I wondered if I would still be living here in two months.

'Where are your raw peanuts?' I asked. I decided I would light the charcoal burner and roast them in the wok. If I hurried now, I could make the *fah sung tong* and leave it to cool while I washed and went to Mrs Maki's house.

Or, in other words, as long as I kept myself busy in the moment, I wouldn't have to wonder what might have happened if Dolly and I had arrived earlier that morning. Would Bernie Hemsworth be alive now – or would Dolly and I be dead too?

And if Bernie hadn't known Dolly and I would be there that morning, whom had he gone there to meet?

Peanuts

———◆———

Shen Shen was famous for the *fah sung tong*, or peanut brittle, they sold in the shop. This simple but delicious sweet was the favourite taste of my childhood, the highlight of the feast when it appeared for Chinese New Year and the lantern festival.

In the old days the black-and-white *amahs* – domestic servants, who always dressed in a white top with a mandarin collar and loose black trousers – boiled down the sugar in the outside kitchen behind the main house, scenting the whole house with sweetness and good luck. But Shen Shen had a modern charcoal burner. And she always added sesame seeds and a touch of sesame oil. This was not traditional, but Uncle Chen loved sesame seeds so Shen Shen added them to everything she prepared. It was lucky my uncle wasn't addicted to something like pigs' brains or their business wouldn't be doing as well.

I spread out the peanuts to roast on the huge black wok before tossing them with salt. Then I put the sugar, vinegar and water to boil, stirring. It felt strange to be using Shen Shen's kitchen utensils when she wasn't there. Though I had spent a lot of my time in the kitchen growing up, I had always been following instructions from someone else. It was a new experience deciding what to do next. I approached cooking just as I approached my lessons in school. What was I trying to achieve? A hundred marks or perfect peanut brittle. What did I need? Facts and techniques or ingredients and techniques.

When Uncle Chen looked out later, I was stirring the melted sugar mix that was just turning a rich amber colour. The crisp roasted peanuts and sesame seeds were already spread out on the buttered tin tray, and Uncle Chen helped me lift the heavy pot and pour the caramelised sugar over it.

'Does it look as good as Shen Shen's?'

'Look good for what? Must taste good. *Wah*, hot! *Aiyoh!* He went off, sucking burned fingers and grinning around the hot caramel in his mouth. It was what I had often seen him do when Shen Shen was cooking. I knew it was his way of acknowledging my attempt to help. (I was even more touched when Uncle Chen asked me to wrap up a packet of my *fah sung tong* for him to take back to Chen Mansion for my grandmother and Shen Shen. He would not have done that unless it had passed his test.)

I scored the peanut brittle into neat rectangles, then covered the tray with bamboo and netting food covers. It would cool and harden while I was at my session with Mrs Maki. It was safe to leave it there until I got back. The legs of the table stood in dishes of water to keep the ants away. And I remembered to add a dash of vinegar to the water to keep off the mosquitoes.

'I have to go out soon,' I said.

Uncle Chen didn't approve of Mrs Maki because he thought all Japanese were monsters. But my grandmother's source, a Japanese hairdresser she had anchored in Singapore by finding him a Straits-born wife, told her Jimmy Maki was one of the moderates.

'Ah, girl! Somebody here to see you!' Uncle Chen shouted.

I assumed it was my best friend Parshanti Shankar. 'I have to leave soon,' I called, as I pushed through the curtain to the shop. But it was Rose Radley.

'They sent me to see how you are,' she said. 'Dolly's in such a state. She's sure you'd already been arrested and executed for murdering Mr Hemsworth. But I went to the Detective Unit and you weren't even there.'

Rose was better-looking and better dressed than Dolly, according to Parshanti, who knew about things like profiles and bone structure and dress design. Rose's clothes were understated and she was not made up like Dolly. With her pale skin, dark hair and eyes, she looked striking with only a slash of red lipstick. She made me very aware of my sweaty face and crumpled cotton outfit.

Unlike Parshanti, most of the young officers in town found Dolly far more appealing than Rose, who always seemed to keep her distance. I could understand that, now I knew she had been attacked by a terrorist assassin who had just killed a government official.

'Rose!' I said, 'How good of you to come. I'm so happy to see you.'

Rose seemed surprised – which was not surprising. I had never been happy to see her before. She studied me, then smiled. 'We were all concerned about you.' She sounded as if she meant it. 'Mrs Lexington says you don't have to come in this afternoon. She can use the notes you made for the Tiger Beer advertisements.'

'I would like to go over it one more time. I'll come after Mrs

Maki's English lesson,' I said. Having lost one job, I didn't want to lose another. 'There's the refrigerator posters for the Orchard Road Market that they want in three languages. I can finish them this evening.'

Not many people could afford the new-fangled American refrigerators that cost at least $270 each, not to mention you needed electricity in your house to run them. But the Borneo Company could afford to pay for the advertising, which was the important thing.

'No, don't bother. She'll put them off . . . or something.'

'Oh, no. Please don't put them off. I'll come and get the outline and requirements later and I can drop off the copy—'

'Mrs Lexington doesn't want you to come in,' Rose said. 'She says Dolly needs to rest. And you should too.'

'Is she firing me?' I asked.

Rose looked taken aback. 'No! Whatever gave you that idea? No, not at all. Don't worry about that.'

She smiled, which gave me the courage to say, 'I heard about what happened to you in Calcutta. I didn't know.'

For a moment I thought she was going to turn and walk out of the shop. I suppose if I had been attacked and almost killed, I might not want to remember it either. But I still hoped to interview her one day. She had actually seen the notorious Chirag Bose in person.

'I'm very sorry,' I said quickly. 'It must have been terrifying.'

'Do you want to know what really happened?' Rose asked quietly. Her dark eyes held mine.

'I know that a man, Dolly's man friend, was killed and you were hurt by Chirag Bose, the terrorist assassin.'

'I didn't know it was Bose at the time,' Rose said. 'They told me later when I described the scar on the man's arm and the mole on his face. All I knew then was he kept asking me why I was there. He said Dolly was the one he was interested in. She was supposed to be with Weston. He said his plan was to kill Weston and take Dolly with him, but now he was going to kill me as well. Oh, I was too terrified to beg for my life!'

I heard an artificial note in her tone that told me she was distancing herself from what had happened. After something so traumatic, who could blame her?

'How— Why Dolly?'

'They met in Calcutta. Dolly was with someone who pointed him out and said, "That's Chirag Bose," and she smiled at him and went over and talked to him. That's how Dolly is. She had no idea who he was. That must have given him ideas. He found out where she lived and has been stalking her ever since.'

'You told Bernie Hemsworth this,' I guessed. 'That's why he gave Dolly the job at the Detective Shack instead of you.'

Rose nodded. 'Bose was the reason we left Calcutta. But he must have followed us. I don't want to frighten Dolly but I believe he's been spying on her. He's obsessed with her.'

My thoughts were spinning, 'Then . . . Bose might have seen Dolly with Mr Hemsworth—'

'And killed him just like he killed Alan Weston!' Rose closed her eyes and shuddered at the memory. 'Dolly was so angry with me for telling Mr Hemsworth that I had to promise her I wouldn't say anything to anyone here. I think she likes the idea of having a secret admirer. She refuses to believe the man is dangerous.'

'She must see he is,' I said, 'Colonel Mosley-Partington knows

Bose is in the area, but he thinks you're the one Bose is after because you can identify him. Did you tell the authorities in India what Bose said about Dolly?'

Rose shook her head, saying she had promised Dolly she wouldn't.

I hadn't promised not to say anything. I wondered if Rose had told me the story hoping I would pass it on.

'I don't trust that one.' Uncle Chen reached for his backscratcher and worked it down his back under his singlet. Sitting silently on his stool behind the counter, he had not moved since calling my attention to Rose.

'You don't trust any *ang mohs*,' I pointed out.

'Some of them I don't trust more than others.'

'Why?'

Uncle Chen just shrugged.

That was the biggest difference between British men, like Bernie Hemsworth and Colonel Mosley-Partington, and locals, like my uncle. *Ang mohs* had opinions on everything and loved to explain their views whether or not anyone was interested. Locals, like Uncle Chen, would not say anything until they were ready to jump in to tell everyone else where they had gone wrong.

In this and many other ways, Le Froy behaved more like a local man.

When Le Froy and I worked together, I had been the restless gut and he the quiet brain. He had no problem being active on duty, but detested turning up to be diplomatic with higher-ups at social functions. If he was more favourably regarded now, it was due to my wording his reports, requests and wire communications for the past year. All he had had to do was sign them.

Now I hoped he would manage to convince the colonel that Indians in Singapore could not automatically be considered terrorists. The longer he waited, the harder it was for officers like Prakesh, Corporal Shorey and the Mukherjee brothers, to do their jobs.

As it turned out, it was already too late.

'My father's been arrested!' Parshanti Shankar burst into the store, setting the door chimes jangling harshly. 'They came to the shop and took him away!'

'Why? What for?'

'They said he lied to them. They asked how many sons Pa has, and when he said there's only Vijay and he's studying in England, the soldier hit him and called him a liar!'

Parshanti

———◆———

Parshanti had been my best friend since we'd met at school in the Mission Centre, but since the death of her fiancé just before Christmas last year, she had withdrawn into herself, not wanting to go out or do anything except mope and write love poems about her beloved Kenneth.

Deep inside, I hadn't thought their relationship would last. It was not the first time Parshanti had fallen madly and passionately in love. In fact, I still believed that if Kenneth Mulliner hadn't died, their engagement would be over by now. Of course I never said so, but Parshanti might have sensed my thoughts, which would explain why we hadn't spent much time together lately.

'My father has been arrested! Taken into detention!'

'Your father? Dr Shankar? Arrested?'

Parshanti, so wilting and despondent for months, was spitting furious: 'You know of any other father I might have?' she snapped. Then, 'I'm sorry. It's not your fault. I keep forgetting you don't work there any more. I went to the station to look for you and Ferdie told me you'd come back here. They kept calling Pa a liar and asking

69

about his relations in India. Asking to see letters and photographs and wanting to see receipts for money he sent them. He hasn't heard from them or sent them anything for years! Not since he went to Edinburgh and them all being so furious about him marrying my mam instead of going home to marry one of their daughters!'

'Shanti, slow down. Who arrested your father?'

'Why do they say he's a liar?' Uncle Chen asked.

Parshanti answered him first: 'Because of the shop sign. "Shankar and Sons". They said he was hiding his terrorist sons! I don't know who they were. Some *ang moh*s from the Military Police, nobody we know. Pa said it's just routine, he'll be home once he answers their questions. But why didn't they just ask their questions there? And they searched the whole house too! The shop and Mam's sewing room and the bedrooms . . . They even emptied out the beads Mam was sewing into Mrs McPherson's dress for the foundation-stone ceremony next week. Had to search the containers, they said, but wouldn't say what they were looking for. It's such a mess!'

Uncle Chen came around his counter. 'Where did they take your father?'

'I don't know! He's not at the Police Headquarters. I went there first. They don't know anything about it either.'

It had to be part of Colonel Mosley-Partington's search for the assassin Bose. He had said he didn't trust the local police: that was why he was using military men.

Uncle Chen slipped out of the back door. He would find out more easily from his network where Dr Shankar was being held than I could. I looked at the time and wished I had let Mrs

Lexington cancel my lesson with Mrs Maki. But it was too late. 'I can't stop now. I have to go and give an English lesson at Selegie Road in forty-five minutes and I don't want to be late.'

'No. You're never late, are you?' Parshanti barked. Then, 'Oh, I'm sorry, Su. I don't mean it like that. Everything's so upside down.'

'Come with me,' I urged, taking her hand. It was cold. I didn't want to leave her like that. 'We can talk on the way.'

'But what about the shop? Should I wait here till your uncle gets back?'

'It'll be all right.' The three pavement cobblers across the road would watch the shop, and anyone who needed something would help themselves and leave their payment on the counter.

'I should look for my mam,' Parshanti said.

'Where is she?'

'I don't know.'

'Then come with me.' I hooked my arm into hers, the way we used to walk home after school. Parshanti was a head and a half taller than I was now, but we fell into our old rhythm of walking, automatically matching our steps.

At the end of the row of shops we took the shortcut that ran alongside the drain down the slope to the trolley stop on the main road. Singapore had the largest trolley-bus system in Asia. It cost ten cents a mile to travel first class and five cents a mile for second, where the main difference was that you could negotiate with the driver if you wanted to bring chickens or goats on board. I paid for two first-class tickets. It was the wrong time of day for office workers to travel, so we had the back row to ourselves.

A fair-haired young man took a seat at the end of our row, smiled at Parshanti and said, 'Good morning.'

She glared at him and snarled, 'What do you want?' so viciously that the poor chap got off at the next stop.

I kept very quiet as the trolley rattled on. The physical camaraderie we shared while walking was gone now. A thick cloud of bad feelings – misery, suspicion, resentment – seemed to hover in the space between us.

This tense, unhappy girl was miles away from the old, silly Parshanti, who was only interested in boys and clothes, and who hid her lipsticks in my bag so her mother wouldn't find them on her. I missed my old friend. And I missed my old self, who had been so thrilled to work at the Detective Shack.

What I missed most of all was knowing that I was doing some good, making a difference in the little ways. Showing the locals that some white men can be trusted and proving to the *ang mohs* (via Le Froy) that local people are not stupid or out to block every move they make. I had been helping my people. And 'my' people covered my family and other locals, as well as my teachers and friends at the Mission Centre and the men in the Detective Unit.

'I'm telling this all wrong.' Parshanti finally spoke up. 'I know it's not your fault. Apparently there was a report saying Pa lied on his papers and might be a nationalist sympathiser. Pa didn't declare he still has relatives in India because he hasn't been in touch with them for years. But they said all Indians have hundreds of relations so he must be lying to cover up for relatives who are terrorists.'

I could guess who had prepared that report. Bald Bernie had loved digging up information and writing reports. When no one in the office paid attention, he sent his findings as letters to the newspapers.

'It's a mistake,' I said. 'Everyone knows your father.'

Parshanti's father was a brilliant doctor, but most Westerners wouldn't trust an Indian and most locals didn't trust Western medicine, so Dr Shankar ran a pharmacy and photograph-developing shop.

'The report made a big deal of Pa being a dangerous, subversive element because he married a white woman. Apparently that shows he thinks he's as good as a white man. I remember Mr Hemsworth hanging around the shop and asking Mam if she was afraid for her life, but I thought he was just being a nuisance.'

'And they think your father killed Bernie Hemsworth because of that?' I couldn't believe it. 'I thought they were looking for the terrorist from India.'

'I don't know what they think they're doing. I asked them what Pa was being charged with, and they said he was in detention without trial. Usually that's for people they suspect of working with terrorists or hunting wild boar with army ammunition, isn't it?'

'I'm sure Le Froy will make sure your father is all right and that it's cleared up.'

Dr Shankar had worked with Le Froy on many occasions. Le Froy could not possibly suspect him of being involved with Bernie Hemsworth's murder, no matter what nonsense Colonel Mosley-Partington came up with.

'This is probably just some red tape they have to go through.'

That made Parshanti flare up again: 'Your precious Le Froy is a big fish in a very small pond and the boats are coming in from the ocean. You'd better not count on him for anything. Wait! Where are you going?'

'We get off at the next stop. Coming?' I pulled the stop cord.

Parshanti climbed off the trolley after me. 'Ferdie thinks you and Prakesh are trying to find out who killed Bernie Hemsworth. I hope you don't. I want whoever killed Bernie to get away with it. I'd have killed him myself if I'd known what lies he was writing about my father. But it's not just Pa. They took in a lot of Indian men for questioning. I'm so glad my brother's not here. Vijay would have done something terrible for sure.'

It sounded like the British were trying to do in Singapore what they had done so successfully in India: turn the local people against each other so they wouldn't join forces against the British.

We walked in silence up the road till we saw Mrs Maki in the miniature rock garden she and her husband had created at the side of their house. She was wearing her wide-brimmed sun-hat as usual. Active as she was, Sakiko Maki was fanatical about the whiteness of her complexion. She had her gardening scissors and was trimming the dwarf trees. She waved to us when she saw us and I went over to the fence, Parshanti following reluctantly.

'You young ladies had better be careful, going around alone. The British officials say Indian nationalists are planning an uprising here, with the help of local Indians. One of their officers was murdered by an Indian terrorist. They say two young women found the body. I told my husband I was sure you were one of them. You must tell me what happened.'

'He wasn't an officer,' I said, 'just an administrator.'

Abruptly, Parshanti turned around and stalked off rudely. The effect was spoiled by the mud squelching beneath her feet, but her feelings were clear. She saw me as collaborating with the anti-Indian hysteria that was starting to build.

Mr and Mrs Maki

———◆———

'I have upset your friend,' Mrs Maki observed. 'She is Indian. I am correct? And the other girl too, whose skin is so white – but not so white as mine. She is part Indian too, yes?'

'Not all Indians are Nationalists,' I said.

'Of course not,' Mrs Maki said. 'I am sorry. But she is so upset, there is some sympathy. I heard about the murder, that you were there. I was afraid you would not come today. You must be upset also. We can converse. No need to study grammar today. You must tell me all about what happened in English. Come, you will have tea.'

Did all Orientals soothe anxiety with hot tea? Well, I wasn't going to complain. The time I had spent with Parshanti had only added to my upset, and now she was gone I felt totally drained and exhausted. It was nice to have Mrs Maki gently fussing over me as I followed her into the house.

Sakiko Maki led me to a cushioned wooden bench between two pots of flowering bonsai. She was not much taller than I was, and couldn't have been more than ten years older. Her shining black hair was cut in a fashionable Western bob but her indoor slippers matched the blue-green wrap she wore over a simple cotton home kimono.

'Is it true that there is an Indian terrorist assassin in Singapore? Is it true that he is here to kill the police chief?' she asked.

'Oh, no. I mean, I don't know. But I don't think so.'

'Perhaps they have caught him already, of course. The very efficient Military Police? They have put very many men in prison. Or is he dead?'

Very many men, including Dr Shankar, I thought unhappily. Though I was still certain he had been taken in only for questioning, 'Not yet. I mean, no.'

Mrs Maki went off in search of tea.

I usually enjoyed my weekly sessions practising English and basic translations with Jimmy Maki's wife. I was surprised my grandmother had not fussed when I accepted the post at Mrs Lexington's suggestion. I'd thought Ah Ma would be against my going anywhere near the Japanese, given the stories of the Japanese invasion coming out of China. Uncle Chen had been very against my taking the job. But it was hard to believe in Japanese atrocities while I was sitting in that very Japanese, very peaceful room.

Ah Ma, always practical, wanted me to learn Japanese and make contacts in their community because she was coming to fear them almost as much as the British colonials. She said a time might come when being able to speak Japanese was more important than speaking English. Her business dealings had already made her aware of Consul General Jimmy Maki. He, unlike most Japanese in Singapore, didn't seem to see all Chinese as ignorant savages.

Meeting the Makis made me think of how people shape their surroundings even as they are shaped by them. I was also coming to understand that, given how much things were changing, the 'rest of my life' might be very different from what I had experienced so far.

The Maki house was furnished with style and art, civilisation and elegance. Here there were no portraits of the new King and his late great-grandmother, the Empress of India. Nor of the Emperor of Japan. Instead there were ink paintings and scrolls of calligraphy. It was a semi-official residence, but had none of the pomposity of Government House. And it felt much more sophisticated than any other place I had seen in Singapore.

Yes, I had grown up in a wealthy family, even if the Chen wealth came from black-market businesses and money-laundering properties. But Chinese wealth didn't translate into luxury by Western standards. It was kind of mixed up: ostentatious in public, messy, shabby and cluttered in private. In Chen Mansion, nothing was ever thrown away but passed on to extended family, then down to servants, their families and friends. There were always more people needing things.

The Maki house was beautiful, like an art gallery or a museum. And, like those places, it felt more like a showcase than a home.

'Call me Jimmy', the consul general had said when we first met. He told me he liked reading English books, especially the novels of P. G. Wodehouse, playing tennis and watching American films, and he worked with the Japanese trade delegation. 'I was chosen for this posting because I speak English. I want you to help my wife speak good English also. And guide her to understand Chinese culture.'

I soon discovered Maki-*san* knew vastly more about Chinese art and culture than I did, mostly in terms of contribution to the Japanese arts.

'Look at the Dazu rock carvings, for example. There are others, too, that I haven't seen. And things we claim for ourselves, like bonsai and calligraphy, came from China originally.'

Of course there were no recognised diplomatic ties between Japan and a British Crown Colony like Singapore. But, given the number of Japanese traders and crews passing through Singapore, a representative whose word was respected and who spoke English was an enormous bonus for the island's administration.

To my surprise Le Froy, despite his suspicion that Japanese spies lurked beneath every sewer hole, had not objected to my working with Mrs Maki either. Not that he had any right to object, since I was no longer in his employ. 'Not all Japanese are aggressive,' Le Froy said, when I told him. 'That is why so many of their more moderate ministers have been assassinated recently. Commoners suffer under levies to support the warrior class. The only way the old samurai families can show usefulness to their nation is in war. So they have to start one.'

Le Froy believed Maki-*san* was one of the pacifists, 'Jimmy Maki is probably safer here than he would be in Japan.' He hadn't commented on the fact that Mrs Maki was a daughter of the samurai class and far more nationalistic than her husband. Le Froy could be as blind as any other man when it came to women.

It was only on that day that Mrs Maki told me I hadn't got the job thanks to Mrs Lexington's goodwill, as I had believed. 'I asked my husband to find the girl who had helped to solve Miss Nakagawa Koto's death last year,'

Nakagawa Koto had been a *karayuki-san*, which translates as 'a woman who has gone overseas' but usually referred to Japanese prostitutes from famine-struck farming regions. They were officially

banned in Singapore, so those still on the island existed without
the protection of the law.

'He could not do anything officially, but he was following the
case. He said it was a local employee in the police force who had
linked the poor woman's death to the case the police were
investigating. Nakagawa Koto was a poor woman whom no one
else cared about. But you helped expose her killer. Thank you.'

I saw Sakiko Maki had cared for the dead woman, too, though
it was unlikely they had ever met. Perhaps it takes another female
to understand such things. No matter how shielded you are by
money and class, women share vulnerability and a bond.

'Here. I want to show you something.' Mrs Maki drew a small
knife out of a sleeve pouch. It was about eight inches long and
looked like a double-edged dagger.

'Nice,' I said politely. Then, more honestly, 'I don't understand
what you mean.'

'Miss Nakagawa Koto had a dagger like this. It is a *kaiken*.
Women carry it for self-defence and honourable death. If Miss Koto
had chosen to die, she would have used her *kaiken* to cut the blood
vessels on the left side of her neck.'

'That's how you knew she did not kill herself,' I realised.

'It is a good thing for a woman to carry, especially in times like
this.' Mrs Maki tucked the knife back into her sleeve and leaned
towards me. 'We women must share our secrets to grow strong.
Now. Tell me about the dead agent you discovered. The Western
imperialists must be very angry with the attack on their police
force. Do they suspect the Indian Nationalists?'

'It wasn't an attack on the police force,' I said automatically, then
thought about it. Could it have been an attack on the Detective

Unit? After all, it had been created to monitor political threats, among other things. Had someone thought Bernie Hemsworth was part of the Detective Unit? He had been spending enough time there. I remembered Colonel Mosley-Partington's words and what Parshanti had just told me about Indian men and boys being rounded up for questioning.

'They think it's a missing Indian terrorist. He killed a man in India then escaped in a plane.' I hadn't believed that theory myself but as soon as I'd said it out loud I was aware that I might have divulged confidential information.

Did this show Bald Bernie had been right to say a local girl couldn't be trusted?

No. If not for him, this local girl would not have had anything to divulge. If he had not given my job to someone too incompetent to handle it, we would not have been sneaking into the Dungeon early in the morning, and he would not have been waiting there to ambush us and get himself killed. Because I was certain that that was what he had been doing there. That he had just happened to be meeting someone else at the same time was too great a coincidence.

Dolly must have told him about our morning trip to sort out the accounts. Her mind was like a sieve: everything that went into it came straight out. Either she had been confiding in him regularly or she had told someone who had passed it on, or Bernie had been paying Mrs Lexington's servants to spy on the household.

That meant that if I hadn't agreed to Dolly's crazy plea for help, Bald Bernie might still have been alive.

'Any news of the missing Indian terrorist?' Jimmy Maki joined us, as he often did. 'How do you do, Miss Chen? I trust you have recovered from the shock of your discovery. Is there news of the missing plane from India?'

'No news yet, I'm afraid.'

Jimmy Maki might have been a peace-loving poet and painter but he was also a Japanese representative. I was becoming as paranoid about the Japanese as Le Froy.

'Tea?' Mrs Maki asked her husband. She patted my hand and I saw the look she gave him. She must have thought talk of the murder upset me and wanted to change the subject. 'All these people flying around in small planes, these days. So dangerous. That American woman is still missing, too.'

'They believe that his plane crashed in Malaya,' Jimmy Maki said, 'but no bodies were found. Plane crashes are not all that dangerous. A skilled pilot can bring his plane down like a crane landing. Look at gliders.'

My thoughts went to Amelia Earhart. 'It must be more dangerous to land over water,'

'No sign of the American woman either.' Jimmy Maki seemed to read my mind. 'We have supplied the Americans with transmissions from Japanese ships that joined the search for Miss Earhart.'

'You sent ships to search?' I was surprised.

'There were already Japanese fishing trawlers, oceanographic survey vessels and seaplanes in the area so they joined in the search. Our reports cover many thousands of square miles.'

'I'm sure that was helpful,' But Amelia Earhart had not been found.

'At a time like this, everyone must help. It is a human rescue mission. It goes beyond nations and politics,' Jimmy Maki said.

Passages

◆

After Jimmy Maki left us, Mrs Maki and I talked for the rest of the hour in English, trying to avoid the subject of death.

Mrs Maki told me about her children in Japan. She had three; an eleven-year-old girl, then a son and a daughter aged six and five.

'It must be difficult being so far away from them,' I said. She clearly missed them. 'Why didn't you bring them to Singapore with you?'

'It would have been good. We could have learned about the culture together and I would have taken them to see films. They like films. But we are in Singapore for work,' Mrs Maki said, 'important work for my husband. He must not be distracted by family needs.'

Most of the cinemas in Singapore were showing anti-Japanese resistance films, brought in by the Shaw Brothers from Hong Kong as a fundraising effort to support the war in China. I didn't think they were the culture Mrs Maki had in mind for her children.

'Who are your children staying with?'

'With duty and safety.'

I tried to ask if her children were being cared for by her relatives or her husband's, but she seemed not to understand my question and we spent some time discussing English terms for family relationships, which we both found inadequate. For example, the English term 'sister-in-law' can refer to your husband's older or younger sisters as well as to the wives of your older or younger brothers.

'My father lost two of his brothers and eleven other relatives in the Great Kantō earthquake of September 1923,' Mrs Maki told me. 'It was the worst earthquake in recorded history. Then there came a forty-foot-high wave. And after that the fires. Most of the houses there were built of wood. The fires roared through them, like devouring monsters, swallowing all the buildings and people in their path and spitting them out as ash. Our family members were among a hundred and fifty thousand people who died then, and in the sickness following. Yokohama and Tokyo were destroyed in that one afternoon.'

'That's terrible.' I found it difficult to imagine that many people in a city, let alone dead. 'So many.'

'Before the earthquake, Japan was a dynamic country. Yokohama, the City of Silk, where my husband's mother's family came from, was a cosmopolitan city of half a million,' Mrs Maki said. 'Since then we have been trying to recover. That was what made us realise that we, as a nation, had to work together to rebuild.'

Mr and Mrs Maki changed my ideas about Japan and the Japanese. Until then, thanks to my grandmother and uncle, I had thought them aggressive, suicidal barbarians.

Mrs Maki invited me to stay for lunch. I enjoyed her Japanese vegetarian cooking, but since Mr Maki was at home I declined.

My presence always created a dilemma for them because as a guest, especially one there as a 'teacher', I would eat with Mr Maki and be served by Mrs Maki, who did not sit down to share the meal, though her servant girls did the actual cooking. It was much easier when Mr Maki was out because I could eat in the kitchen with his wife.

Instead I started on the walk back to Uncle Chen's shophouse. I wasn't in a hurry and I didn't want to pay for another trolley ride. If Uncle Chen had left for the East Coast Road house by the time I returned, I could prepare a simple dinner for myself and collect my thoughts. And perhaps I would slip over to the Detective Shack and see if there was any news.

Singapore's Detective and Intelligence Unit had been set up to crush Chinese Nationalists from China, Indian Nationalists from India and Communists from anywhere, in addition to keeping the local population in order. Now there had been a murder on its premises, which would upset the Home Office more than any number of deaths elsewhere.

All the files in the Dungeon were compromised, I thought. Bernie Hemsworth's murderer could have read or even taken some away with him. I could have worked out what was missing faster than anyone else, but it wasn't my job any more. I wasn't even sure I would be welcome there, but I hoped to learn that Dr Shankar had been released. That would give me a cheerful excuse to visit Parshanti.

But there was no news for me at the Detective Shack. The round-up of local Indian men had been carried out, of course, by the Military Police and all I learned was that even local policemen had been taken in for questioning.

Chief Inspector Le Froy and Colonel Mosley-Partington had been summoned to a meeting at Government House. The higher-ups clearly thought they were dealing with an international terrorist. It didn't bode well for us national non-terrorists.

Detective Shack

◆——

The next morning I left Uncle Chen's shop after the morning rush had subsided and walked to Shankar & Sons, Pharmaceuticals and Photographic Prints. That was what Parshanti's father's shop was called, even though her only brother, Vijay, was at university in Edinburgh and had never worked in the business. A family friend had made the sign for Dr Shankar and thought having more sons made him sound prosperous and reliable. Instead, it had made him look like a liar to the Military Police.

The shop door was closed and locked and no one answered from the rooms above when I called. I attracted several curious looks from people in the neighbouring shops. They stared and whispered rather than telling me where the Shankars were and when they would be back, as neighbours normally did, even if they were only guessing.

Something had made them uncomfortable. I guessed Dr Shankar being questioned over Indian terrorist connections had been an event for the street. Perhaps the family was upstairs with the windows shut, sick of answering questions. I walked on to the Detective Shack without leaving a note.

I hoped to catch Prakesh on his own: he might be persuaded to tell me whether Dr Leask had found anything in Bernie Hemsworth's autopsy. After all, he needed my help with whatever he was working on: it would be a fair exchange.

But as I reached the Detective Shack, I saw Chief Inspector Le Froy coming from the other direction so I waited outside for him.

'It's procedure,' he said, as soon as he saw me. 'They'll keep him for one more night at the most.'

Then, seeing my momentary incomprehension, he shook his head wryly. 'Good morning, Su Lin. How are you? Recovered from the shock of yesterday?'

But my thoughts had caught up. 'The Military Police still have Dr Shankar under detention. Chief, you know Dr Shankar. You've worked with him. You can't think he had anything to do with murdering anybody.'

Le Froy held open the office door without answering. I went in, though I hadn't intended to stay if I found him there. I knew Prakesh would not tell me anything if the boss was around.

'How are you?' he asked again. 'Have you seen Miss Darling? Do you know if she means to come back to work? Has Mrs Lexington said anything to you about leaving Singapore?'

Since when had Le Froy started making small-talk? Was he just trying to distract me from Dr Shankar? Or had he found out something?

Inside, Prakesh was looking grim and de Souza glum. De Souza's face lit up on seeing me, which gave me a nice feeling. 'Are you coming back to work, Su? We miss you. We need you.'

'Why are you asking about Mrs Lexington?' I asked Le Froy. I was not good at small-talk either. 'Who told you she might leave Singapore?'

'Do you know why she and her girls left Calcutta?'

'The Indian independence movement was getting too violent. And a man was killed not far from their house. I was there when Colonel Mosley-Partington told us.' I didn't mention Bose's fixation on Dolly because I meant to get her to tell him herself – after she'd told me all about it, of course.

'The Calcutta branch of the Anglo-India Virtuous Women's Family League started a petition against Mrs Lexington and her girls remaining in the city after the League president's husband was caught *déshabillé* on her premises by an enthusiastic administrator needing his signature.'

'Guess who that enthusiastic administrator was?' Ferdie de Souza said, with a wry grin.

I gasped. 'Not Bernard Hemsworth?'

'The very one.'

'That's why she and her girls had to leave Calcutta, then India in a hurry. Colonel Mosley-Partington helped facilitate the move, but believed they were returning to England. It's all in Hemsworth's notes. Pity no one was listening to the stupid man.'

That was true. But if a man says one true thing among ninety-nine stupid things it is the same as saying a hundred stupid things.

'You can't be suggesting Mrs Lexington killed Mr Hemsworth in revenge,' I said. 'That's as likely as Dr Shankar killing him. Why are the Military Police still holding him? Can't you do something?'

'And there were rumours the girls were Anglo-Indians passing as expatriate Europeans. Which, of course, prompted Hemsworth into writing more outraged letters. According to him, interracial marriages destroy racial purity.'

'Parshanti said he questioned her mother,' I remembered.

Dr and Mrs Shankar would be used to people like Bernie Hemsworth. The young Indian medical student marrying his Scottish landlady's daughter had upset both their families.

Given Rose's dread of Indian men, it must have been Dolly who was suspected of being Anglo-Indian. Or had Rose's fear of Indian men only come about after the attack – and might she have been attacked by a lover who wanted to silence her after she'd passed information to him? Could Chirag Bose have been that Indian lover? Had Rose lied to me, as she must have lied to the Indian authorities, about not recognising him?

The most honest women lie even to themselves when it comes to men.

'Doesn't make any difference what the rumours say. Pretty young women have short memories,' Prakesh said. He sounded bitter, though surely he had flirted with and broken far more hearts than most women.

'Regardless of what happened in India we have to find out what happened to Hemsworth here,' Le Froy said. His voice was bland and business-like. He had delivered his warning about Mrs Lexington, and if I didn't believe him, it wasn't his business to persuade me.

Perhaps he thought I should have sensed something of the sort myself. Or that I had kept quiet about my suspicions because I was so grateful to her. But it wasn't a big a deal to me. Many *ang mohs*, especially Christian men in positions of power, associate prostitutes with sin. Asian women see prostitution, like marriage, as a business and a means to survive.

'What's wrong?' I went over to Prakesh when Le Froy had disappeared into his office.

'They took him for questioning,' de Souza said.

'I offered to help translate, because the so-called expert translator Colonel Mostly Pig-headed's people brought in is hopeless. The man has an Oxford degree in classical Asian philosophies and can read Sanskrit but can't understand Tamil, Urdu or Hindi.'

'But Colonel Mosley-Partington accused Prakesh of trying to infiltrate the investigation and charged him,' de Souza said. 'The chief went over and swore that he would join the Indian Nationalists himself if they didn't let Prakesh go.'

Even Prakesh laughed at this. 'I believed him!'

'It's not funny! You might both be in prison! And Dr Shankar is still being held? This is so crazy. When will he be released?'

'Soon,' Le Froy said, coming out to remove a paper from the wireless machine. 'By tomorrow most likely.'

'And tomorrow you *ang mohs* will say, "Tomorrow," and then again "Tomorrow" until one day you say, "He's in prison for so many years already, *what*. Leave him there, *lah*. What for change things?"' Prakesh had always been vocal about our colonial overlords. But he was usually funny rather than bitter. And I had never known him to say anything directly to the chief's face before.

De Souza looked shocked. His eyes went from Prakesh to Le Froy and back to Prakesh. He looked like a man who knows it's his duty to throw his body onto a grenade to save the rest of the team but who can't decide which of two grenades is more dangerous.

Le Froy looked at Prakesh for a long moment. I saw Prakesh stand up straighter, as though his body was anticipating a blow. But Le Froy just gave a half-nod and went back into his office without saying anything. The door closed gently behind him.

I let out a breath. I had been afraid for Prakesh. I realised that meant I had been afraid of what Le Froy might do. Or, rather, what he might not do. I had always believed he and Parshanti's father were close and trusting friends. Dr Shankar would have done anything he could to save Le Froy's life. Was the chief inspector putting his work and position above friendship?

'We are all on edge,' de Souza said. 'You're not the only one upset about Dr Shankar. Mrs Shankar came here earlier. She was crying. Le Froy went to see about getting them to let the doc go home for a meal and a bath if they weren't going to charge him, but the colonel is running this show. Word is that, since he doesn't like the chief, he's going after Dr Shankar because he is the chief's good friend.'

I loved Mrs Shankar. She and Mrs Lexington were both white women, but apart from that they were complete opposites. Mrs Shankar was outwardly bossy, noisy and assertive, in her brightly coloured batiks, but inside she was completely and unquestioningly devoted to her intelligent husband. Convinced of his brilliance, she was happy to support him. Mrs Shankar could run a household on very little. In contrast, Mrs Lexington in her dark silk dresses with lace collars and cuffs, and tea cakes, had inside her the heart and soul of a business tycoon.

I turned to Prakesh. 'The best way to clear Dr Shankar is to find out who really murdered Bernie Hemsworth. You don't believe Bose did it? Help me to prove it.'

'If you find out who killed that fellow I'm going to shake his hand!'

It wasn't any use trying to talk to him in that mood.

'Can I look in the Dungeon?' I peered at the key on its hook. I really didn't want to go in there, which was exactly why I felt I should. Bald Bernie's body would have been taken away and I didn't want my feelings about the place to turn into a phobia.

'If you're helping with Dolly's work until she comes back or quits, you should go and make sure the guys from HQ didn't mess up your filing system,' de Souza said. He tilted his chair to reach the key and tossed it over to me.

———◆———

It didn't look like much had been disturbed in the Dungeon since Dolly and I found Bernie's body there. The corpse had been removed, of course, and the stool it had been perched on. The damp rings on the table were long dried, any marks lost among the many the wood had suffered before. Aside from that, I didn't even see traces of fingerprinting powder.

How had someone strangled and stabbed Bernie in the Dungeon without making a mess? Even he would not have sat quietly and allowed someone to strangle him. He must have been drugged first, though that wouldn't have been easy either. Bernard Hemsworth had been very particular about what he ate. For instance, he refused to eat anything from roadside hawker stalls for fear of catching worms.

That suggested whoever had given him the drug was someone Bernie had trusted – therefore not a local.

'Hey,' Prakesh came in and closed the door behind him. 'No use looking. There's nothing to see here.'

'Have you seen the autopsy results? Did Dr Leask find he was drugged first? What's happening at HQ?'

Even if Colonel Mosley-Partington was in charge, he would need local men to do the work on the ground, and they would talk.

'They are busy. The colonel thinks he's got as many men here as he had in India. He's making them send out search parties into the jungles around Bukit Timah Hill and Pandan Valley. Latest thing, now he wants teams to go through the mangrove swamps. He thinks that Indian terrorists are hiding everywhere. But he doesn't want any Indians in the search parties in case we warn the terrorists.'

'That's crazy. I'm sorry.'

'I'm not. Who wants to be eaten alive by mosquitoes? No news on the autopsy. And nobody has time to go through all Bald Bernie's things. Especially his notebooks. The guy had tons, but nobody can understand them.'

'I could take a look,' I offered. 'I'm good at working out bad handwriting.' Even Mrs Lexington had been impressed by how I could make out what clients meant when they couldn't decipher their own scrawl. I was careful not to reveal I was analysing them rather than their handwriting. There are really very few variations between business expatriates, and once I categorised a man, I could guess what his reports and letters would say.

But I had been so taken up with hating Bernie Hemsworth that I hadn't tried to understand him. His notebooks would give me a chance to find out who he really was and what he had been up to. They might also point to what had got him killed.

'I thought you would never ask.' Prakesh grinned. I realised this was the favour he had meant. 'You can put them in here.'

He hauled out a large, faded carpet bag from under the desk and shook it out. 'My mother's old one. If I don't put it back, she will blame one of my sisters for giving it away.'

'I'll bring it back,' I promised.

'Serves them right if you don't. They keep giving away my trousers.'

Prakesh pushed aside a stack of dusty files, then pulled out the box behind it. It was full of notebooks and papers.

'Bernie's notebooks? Why did you hide them?'

'I didn't. I just found out where Bernie hid them. If the Military Police had searched this place properly they would have taken them.'

Then again, why would they have paid any attention to another box of papers in a storeroom full of them?

Prakesh put the whole box carefully into the carpet bag and zipped it up. 'I don't have to say it but this is confidential.'

'I know.'

I had meant to go round to the Shankars that evening and insist on seeing Parshanti, whether she was feeling up to it or not. At least I could do something practical, like cleaning and preparing a meal for them: at such times, it's hard to think of housework, which just adds to the general misery. But now I knew the best thing I could do for Parshanti was to find a way to clear her father.

Bernie's Notebooks

◆

At first glance I couldn't make head or tail of Bald Bernie's notebooks. I understood why Prakesh had come to me for help: the notes seemed to be enciphered. But once I dug in, I saw Bernie had not used a code so much as a shorthand of his own invention, with symbols and abbreviations. In addition, he had written each page from right to left, instead of from left to right, and had started at the back of each book and worked his way forward.

Given my interest in words and script, I found this fascinating. Or I would have, if I wasn't falling asleep on my feet. I was glad Uncle Chen had already left for Katong when I got back to the shophouse so I didn't have to answer questions about the carpet bag and its contents.

I would keep the shop closed, front and back, and work on them next day, I decided. Because of the 'no selling on the Sabbath' law, customers were served from the back doors of shops on Sundays, but Uncle Chen's regular customers knew about the coming baby and would not be surprised to find themselves locked out.

I wondered whether His Majesty's anti-terrorist search parties were working that Sunday, when the colonial administrators were not allowed to.

I had stopped attending Sunday services at the Mission Centre. Since the influx of Anglo-Indians and Europeans fleeing troubles on the subcontinent and in Europe, there had been several calls for separate services or, at least, segregated 'clean' seating areas for Europeans set apart from locals. Apparently locals could be trusted to clean church pews but not sit on them. I suspected Bernie Hemsworth had written at least one of those letters. He had clearly believed racial purity and religious uprightness were linked.

It was unlikely these measures would be introduced. Governor McPherson had told the *Malayan Morning News* that he and his wife would sit in the local section if segregated services were introduced. But the movement had made local Christians uncomfortable attending services, which might have been its goal.

Bernie Hemsworth had certainly made a pest of himself in many areas. But so ineffectively he seemed hardly worth the effort of killing.

I was surprised to find, between the pages of one of the notebooks, an envelope containing feathers. I picked one up that was yellow, orange and red topped with white fluff. I had seen similar feathers in one of Dolly's brooches. She embellished headwear, bags and sometimes jewellery with feathers and beads. Further on, there was a photograph of her in one of her decorated hats.

This would have established a connection between the two had it not been autographed, 'To my loyal friend Alan'.

Was it in Bald Bernie's hands in relation to the investigation into Alan Weston's death? But a signed photograph was a strange clue.

Surely it should have been returned to Dolly after being discreetly recorded. I wondered if Dolly knew Bernie had her photograph. She had never mentioned it in her frequent gripes about him always hanging around and wanting to walk her home.

Or could he have stolen it from Alan Weston? Before or after his death?

Colonel Mosley-Partington was set on finding Alan Weston's killer. But what if that murder had already been avenged with another?

Appealing as the idea was, I couldn't see Bernie as a murderer. Most likely he had taken the photo from Evidence, hoping to pass it to her at the right moment. But, being as fastidious as he was, the 'right' moment had never come.

In his notebooks, the most commonly used abbreviations were 'pol' for politics, police and policy, and 'guv' for governor. But 'guv', I soon realised, referred to Colonel Mosley-Partington as well as to Governor McPherson, Bernie's father, and the former headmaster of one of the schools he had attended.

And Dolly was represented with a little heart. That was telling, I thought. If he had loved Dolly, might he have invented reasons to keep her under surveillance to justify being near her?

As I got used to his shorthand, I found he wrote with an observant spite and self-righteousness that might have made him successful as a gossip columnist, like Louella Parsons. For instance, he had compiled detailed notes on me. The man had been investigating the possibility I was having a liaison with either Sergeant Pillay or Sergeant de Souza or possibly both of them!

But he had finally concluded it unlikely that I was there for carnal reasons – being skinny and limping has some benefits.

Instead he had decided I was the chief inspector's source for local news and Chinese gang activities. He had written 'Double agent?' and underscored it twice. I felt flattered.

Yes, I was sorry Bernard Hemsworth was dead. The same way I would be sorry for a snail I had accidentally stepped on. It's nothing personal, but unnecessary death is always a waste.

I was no stranger to death, having lost both my parents before I was five. That kind of death you blamed on the gods and accepted because who else could you blame? Bald Bernie's death had been deliberately caused by human hands. I wanted to find out whose hands they were.

Prakesh had not liked Bernie, but I could tell he was sorry not to be part of the official investigation. The case was under Colonel Mosley-Partington's direction and the colonel didn't want Indians on the team, citing conflict of interest. This cut out a good quarter of the men available, and normally deskbound men were being sent out to do jungle searches. They would hardly have time to go through Bernie's personal files as they would otherwise do. Prakesh had included whatever he could find with the notebooks so I would do their job for them. And I would do it better than they could have done. Very often, true understanding of a man affords the best clue to finding out what has happened to him.

It became increasingly clear to me that Bernard Hemsworth was one of those British civil servants exported to the colonies as 'administrators' because nobody knew what else to do with them. Most of them were harmless, without enough initiative to be entrepreneurs or criminals.

The first time I'd met Bernie Hemsworth at the Detective Shack, he'd praised me for my English-language skills (as one might praise a trained monkey harvesting coconuts) and said he was impressed by my typing speed. Then he spent some time trying to find out who was really doing the office accounts. He refused to believe a mere woman, an 'uneducated' native, could have set up the accounts and filing system.

I was flattered until I was fired, Bernie pointing out that I had only a General Cambridge Certificate and had not been vetted by security. He found my shock amusing: 'All women are good at typing. You have smaller fingers and all that piano-playing makes them agile. But typing isn't important. This is *government* work. You can't do it without the qualifications.'

He went over Le Froy's head and reported my presence in the Detective Unit as a violation: 'Given the sensitive matters passing through the office, it is a dangerous oversight to allow an untrained, unqualified local access to sensitive information.'

At first I thought he wanted my job for himself. But he announced he had arranged for a respectable white woman, a trained secretary – Miss Radley – to take over my post at the Detective Shack. Yes, I remembered it was Rose he had proposed for the job. But then he had arrived with Dolly. Had he been in love with Rose first, then transferred his affections to Dolly? Or might he have mistaken one for the other, showing how little he knew them?

At the time I had been too concerned about losing my job to wonder.

'What am I doing wrong?' I demanded. 'You can't have complaints about my shorthand or my filing. Is it my typing? You won't find anyone who types faster and more accurately than I do.'

As far as I could see, the only qualifications Dolly had were the colour of her skin, and a letter signed by Colonel Mosley-Partington putting Bernard Hemsworth in charge of auditing employees and payments at the Detective Unit.

I accepted my dismissal, of course. I was Straits-born, female and not stupid. Bald Bernie couldn't have known how much I hated him as he held the door open for me to carry my things out. I didn't even spit at him when he went through my basket to assure himself that I wasn't making off with any office stationery.

I had hated Bernie Hemsworth so much that, when I first saw him dead, I felt my black thoughts had caused his demise.

More to the point, his notebooks showed he had been tracking Dolly's movements and visitors. There were carefully written accounts that included dates and durations of visits. And he had kept careful accounts, noting items such as '$2 – Information. 20 cents – mosquito balm.'

Had he been paid to watch Dolly or had he been paying someone to spy on her? Or someone else?

He also carefully noted occasions when Dolly refused his offers to see her home. That seemed to him so 'highly suspicious' that he had followed her. I didn't find Dolly's rejections suspicious at all.

Between the pages of the notebooks there was a strange assortment of things. Several lists on yellow foolscap bore strange combinations of alphabets and numbers, a pawnshop ticket, lists of dates. There was also an Ordnance Survey map of the Central district where Mrs Lexington's house was situated, showing the shaded forested regions that stretched out to link Fort Canning to the central rainforest jungle at the mountainous granite heart of the island.

Had Bernie been spying on Dolly's movements outside the Detective Shack?

And, to my surprise, a book of poetry: *Poems Every Child Should Know* by Mary E. Burt. At first I thought it was an old school copy he had brought with him to Singapore. Administrators often bring out the strangest things, baby photographs (of themselves, not their children) and stuffed zebras, for instance. But then I found the Mission Centre Library chop on the inside front cover. And the library loan card was still in its paper sheath on the back cover, showing it had not been legitimately borrowed.

I wondered if he had found it somewhere else. He hadn't seemed the sort to be interested in poetry, much less to pinch a poetry book. I would ask the Mission Centre if they had had any trouble recently. For some reason, drunken young officers thought it 'tremendous fun' to break into buildings to steal ladies' underwear and policemen's whistles. Finding neither, they might have resorted to library books.

Even more strangely, there were what looked like pieces of parchment, carefully trimmed into rectangles and pressed between pages of *The Annual Report of the Colonies*, Malaya 1933.

And then I struck gold. At the back of a jotter book that held rainfall estimations in the front was an Elliot Road, Calcutta address. And beneath it, the address of Mrs Lexington's rented house at Fort Canning. I would have to check it, but I wouldn't be surprised if the first address didn't belong to the house where Dolly had lived in Calcutta.

Dolly had mentioned getting anonymous letters in Calcutta, and that they had started arriving again in Singapore. She hadn't taken them very seriously. She was used to men who tried to get her attention in that way, she'd said. I'd had the impression they were love letters, containing poetry, from someone Dolly wouldn't have minded getting to know better.

'He doesn't sign them, of course. It's all so mysterious and romantic!'

What if she had told Bernie Hemsworth, and he was trying to track down who had written those letters to Dolly? That would explain his having both addresses with him.

And Dolly should have seen enough of his handwriting to identify him as her anonymous correspondent. Even if he had disguised it, I was sure I could. I would have to get her to show me those letters.

What exactly had Dolly said? 'I thought we left the anonymous letters behind in India. It was a pity because they were fun. Sometimes he would send a pressed flower. That was nice.'

'Pressed flowers are bad *feng shui*,' I told her.

'Don't tell me you believe all those silly superstitious things, Su. Flowers are romantic. And, can you believe, I got another two letters in Singapore. I was so thrilled! He's found me here, hasn't he? And locally posted too. Shows he's serious! I wanted Rose to go round with me to the Royal Forces Hall to see if we recognised anyone, but she wouldn't. She's better at faces than I am, but she's such a spoilsport!'

Dolly wouldn't have liked to get love letters from Bald Bernie. But other than Bernard Hemsworth, who else could be sending anonymous letters to her? And why had he followed her to Singapore?

I treated myself to a large pot of chrysanthemum tea and sat down to study the notebooks. They were the only handle I had on who Bernie Hemsworth had been, and who might have wanted to kill him.

His laboriously careful entries in pencil and fountain pen

showed a man who was ingenious without being clever. All through his life he must have mistaken the gift of ingenuity for intelligence. He was fed up with a world that ignored the schemes he designed to showcase his cleverness.

When I dislike someone, it's too easy to paint them in the darkest shades of black.

I didn't think I was wrong in this case. Still, I wanted to work out who Bernie Hemsworth had thought he was and what had brought him to this point in his life. He might help me find out who had ended it.

But first I collected a bowlful of peanut brittle corners and scraps. I needed something sweet to protect my mind if I was going to tackle the pieces of Bernie Hemsworth's life.

A Short Life of
Bernie Hemsworth

I divided Bernie's life into sections: Family, Schooling, First Romance, India, Singapore, Dolly, and Diamonds. Yes, Diamonds.

Family

Bald Bernie's problems began in his own family. His father had always favoured his elder brother because Tom was brave and sporting, while his mother indulged Bernie because he was younger. His sisters gave him treats for smuggling letters to their beaux, but once they were married, they hadn't much time for him.

But Bernie's father had taught him a valuable lesson he never forgot.

When his sister Louise refused to marry the man, a duke, her parents approved of, 'because he doesn't like dogs', his father had taken his gun and shot his wife's Pekinese right there in the drawing room. Then, as his wife and daughters screamed, he put a second bullet into the creature's head.

'That's the only way a man gets respect from women and dogs,' he'd said.

Bernie never forgot his father saying that.

His sister married the dog-hating duke and died two years later from a fall down the stairs. His mother never nursed another dog.

Schooling

School had been a nightmare for Bernie. The other boys made fun of him because he didn't like sports and was scared of horses and dogs: a horse had bitten him once when he was a small boy, but no one had cared.

His schoolmasters were unsympathetic, even though Bernie followed the rules and drew their attention to boys who failed to. They didn't seem surprised when Bernie failed his exams.

Then when Bernie left school, his father did nothing to help him find a position. And his sisters' husbands, who might have used their influence to help him, did nothing either.

First Romance

Bernie met Jessica Thiery while staying with his brother Tom's family in Cheltenham. Jessica was the younger sister of Emily, Tom's wife.

Bernie decided to make Jessie fall in love with him and marry him. She had a weak chin and thick legs, but if her parents gave her the same amount as they had settled on her sister, he would be able to buy a townhouse like his brother's once they married.

He thought Jessie would appreciate his honesty, but he was wrong. She declined his offer.

He warned her that when he made his fortune she would be sorry. With her weak chin and thick ankles, she would probably still be a fat old maid when he was knighted for services to the Crown. He gave her another chance to be Lady Hemsworth rather than spend the rest of her life crying into her pillow because she had turned down Sir Bernard Hemsworth.

Instead of being grateful, she laughed at him.

Bernie remembered his father's words. He didn't have a gun, so he took the fireside poker and tried to hit the family cat with it. The cat leaped away and escaped but the poker smashed the vase on the table, which turned out to be Emily's favourite Winterton Ware vase, a gift from her grandmother, the dowager duchess.

At least, after the fuss Jessica's family made, Bernie's father had finally wangled him a post in the foreign service, and he was sent out to India.

India

He found India as bad as London: all the people were so lazy and disorganised. This was when Bernie had recognised his calling. He started taking detailed notes for the manual he meant to write on governing native populations. If you didn't organise the natives and keep them in order, sooner or later they would get ideas and try to break out. Native workers needed to be corralled, like horses and cattle. They were no use if they couldn't be controlled. A good administration must organise the ones who were willing to be trained and productive, and shoot the rest or they would come back in greater numbers.

He submitted letters on the subject and things looked up for him when Colonel Mosley-Partington took him on.

Alan Weston was already working for the colonel and Bernie tried to befriend him, but Weston had been a snob. Bernie couldn't tell if Weston looked down on him for not having been to Oxford, or for not having a commission, but he had turned down Bernie's offer to move into his digs and supervise the housekeeping in exchange for rent. Even after Bernie had pointed out that his collars were dirty and his shirts poorly pressed at the seams.

As for Weston's murder, he thought the man had asked for it. If Weston had gone directly to the airfield, as instructed, Bose wouldn't have been able to attack him. Rules existed for a reason, and bounders like Weston never saw that. It was also Colonel Mosley-Partington's fault for not trusting Bernie instead of Weston with that top-secret commission.

At least the colonel had seen his mistake. He counted on Bernie now.

Colonel Mosley-Partington was clearly bound for great things, and Bernard Hemsworth would rise with him. And the colonel had picked him for this special mission.

He had proved his worth by tracking Mrs Lexington and the girls to Singapore. And it was he who uncovered proof that Chirag Bose was obsessed with Dolly.

Singapore

At first, to Bernie, Singapore seemed better ordered than India, probably because it was such a small island. But then he saw the natives walking around and giving themselves airs, as though they were as good as white men. He was in Singapore on a mission, but it was his duty as an agent of His Majesty to put right such things as came his way.

He warned Chief Inspector Le Froy that Indians should not be allowed to handle firearms. What had happened in India was a lesson. But the chief inspector had not done anything, not even when Bernie had explained that local Indians, like Sergeant Pillay, should be restricted to patrol duty, not allowed indoors and especially not around women. It was easy to see why Colonel Mosley-Partington didn't think much of Le Froy.

And health care in Singapore was appalling.

Dr Leask was hopelessly disorganised. When Bernie had gone to get some mosquito balm from him, Dr Leask had refused to stop tending a local woman with a swollen stomach and told him to go to Dr Shankar at the pharmacy. Bernie was appalled to find a native calling himself 'Doctor' and presuming to treat white men.

He had gone into the bounder's history and been proved right: Dr Shankar's marriage to a white woman clearly showed he refused to accept the position God had assigned to him. Such a character was dangerous, because it was capable of anything.

Dolly

Bernie Hemsworth had met Dolly Darling in Calcutta when he accompanied Colonel Mosley-Partington to question Rose Radley after Alan Weston's death.

He had liked her, even when she teased him to give her his Chesterfield cigarettes and kept pinching packets out of his pockets. He didn't approve of women smoking. It was an affectation, like women going out to work. Women ought to be proud to be homemakers. They were the heart of the empire. Every working man should be able to come home to an ordered house and a good meal at the end of the day. How is that possible if women are running around playing with typewriting machines?

But since he had to keep an eye on her, he had come up with an ingenious way to do it.

Dolly had been happy to move into what Bernie had described as free, private, luxurious accommodation in the Detective Unit until she saw the small, stuffy upstairs room. He had not examined it himself, assuming that, since Le Froy had been keeping his local mistress there, the space would have every comfort missing from the office downstairs.

Which showed it was just a blind. The crippled local girl could not have made it up those steps. And now she had moved in with an uncle who had black-market and loan-shark connections. Possibly she had been sent to spy on the police and Le Froy should thank him for rooting her out.

Dolly continued boarding with Mrs Lexington, and he had made arrangements there.

He knew the colonel didn't trust that woman and he didn't either. Mrs Lexington reminded him of his aunts, his father's sisters, who were always telling his father to be stricter with him.

Diamonds and His Mission

But all that would have to wait till the mission was completed and Bernard Hemsworth got the credit and recognition for recovering the diamonds. Yes: Bernard Hemsworth was going to retrieve and return the diamonds stolen from Alan Weston when the man was killed. Except one, perhaps. That would do nicely for Dolly's engagement ring. He was sure it could be managed. And he already knew which one she preferred.

Colonel Mosley-Partington would have to fix up a new background for Dolly. Bernie knew he could, and the colonel owed it to him for all he had done. Dead missionary parents in New Zealand, something like that, and no living relatives.

———

I still didn't like the late Bernie Hemsworth, but I thought I understood him better now. I even felt sorry for him, not because he was dead but because he had tried so hard and so clumsily to fit in and be liked.

And now I knew Colonel Mosley-Partington had brought him to Singapore to hunt down Bose for the diamonds that Alan Weston had been carrying, not just because he was a terrorist. But why were they so certain he was in Singapore? Why was it all so hush-hush?

And where were the missing diamonds?

A slip of paper fell out. Bernie had written, 'Found his poetry book!' on one side of it. Scribbled below that, in a different handwriting, 'Archive room, 5 a.m.'.

Bernard Hemsworth had made an appointment with his murderer.

But reading about him and the poker had made me wonder: what if Bald Bernie hadn't been killed by the same man who killed Alan Weston? What if he had killed Alan Weston and someone had killed him the same way in revenge?

Detective Shack

◆

The next morning I woke out of a convoluted dream in which Bernie Hemsworth killed Alan Weston out of jealousy over Dolly, and was killed by Dolly, who then killed herself because she had loved Alan Weston. It left me with a lingering feeling that Dolly was both in danger and dangerous, but I ignored it.

After reading my notes in the Detective Shack, Sergeant Pillay wondered much the same thing: 'Like his old man killing the dog,' Prakesh said, 'maybe he thought he could scare Dolly into liking him. Was Dolly really in love with Weston?'

'No, I don't think so.'

I had watched my poor dear friend Parshanti going through all the stages of love and loss, and what I had seen of Dolly suggested she was yearning rather than mourning.

'She has someone on her mind now. Not Weston, not Hemsworth. She's hoping, not mourning.'

Whoever it was, Dolly wasn't sure of him yet, but he had given her reason to hope.

I had come to the Detective Shack as soon as Uncle Chen

arrived at the shop, bringing with me a waxed brown-paper packet of warm turnip cake he had brought from Chen Mansion. The *lo bak go* that comes out of my grandmother's kitchen is not to be missed. It was almost like it had been in the old days.

I didn't want to get Prakesh into trouble for passing me the notebooks, but I thought Le Froy ought to see the issues they raised.

As it turned out, only Sergeants Pillay and de Souza were at the Detective Shack. Dolly had not come to work since Bernie's death and Constable Kwok had been conscripted into the search for Bose.

'I don't think Miss Darling wants to work here,' de Souza said. 'She didn't know how to do what you did. Why don't you come back now Hemsworth isn't around to make a fuss?'

'I don't think it's as easy as that,' I said. 'Where's the chief?'

'Government House meeting. Confirming the security for the Supreme Court building launch.'

'I thought that was fixed months ago.'

'Hemsworth filed a report that the coolies squatting in front of the building site could be undercover agents. He tried to take down their names but they were uncooperative.'

'Those men are just hoping for work. Even though they didn't get picked by the contractors first time round, they want to be nearby in case any small jobs come up.'

'You know that and we know that and the rest of Singapore knows that, but Bald Bernie said they should be investigated and arrested or given a good hiding so they clear out and stay away.'

'That's crazy.'

'Plus Bald Bernie said they would steal tools and material and wreck the equipment.'

I had always thought Le Froy had a low view of human nature. Bernard Hemsworth's, it seemed, had been even lower.

'At least the chief thinks anybody is capable of anything.' De Souza seemed to have read my mind. 'Hemsworth thought all Asians are bad. There's a difference.'

'Anything from the autopsy results?' I asked. 'Has Dr Shankar said anything?' Dr Shankar often had more interesting ideas than the overworked Dr Leask.

'Dr Shankar is still being held,' Prakesh said, without looking up from my notes.

'What? Over the weekend? Why?'

'Dr Shankar, taken in for questioning, was reticent and unhelpful,' Prakesh recited, in a British accent.

'But that's crazy! Dr Shankar? And Le Froy's letting that happen?'

'His Majesty's government granted special diplomatic status to the colonel,' de Souza said. 'Le Froy has no say.'

'Alan Weston was killed in Calcutta in the same way as Bernie was here, so they think the same person is behind it.'

'Dr Shankar wasn't in Calcutta,' Prakesh slammed a fist onto the table, 'so he can't have killed that man Weston. They are still holding him because he's Indian.'

I could understand Prakesh's anger. I was angry too, and not just for Dr Shankar. We who lived here, and knew how things worked at ground level, had no say in our own lives. Instead decisions were made by outsiders who considered themselves above, in every sense, the mud we lived in.

The Mission Centre ladies like to say we can all change our lives for the better. But I knew that if you tried to make any real changes, you might find yourself in gaol on trumped-up charges.

Was that the real reason Dr Shankar was still in detention? Because Bernie had accused him of being a doctor and a husband, while being Indian, in his reports?

But being bitter and cynical was not the solution and I wished I could make Prakesh see that.

'Now you distrust the white people,' I said. 'When the white people are gone you will start to distrust the Chinese. There will always be someone to distrust if you're going to be prejudiced.'

'I'm not prejudiced,' Prakesh said. 'I have nothing against people being different. It's those people thinking we're useless because we look different from them that I can't stand. Like that bugger Mostly-Barkington, coming here and giving orders, like he's the King of England and the Emperor of Japan rolled into one.'

Those words could have got him thrown into prison for treason.

'Can you ask Miss Darling when she's coming back to work?' De Souza changed the subject. 'If she's coming back. If not, well, maybe ...' But we knew it was not up to us. To change the subject, he nodded towards Prakesh, who had gone back to frowning over my notes. 'Anything interesting? Useful?'

'Bernie Hemsworth wrote a lot of complaints about trees he calls "diseased",' I said. 'Especially around the quarters where white people are staying. I think he's talking about Mrs Lexington's place on Fort Canning Hill where Dolly is staying. But I've visited the house and I didn't see any diseased trees.'

'Diseased as in root rot or fungus?' de Souza asked. He hadn't any great interest in trees, as far as I knew, but when your island is full of nutmeg and rubber plantations you grow up aware of these things. 'Are the leaves turning black or yellow?'

'He doesn't mention the leaves. Just says the trees look like they have leprosy and have been poisoning birds. He wanted them chopped down before whatever is infesting them spreads to other trees and maybe people.'

'Poisoning birds?' De Souza shook his head and gave up.

'You believe the colonel wanted Hemsworth to use the women from Mrs Lexington's group to track down Bose?' Prakesh's finger marked his point as he looked up.

'I don't think he acted on his own. He had lists of questions to ask them – who had been on the ship coming out with them, how much luggage they had and so on.'

'He was watching Rose at first, because she identified Bose as the man who had attacked her. It made sense that she was the one Bose would be after.'

'According to his notes, he wanted Rose to take my job here. But Rose said she was still too shocked by the attack. She must have found out somehow that you worked here, and she said she couldn't work in an office with an Indian man. So Bernie agreed Dolly could take her place until he managed to get rid of Prakesh.'

Sergeant Pillay looked furious and I hurried on. It was all in my notes, but Prakesh listened faster than he read, and I wanted him to have the whole story before he blew up. 'But then he found out Dolly had met Bose. In fact, they had some kind of understanding, according to Rose.'

'What?'

'Rose said Dolly was terribly upset when Bose's plane disappeared.'

'Rubbish. That woman is making things up,' Prakesh said. 'If Miss Darling knew Bose, the colonel would have arrested her. He's going round arresting people for knowing Bose's name, never mind knowing *him*.'

'Do you believe that?' de Souza asked me.

'I think Bernie did. I believe he thought Bose had already contacted Dolly in Singapore. That was why he was trying to get Dolly to confide in him. Then he fell in love with her himself. He sounds like he wanted to "save" her from Bose. But Mrs Lexington told him Dolly couldn't be meeting Bose without her knowing.'

'She should be so lucky,' Prakesh said. 'Su Lin, I don't think you should go on working for Mrs Lizard Skin. That lot, they are not like your Mission ladies, you know. Keep your eyes open. Make sure she pays you in cash.'

'Talking of money, Bernie heard Dolly ask about pawnshops here and he put together a list of them. That was less than a week before he died.'

I had been uncomfortable about putting that down on paper. Several of the pawnshops – practically all those on the list – were owned by my grandmother. Chen Tai had bought them as a service, 'poor people's banking', when the Great Depression in the West had caused the local economy to crash and pawnbrokers couldn't return deposits. Of course, once the economy recovered, they generated a good income, as did all of her businesses.

'She asked me,' de Souza said. 'She wanted to know if they would understand English.'

'What did you tell her?'

'Said I didn't know because they were all run by gangsters.'

'Oh, Ferdie.' I laughed, but that would have been enough to start Bernie on another witch hunt.

'Don't worry. He asked Dolly what she wanted to pawn. She

said nothing – she'd heard they were a good place to pick up bargain jewellery.'

'I don't think he believed her,' I said. 'He was following her around. Watching who she talked to.'

'He didn't like Prakesh talking to her.' De Souza laughed. 'Didn't even like him walking past her desk. He was okay with me until he saw me crossing myself – just automatically, you know – and said that, as far as he was concerned, Catholics were even worse than heathen. And he accused Kwok of being a nancy-boy.'

'What?'

'According to him, us Catholics are damned because we think we can buy our way into Heaven. And he called Kwok a sodomite because he carved a dragon out of a watermelon rind.'

I hadn't known how bad things had been in the office. Dolly had only complained about the work she was expected to do. 'I'm sorry about that, Ferdie.'

'Frankly, you were lucky to be out of here. I thought Kwok was going to stick his knife into him!'

'I think Bernie was collecting material to justify firing you,' I told Prakesh. It was difficult not to feel just a little glad the man was dead, so I gave up trying. 'Oh, and I almost forgot. There was this paper inside the cover of the leather notebook. I don't know if he was hiding it or that was just where he kept it. A lot of numbers in columns in his handwriting, so it's not a pawn ticket.'

I showed them the slip of paper I had found. De Souza shook his head. I saw it meant something to Prakesh but he only said, 'Maybe he was weighing his food, trying to lose a few pounds. He needed to.'

'Tell me,' I said. 'You're not being fair.'

But Prakesh had his stubborn face on.

'Prakesh, come on. We have to work this out and get Dr Shankar released.'

'That is what I'm trying to do,' Prakesh said. 'For once, trust me as much as you would trust a white man.'

He left before I could answer, without signing out in the log book.

'He's struggling,' de Souza said. 'We all are. Please find out if Miss Darling is too upset to come back to work. We really do need you here. Not just for the *lo bak go*.'

I reminded myself that I didn't have to work there to bring them turnip cake.

Barber

———◆———

Sergeant Prakesh Pillay saw the significance of the scribbled numbers on Su Lin's scrap of paper at once. When he left the Detective Shack, he was angry with himself for not having spotted it when going through Hemsworth's notebooks. But now he had it in hand, he turned away from the business district to a quieter, more rundown part of town.

He was going to the barber.

———◆———

As always, a group of desultory men was sitting around, drinking cold tea and listening to cricket on the wireless.

'I'm looking for Rajesh. Is he here?'

'Take off your shirt,' the barber ordered.

'I haven't time. I must see Rajesh!'

'Body hair is not in fashion, these days. If you're shy go behind the curtain and take off your shirt. Don't waste time, boy.'

Vijay Merchant was batting and none of the old men looked

round. Prakesh went behind the curtain, undoing the buttons of his khaki uniform shirt, his mind crowded with thoughts. He had once believed he could make a difference in and through the police. But now they were shutting him out of an investigation that was clearly intended to convict an innocent and good man.

The barber would know what to do.

Rajesh turned on a second short-wave wireless, which produced a lot of static and a little gramophone music, then whipped out a noisy trimmer that he waved over Prakesh's chest and back without actually touching him. 'You shouldn't have come here. It's not safe.'

'I have proof they are after the diamonds,' Prakesh said. 'And that the diamonds are here. In Singapore.'

One side of the paper bore the specifications of one of the stolen diamonds: the numbers recorded the quality and weight of the cut stone and approximate transaction price expected. Until now, the presence of the stolen diamonds in Singapore had been mere speculation. Especially as there were no records of where they had been mined or cut.

The other side had a pawnbroker's assessment of one of the diamonds, copied carefully in Bernie Hemsworth's round fussy handwriting.

'These numbers are from the Panna district of Madhya Pradesh. But the mines there have been closed for more than five years, and these numbers are new.'

'Where did you get this paper?'

'It was among the dead man's things. Hemsworth.'

'So he was here looking for the stolen diamonds. Did he find them?'

'He must have found at least one. Can you tell which pawnshop?'

'Not from this. But it's here. See the conversion from Straits dollars to Indian rupees and British pounds? These are current rates.'

Prakesh knew from local supporters of the Indian Nationalists that the Japanese were willing to trade arms for the diamonds they were certain would soon surface. Not because they wanted diamonds but because the Indian Nationalists needed arms, food and fuel, and the Japanese wanted the connection.

Prakesh was working undercover within the local branch of Indian Nationalist sympathisers, though they all knew he was a police officer. There might come a time when he had to choose allegiance, but not yet. Le Froy was aware of his sergeant's sympathies and glad to keep negotiation channels open. Neither had spoken of this since Colonel Mosley-Partington had taken charge.

As far as Prakesh was concerned, it all pointed to Dolly. She had been a friend of Alan Weston. She must have known he was carrying the stolen diamonds. And now he was sure he had proof that Dolly had – or knew who had – killed Weston and taken the diamonds.

'Are you going to report this?'

If it had happened last year or even six months ago, Sergeant Pillay would have brought the information to Chief Inspector Le Froy without a second thought. But doing so now might land him in prison next to Dr Shankar – or worse. He didn't know whether Hemsworth had been protecting or investigating Dolly Darling, and the man was dead now.

'I'm going to find out what Dolly Darling knows first,' Sergeant Pillay said.

'How will you get her to talk?'

'There's that big party tomorrow night. No one will notice her slip away to meet me to talk. If she doesn't, I will pass this to Le Froy for the colonel.'

Dolly

'How nice to see you, Su Lin. Please come in. We were all wondering what had happened to you. Have you got over the shock yet? Poor Dolly is still that upset!'

On leaving the Detective Shack, I'd taken a bus, then walked slowly up to Mrs Lexington's. The house she rented was the highest along the curve of Fort Canning Rise, above it the central jungle continued all the way to Bukit Timah. It was much too large for a single woman, but perfect for Mrs Lexington's Secretarial Services, which occupied the downstairs rooms while the three women lived upstairs.

Mrs Lexington was a lot friendlier and more practical than most married expatriate women, who were always complaining about the weather and their husbands.

She didn't stand on ceremony. I liked that she had made it clear to Bernie Hemsworth that she didn't want him hanging around the house, not even the downstairs office. She had given me a desk to work at, and I had the use of the two modern Underwood typewriters, all the bond paper I could need and fresh carbons every week or more often if the typing load was heavy.

'I'm so glad to see you! Rose said they were sure to arrest you, cut off your fingers and torture you to death. Oh, I wish we'd never come here!' Dolly burst out when Mrs Lexington brought me to her.

Dolly and Rose were sitting on the side porch where there was a bit of breeze. That was the advantage of being high up Fort Canning Rise instead of down in the stifling town. The house overlooked what had once been a peaceful graveyard, but was now a massive construction site, which was probably why so many of the black-and-white houses on Fort Canning were then unoccupied.

The previous governor had commissioned an artillery fort, with officers' quarters, secure gunpowder storage and a hospital, 'before we feel the need'. But he had not defined the need, and once his attention shifted, work had stopped. Governor McPherson had not continued the construction, saying funds were needed elsewhere.

Now it was a peaceful space where bulbuls, squirrels and ground lizards basked incongruously among the construction equipment that young trees and ground creepers were already starting to cover. Nature is strong here on the equator.

———◆———

'Of course I'll go back to work,' Dolly said, when I asked her. 'I'm just not ready yet. I'm still too shocked. That nice doctor whatshisname – sounds like he's leaking – said so. He said I should take as much time as I needed to recover.'

'Dr Leask?'

'Something funny like that. They'll still have to pay me, though.

I'm on medical leave. The doctor prescribed lots of rest. In England you get medical leave with pay.' She looked at Rose as she spoke and I guessed that was where she had got the information.

Dolly looked fine to me. She was carefully made up as usual and had her craft basket by her side. I saw no point in the pretty trinkets she made, but many other expatriate women pressed flowers and painted in watercolours, which made as little sense to me. My grandmother liked to play mah-jong to keep her hands occupied while she assessed the value and weaknesses of people being discussed. But playing with her pretty things seemed to occupy all of Dolly's brain.

'What are you making?'

'A hatpin, I think.' Dolly held up her latest creation to show me. It was a confection of ribbons, beads and feathers. 'Women wear them in their hats. Or stick them onto their bags. Do you like it?'

'It's quite beautiful,' I said honestly.

'I'll give it to you, then.'

'Oh, no! I mean, you should keep it for yourself. I don't wear hats or carry bags.'

'I may wear it as a brooch, I think.' Dolly held it against her dress.

'Pretty feathers.'

'You like them? Look at these.' She took a small cloth pouch out of her basket and passed it to me.

It was full of feathers. Coloured feathers.

'Pretty, aren't they? Rose says they likely all came off sick birds, that there's germs and vermin on them and we'll all get ill if I keep them in the house. But I wash and dry them, so it's safe.'

'They're lovely. Where did you find them?'

Dolly hesitated. 'Someone gave them to me.'

'Mr Hemsworth?'

That would explain the red and yellow feathers among his things.

'Why would he? And why shouldn't he have? Anyway, they don't cost anything and he said he just found them somewhere, so why shouldn't I take them from him? He wouldn't ever tell me where he got them. If he picked them off someone's pet parrot or something it's not my fault!'

In other words, yes, Dolly had got the feathers from Bernie Hemsworth. And, no, she couldn't give a simple answer to a simple question. But why was she so defensive about a few feathers?

I saw a pained expression on Rose's face. I wondered if she knew whose pet parrot Bald Bernie had plucked – but she saw me looking and smiled wryly. 'I've never understood people who wear feathers and furs,' she said, in her low, rich voice.

Rose wore no make-up other than lipstick on perfectly shaped Cupid's-bow lips, striking dark red against her white skin. With her very black hair wound tight in a coiled plait, I thought she looked much more sophisticated than Dolly, with her coloured eye shadow, rouge and artfully arranged curls. Dolly, who was looking petulantly at me now.

'I just meant they're pretty,' I said quickly. 'Really pretty. I thought maybe you brought them from India. Or from England.'

Dolly recovered her good humour immediately. 'Oh, no. You never see birds like that in England. Just a lot of pigeons and crows. Black and grey feathers. Like flying rats, almost. Nasty, greedy, bad-tempered things.'

'Do you miss England? It must be hard being so far away from your family after such a shock.'

'Not likely.' Dolly snorted a coarse, unladylike laugh. 'I couldn't wait to get away. England is old, tired, overcrowded. I had no chance of getting ahead there. Unless you're born rich you won't get a chance at nothing.'

The attention Dolly had got after the murder had perked her up. Far from being ill from shock, she seemed in excellent spirits. If Rose hadn't suggested she might be paid for not working, I believed she would already be back at the Detective Shack.

Mrs Lexington was very particular about spoken English and I had heard her correcting Dolly's speech before. But Mrs Lexington had gone to her kitchen in search of cold drinks and Rose didn't bother.

It is difficult for native English speakers to understand the rules of their language as well as a foreigner can when they have studied it thoroughly. I had studied English speakers and could tell that Rose, Dolly and even Mrs Lexington hadn't received the education someone like Le Froy had. That made sense given what I had learned of them from Colonel Mosley-Partington. I didn't judge them for what they did with the English language ... or what they did with English men.

'It's lucky you met Mrs Lexington in India,' I said.

'Dolly has a way of making her own luck.' Rose smiled as she got up to go back inside the house.

'Whew!' Dolly said, as soon as Rose was gone. 'I'm so sick of how that one's been sticking to me all the time. You'd think I was the one that almost got done in!' She giggled. 'Look at this.'

I leaned forward over the pretty feathered pin she held out.

'I got in the family way,' Dolly whispered, her head close to mine. 'That's why I had to leave London. He didn't want it. Didn't want to have anything to do with me. My old dad wanted me to get a settlement out of him, but even if he'd paid up, the money would have gone down Dad's throat. No, I got him to buy my passage out east. Lots of single men in India and I'd be a widow wanting a fresh start with my child. I had it all planned out, you see. That's how you make your own luck. She knows, of course – Mrs Lex, I mean. But I'm not supposed to talk about it. You won't tell, will you?'

'Of course not. What happened to your baby?'

'Oh, I lost it.' Dolly sounded regretful. Not crushed and broken, like Uncle Chen's Shen Shen had looked those times when it was whispered that her women's cycles had started again, that there would be no grandson coming. Nothing was ever said out loud, of course. Even if a child was born, its arrival was not mentioned until it had lived for a month. And at that infant's first-month announcement, it was described as a year old, so that any wicked spirits or jealous gods would not see it as vulnerable or worth stealing.

'Mrs Lexington helped me lose it.'

She held out her hand for the feathered pin and I handed it to her even as I remembered to shut my gaping mouth. Was Dolly aware of what she had just said? Of course she was. It was her body that had been carrying the lost baby.

'I suppose there won't be any more, now it's gone. I can feel it here where it was, a small ache.' She pressed a hand to her belly.

'Do you need to see a doctor? Or the pharmacy? The pharmacist, Dr Shankar, is very–' I stopped, remembering Dr Shankar was still in detention.

'Pharmacists aren't doctors, silly. Anyway, Shankar can't be a pharmacist, he's Indian. He probably just works there. But he was so sweet and helpful when I told him about the rash in my lady parts just after we got here. He gave me a cream that cleared it up. You were right, by the way.'

'About the baby?' I said stupidly, my mind still on Shen Shen desperately wanting babies, and the people who had whispered that if I had been given away, or drowned in time, the bad luck I brought into the family might not have killed my parents. I liked Shen Shen and I desperately hoped she would have a healthy baby this time – even if it was only a girl. And even if it meant I would never be able to go back to live at Chen Mansion again.

'About the feathers, silly. You're right about the best ones all coming from Bald Bernie. But Mrs Lex didn't like me taking any-thing from him, so I didn't want to say. Rose said it only encouraged him. But, if you ask me, she could be a little more encouraging herself.'

'Did you tell Mr Hemsworth we were going to the Dungeon early to do work that morning?'

'Of course not. Why would I? You said it was a secret. Anyway, the police already asked us that – don't you remember? We both said, "No."'

'So nobody else knew except you and me?'

'I knew. Dolly told me what you two were up to.' Rose was standing in the doorway, leaning against the frame. I wondered how long she had been there, listening. 'Dolly asked me to go along to keep her company while you did her work. And I had to tell Mrs Lexington when Dolly wasn't around for breakfast. But neither of us rushed over to ask Mr Hemsworth to surprise you there.'

I was sure Rose had tried to dissuade Dolly. Rose was far more cautious and conservative than Dolly. And I could tell she had disliked Bernie Hemsworth as much as I had. Though probably with far less reason. She wouldn't have said anything to him.

Dolly had spread out her feathers and was looking at them. 'I might make a sash to wear at the foundation-stone party,' she said. 'I can use those red and yellow feathers and sew them onto the fabric left over from making that yellow dress, so I can wear them together to the party. There should be enough. What do you think, Rose?'

'I thought that was supposed to be my yellow dress,' Rose said. 'I paid for the material.'

'Of course it is, Rosy-Posy. But you'll lend it to me, won't you? I don't have a thing to wear to the foundation-stone launch and you know you don't look good in yellow. Everyone's going to be there, right? The governor and all the important brass from the colonial office.'

'And the people from the Detective Unit,' Rose said. 'If you want them to think you're still in shock and not ready to work, maybe you should stay at home.'

'Oh, no! No, I can't! I haven't been to a party for ages! I'm dying of boredom here!'

'I'm sure they'll understand you need some time off,' I said. 'I'll speak to them.'

'Oh, thank you, Su Lin!' All of Dolly's moods were exaggerated. Now she got up and flung her arms around me, almost knocking me over. 'Do you think there'll be dancing?'

'They may not want you back,' Rose said, 'now they know you had to get Su Lin in to help you because you couldn't do the work.'

'Well, you couldn't even go into the office!' Dolly snapped. 'And as long as Sergeant Pillay is there, you'll never be able to, will you?'

Rose glanced quickly at me. I assumed Dolly had told her Prakesh and I were friends.

'It must have been awful for you. But if you get to know some people—' I could introduce her to Parshanti, I thought. Parshanti was only half-Indian, and female, and would be less frightening than Prakesh.

Rose shook her head. 'I try not to think about it.'

'But why do they think the man who attacked you is in Singapore? And that he'll try to get in touch with Dolly?'

'That's what men do, when it comes to Dolly,' Mrs Lexington said, reappearing with a glass of iced tea for me. 'I don't think they know why.'

I hadn't realised how thirsty I was, but that tea went down in one deliciously cool draught.

Dolly, smiling to herself, winked at me. There was something else she wanted to tell me but couldn't say with the others there.

'I wonder where all those feathers came from,' I said. Bernie hadn't struck me as any kind of naturalist.

'Mr Hemsworth must have found them somewhere. He was always wandering around outside.'

The fastidious Bernie Hemsworth wandering around outside? I couldn't see it.

'You're going to the foundation-stone-laying ceremony tomorrow, aren't you, Su Lin?' Mrs Lexington went on.

'I suppose so,' I said, without thinking about it. Everyone was expected to be there, looking appreciative and supportive.

'I hope it won't be too much for you,' she added.

I wanted to ask Dolly if she knew that Colonel Mosley-Partington believed Bose might try to contact her. But she wasn't likely to tell me the truth while Mrs Lexington and Rose were there.

'Would you like to walk with me down the hill?' I asked Dolly.

'It's not safe,' Rose said quickly.

Dolly started to protest, but Rose said, 'If they ask her how you are, do you want her to have to tell them you were well enough to go walking?' and Dolly subsided.

Poor Rose. Now I knew what had happened I could see her nose was slightly crooked and there was a faint scar on her left temple. It wasn't surprising she was afraid to go walking.

Dolly actually seemed happier than she had before. Rose and Mrs Lexington were much more tense and nervous, keeping close to her all the time, as though afraid something might happen to her.

It must be nice to have people so concerned about you. No one cared that I was spending my nights alone in the shophouse.

'Do you know Bernie may have been watching you?' I asked.

'Oh, yes. He told us Colonel Mosley-Partington asked him to watch us, especially me. It was for our protection, in case the killers came after us.' Dolly said easily. 'He thinks – thought, I mean – that Alan told us about his top-secret mission back to England, but he didn't.'

'Have you heard anything about who killed poor Mr Hemsworth?' Mrs Lexington asked me. 'Or what he was doing there that morning?'

But I had nothing to tell her.

Mr Meganck and
Paper Bark Trees

I was thinking about Bernie Hemsworth and the feathers as I left Mrs Lexington's house.

Bernie had not seemed interested in birds. I knew some *ang mohs* were fascinated by them, even those too small to be worth eating. Mr Meganck, who tutored the governor's sons, was a keen bird-watcher. He was often seen standing outside the Fullerton Building post office, staring up into the crown of the old rain tree, muttering things like 'White-crested laughingthrush', or '*Gerygone sulphurea*', which is a yellow-breasted fly-eater that warbles scales of three to five notes – I met him once and was treated to a half-hour roadside lecture and whistled demonstration. You learned not to ask what Mr Meganck was looking at if you were in a hurry because he could talk about beak curvatures and wing spans for hours.

The only time I heard Bernie mention a bird was when he complained that the chicken in the chicken rendang served at the Greeters Club wasn't crispy.

Chicken rendang, a savoury dry curry cooked in coconut milk, has never been crispy. But in Singapore a white man's complaint overrides tradition. From then on, Greeters Club chicken rendang was dunked in seasoned tapioca flour and fried to crispiness in lard before being served alongside a dish of curry gravy. It wasn't an improvement.

———◆———

When I left Mrs Lexington's house, instead of retracing my steps down the Fort Canning Rise I walked around and beyond the house, following the path that ran uphill along the fencing. Wild grass and tapioca grew on the other side, already sending exploratory seed heads and tendrils through the metal mesh. Beyond them, trunks of trees rose and forked, shadowy between the thick canopy above and dense thorny tangle below. I don't know what I was hoping to find but I felt drawn onwards and upwards.

From the house porch I had seen the edging of jungle above, beyond the exposed earth of the construction site. I wanted to find out what you could see of the house from up there, that vantage point among the trees. Sometimes when you don't understand why something makes you feel uneasy, your inner wisdom is telling you to find a different perspective.

Unseen birds called, insects buzzed and clicked as I followed the uneven path upwards. From somewhere in the distance came a monkey's scolding cry. I stopped when I reached the first clump of trees. There was a small clearing beyond them, and from there I looked down on the porch and side gate of the black-and-white house as well as the curve of its front driveway.

From the other side of the clearing, a trail led deeper into the primary forest.

Something about the place made me uneasy. Dry leaves crushed underfoot, climbing vines pushed aside. Had someone else been there recently?

And then I heard voices further up the trail. High, happy boys' voices. Walking towards them, I recognised with pleasure the tall, thin man in intense discussion with two small boys. They were Caucasian, but tanned a healthy brown and carrying backpacks and nets.

Their serious tone reminded me of the Mission ladies planning a major fundraising dinner. Apparently their conversation had to do with the dietary requirements of the three-horned rhino beetle. The boys seemed to be making passionate presentations rather than arguments.

'They feed on dead leaves and old fruit.'

'Not just old fruit. They eat fruit and seeds and even fungus!'

The tropical rainforest felt familiar and welcoming again.

'Hello, Mr Meganck.' I stepped forward, my uneasiness forgotten. 'Hello, boys.'

Greg and Pat McPherson looked round at the interruption. Mr Meganck put a hand on each of their shoulders. 'You're both right. The beetles are herbivorous. The adults eat nectar and sap. It's the larvae that eat decaying plant matter. Larvae and adults often eat different foods. Good to see you, Miss Chen. If you're interested in fruit we found a couple of rambutan trees.'

'They're not very big.' Greg, the older boy, held open his bag to show me a collection of the hairy yellow and red fruit. 'But they're really sweet. Would you like some? They're good if you're thirsty.'

I declined.

'Why don't you two take a rambutan break? Remember to disperse the seeds and shells over a wide area—'

'Like monkeys do!' the boys chorused, and rushed off.

Mr Meganck turned back. 'Is something wrong, Miss Chen?'

'Wrong? Oh, no. I was at Mrs Lexington's house. I thought I would take a walk on the slope behind. Is this a nature lesson?'

'It started with a history lesson on Borneo, actually. With a little physics and mathematics thrown in. Geometry makes more sense when you're calculating the height of trees.'

He was a good teacher, I thought. The boys looked happily tired.

'Do you bring them here often?'

'It's one of our favourite trails. We walked over from MacRitchie. Oh, it's not that far. Much shorter than following the roads around. And much more interesting, what you come across. But we only make our excursions during the day and there are three of us so it's quite safe.'

Wild pigs and monkeys can be aggressive if you unintentionally approach their young, but something in the way he said this made me ask, 'Have you ever seen anyone else in the jungle around here?'

'We saw signs that someone has been here, hiding.' Mr Meganck glanced at the boys, who were still engrossed. 'Not a local hunter. Someone unfamiliar with the area. We tracked him, using Baden-Powell's *Scouting for Boys*, but we haven't seen him. We found the trees where he watches the house, though. A wicked, despicable man.'

The vehemence in his voice shocked me.

'Who?'

'The man watching the house.'

I thought of Chirag Bose. 'How do you know he's wicked?'

'More than once I've found a dead lorikeet with its coloured feathers stripped off. The colourless down was left. Who would do that to a dead bird? Feathers to attract a mate. No more use once the bird is dead. I suspect someone was killing them with cigarette stubs.'

'Killing birds with cigarettes?' There was a feverish gleam in Meganck's eyes that made me wonder if he was mad.

'The lorikeet is a parrot and, like all parrots, curious about objects. Nicotine poisoning occurs when a bird chews apart a cigarette. The stub contains a quarter or more of the nicotine of the whole cigarette. Several times I found stubs all over the place. Not now,' he added, as I looked around. 'I cleared them up. But whoever left them here was responsible for the deaths of at least five birds. If I ever get my hands on him . . .'

Mr Meganck spoke swiftly and quietly, so coldly furious that, for a moment, I was afraid of him. Le Froy always said every real man has something he would kill to defend. I saw it was true of Mr Meganck.

'Where were they?'

'Over there, behind the cajeput trees.'

'Cajeput trees – not those paper bark trees?'

'Ah, yes. The tiger balm trees, cajeput trees, paper bark trees. Self-explanatory, given how sheets of bark peel off. "Cajeput" comes from *kayu putih*, meaning "white wood", for much the same reason. It's a good wood for fuel and useful for poles and construction. And because of its texture, the soft bark is used for insulation, making mattresses and pillows and as a packing material.'

It wasn't just birds Mr Meganck could hold forth on. I saw why he loved teaching. He wanted to share his fascination with things.

It could have been either Bernie or Bose who had been smoking and spying on the house, I realised.

'The governor's been receiving letters saying birds are eating the diseased cajeput bark, getting infected and losing their feathers. I assured him there was nothing to worry about.'

'So those trees aren't diseased? Not in any way that might infect people – or birds?'

Mr Meganck laughed. 'Of course not! Birds moult their feathers regularly, just like humans shed their hair and wear out their clothes. It's natural. And the cajeput has healing properties. Steam distillation of its leaves and twigs produces the oil that is a key ingredient in Tiger Balm. Yes, it is poisonous if swallowed in large quantities, but so are grapes. You don't see people calling for a ban on grapes on the island, do you?'

'You never saw the man watching the house?'

He shook his head. 'Just signs someone was here in the night. Sometimes I come here in the early morning – there's a pair of brown hawk-owls nesting in the area. If you come early enough you'll hear the change in their "coo-coo-coop" calls. But you have to be here just after dawn.'

'What kind of signs?'

'Cigarette stubs and cigarette papers on the ground. Someone tearing off sheets of bark. At least two different people, I'd say – different brands of cigarette. Very bad practice. Apart from the damage to the birds, you don't want monkeys or ground lizards getting a taste for processed tobacco.'

Had the watcher in the trees been Bald Bernie? He had smoked, but he had always stayed out of the sun, behind screens and as far away as possible from snakes, mosquitoes and mud. Or Bose? Here to stalk Rose or Dolly?

But the letters Bernie had written about the 'diseased' trees and poisoned birds suggested he had been here. Looking at the peeling bark on the trees, I could see how they might give that impression. And Mr Meganck had also found dead birds. Bernie hadn't known the poor creatures had been poisoned by his cigarettes, not the trees he complained about.

I could imagine Bernie watching the house from the clump of trees, not bothering to hide himself. Why should he hide? If the women saw him, so much the better. They would know he was keeping an eye on them. They ought to be grateful.

If finding dead birds under the paper bark tree had made Bernie think that the trees were diseased and dangerous, could he have taken the lorikeets' feathers and given them to Dolly?

Rose might have noticed someone watching the house, I thought. There was nothing wrong with her eyesight, unlike Dolly's. Dolly needed spectacles but was too vain to wear them. That was the reason for the vague, vacant gaze that men like Bernie found so appealing.

'You should come back when the trees are in flower. The lorikeets, the flying foxes, they all love the paper bark trees,' Mr Meganck said. He was gentle again, but I could not forget the cold rage I had seen in him. 'The nectar is a magnet to them. It will be magnificent. As long as the man with his cigarette stubs doesn't come back.'

Prakesh

———◆———

Sergeant Prakesh Pillay wasn't at the Detective Shack. I didn't want to wait there for him so I went round the corner to Shankar & Sons to see if Parshanti was in – and found Prakesh outside.

'Prakesh! I'm so glad you're here. I want to talk to you. Bernie Hemsworth might have been watching the women in Mrs Lexington's house. And if it wasn't him, it might have been that Indian terrorist, Bose! That means he really is in Singapore. If we can prove that, they'll stop picking on local people and go after him.'

I went up to the shop door. 'Come on, let's go inside. Parshanti will want to know.'

'We can't go in. It's closed. They're still holding Dr Shankar.'

I pushed at the door. He was right, it was locked. I was surprised. The shop door was usually left open, like Uncle Chen's shop, though Mrs Shankar's sewing customers preferred to go round to the back.

'We should go and tell them about Bose in the jungle above Fort Canning!' Unless of course it had really been Bernie.

'Don't talk nonsense. Why would Bernie be watching the house? If he wanted to watch them he would be in the house.'

'He might have been watching to see if anyone went to the house at night, but they were too smart for him and saw him. Maybe that's why they killed him.'

'Anyway, Bose isn't here. He went down in his plane over the sea. Case closed. I can't believe you're swallowing their propaganda. They are making up stories about Indian terrorists and Chinese Communists just to frighten you – so that you don't see they are the ones you should be scared of!'

I studied Prakesh. His posture was oddly cramped and he seemed to be dismissing my words before I finished saying them, 'What's wrong with you? What's wrong with your shoulder?'

He was favouring his right arm and shoulder. I reached out to touch what looked like a bruise on the right side of his neck. He flinched and pushed my fingers away,

'Nothing. It's nothing.'

'Prakesh—'

'Don't touch me!' He jerked away painfully and glared at me.

'Prakesh, what's wrong? I don't understand. Are you hurt? Let me see. What happened? Do you need to see Dr Leask? Or a *bomoh*?'

'Just shut up!'

'Su Lin,' Parshanti said.

She came down the narrow external stairs that led directly to their family quarters on the second floor. I was pleased to see her. I reached out and squeezed her hand affectionately. She didn't resist but there was a strange sideways focus to her attention. Like she was concentrating so hard on something else that she barely noticed us.

It was because Dr Shankar was still under detention, I thought. If I had a father in prison I would be sitting outside the gaol every minute of every day until he was released. I was sure Parshanti felt the same.

'They still haven't charged Dr Shankar with anything, have they?' Even Colonel Mosley-Partington with all his connections would be laughed out of court if he tried. 'I heard Mrs Shankar has been allowed in to see him. How is he?'

Parshanti ignored my questions, which I'd realised were stupid as soon as I'd asked them. Dr Shankar was still in prison. How could he be?

'Prakesh is hurt, but he won't tell me what happened,' I said.

'Sergeant Pillay was taken in for questioning by Colonel Mostly-Poopington and his military. They were a little rough,' Parshanti said.

'What?' It was my turn not to believe what I was hearing.

Neither of them replied. It was as though they were both listening in to the wireless, but I lacked the necessary antenna.

'How do you know that?' Prakesh demanded, glaring at her.

'My father told Mam when they let her in to see him. He said they kept you in there for hours. He wanted me to check on you to make sure you were all right. And to tell your family where you were if they didn't let you out. That's why I sent you that message.'

I couldn't believe what I was hearing. 'Why would they question you again?'

'They want me to tell them where Chirag Bose is hiding. They think I'm a spy betraying the Crown. I'm beginning to think that might not be such a bad idea, given how the Crown is treating me.'

I realised my talking about Bose being in the jungle spying on

Mrs Lexington's house would start them off again. 'They think you're one of the Indian Nationalists in Singapore trying to link up with the Japanese? That's crazy!' I meant to provoke Prakesh into laughing and telling me he would never do such a thing. But he didn't laugh.

'It's not like that,' he said. 'All they want is to work for the good of all Asians, not only Indians. You can't see what the colonials are doing to us here because you've been completely brainwashed by them. You think that British people are gods. You think that we should all bow down and worship them!'

'Of course I don't,' I said, stung.

'But you accept without question that only white men are smart enough to run this island. Only white women are clean enough to go into hospitals to help the sick. Only white doctors can be trusted—'

'That's not true. Dr Shankar is a very good doctor. You know as well as I do that he's the best doctor around here.'

I stopped. Hearing my own words made the injustice to Dr Shankar seem even worse. He was truly the best doctor in Singapore and Johor in his medical skills and his care for his patients. But the *ang mohs* looked down on him. He should have been running his own laboratory in the hospital – running the hospital, even. But that would never happen as long as only white doctors could treat patients.

Prakesh put a gentle hand on my arm. 'Su Lin, I'm only trying to make things better for us. For everybody. You shouldn't try to stop me. You should help me.'

'Help you to do what? What are you doing? Are you breaking the law?'

'Bad laws should be broken.'

'No.' That at least I was certain of. 'If you want to be part of a society you must obey its laws or change them.'

'The laws here are designed to keep us in order like sheep. Like dogs, at best. Well fed till it's our turn to be eaten or sent into the dogfight.'

'My father hasn't been charged with Bernie's murder,' Parshanti said. 'Nobody will say exactly why they are holding him, but they are. At least Le Froy made them let Mam and me in to Military HQ to see him. They tried to make Pa say he and Prakesh had been working together.'

'They work together all the time,' I said, thinking of the times Dr Shankar had helped with police cases. Parshanti's father was much more open to new technology and chemical tests than the less experienced, and far younger, Dr Leask.

'They accused Pa of faking his medical degree. Then they said he hated white people for not letting him practise when he had a degree. They even said he married a white woman so that he could upset the laws of nature by dominating her. Mam was so furious when she heard that, she was all for applying her secateurs to the colonel's man parts so he would never dominate another she-donkey.'

I couldn't help laughing. Even Prakesh smiled.

'At least they let me go,' he said. 'They're using Hemsworth's report that Dr Shankar tried to poison him to hold him.'

'If Pa had wanted to poison Bernie, he wouldn't have strangled and stabbed him into the bargain.' Parshanti snorted. 'He had a rash, and Pa offered him some prickly heat powder, that's all.'

'Prakesh, that piece of paper I found in the back of Bernie's notebook. Did you find out what the numbers mean?'

Prakesh hesitated. I could tell he meant to put me off, but Parshanti said, 'What paper? What numbers?' and I saw he wanted to give her something to make her feel better.

'Maybe. The numbers seem to refer to one of the missing diamonds. But there's something odd about them. They don't belong to any of the mines currently registered in India. The facet codes suggest it was cut in Surat but, again, not by an official agency. And if you believe the measurements, it's much larger than the diamonds usually sent to Surat.'

'Then where did it come from?'

'Who knows? South Africa? Brazil? Russia? A lot of places run illegal mines. But if it's one of the missing diamonds, they may all have come from illegal mines in India.'

Dolly wanted to find a pawnbroker, I remembered. Could she have brought in that diamond? Where had she got it?

They started to walk off together without me. Parshanti had not come down because she had seen me in the street: Prakesh had been waiting for her.

I wanted so much to talk things over with one of them. I couldn't bring it up with Le Froy, who seemed so distant, these days, especially if it would get Dr Shankar into more trouble. And I couldn't talk to my grandmother. Ah Ma counted on me to explain the doings of foreigners to her. And I couldn't involve Uncle Chen, who barely held himself in control. Unlike Le Froy, Uncle Chen would jump in and act too fast.

'Are you going to the foundation-stone ceremony?' I called after them.

Only Prakesh answered, without stopping. 'If I'm still on duty. If they don't decide it's too dangerous to have locals and Indians there.'

Once I had thought Prakesh was soft on Parshanti but now I knew that was not why they were going off together. I didn't want to think about where they were going.

Besides, what information did I really have? Cigarette stubs and papers showed that someone, probably Bernie, had been watching Mrs Lexington's house.

Had Dolly taken that diamond to a pawnbroker? Did she know more than she let on about Alan Weston's death? Where was the diamond now?

And had Bernie had been killed because he found out?

Dolly was central to this, somehow. She had known Bernie Hemsworth and Alan Weston, as well as Chirag Bose.

And as for how Bernie had known we would be going to the Detective Shack that morning, who had been in a better position to tell him than Dolly? I had been with her since early that morning, and I could swear she had not been out killing anyone in the night. Her clothes had been too fresh. No matter how carefully you kill someone, it leaves traces on your skirts if not on you. I hadn't spent years helping with the household laundry for nothing. But had she arranged to meet Bernie, and for Bose to kill him, while I provided her with an alibi?

I had assumed she was innocent because I couldn't imagine her being devious enough to lie and scheme. But what if I had under-estimated her?

Maybe Dolly had been fooling us all and laughing at how stupid we were.

As Le Froy had always told me, 'You are clever. But when clever and cunning clash, cunning usually wins – at first. Someone like you has to learn to survive long enough to win in the end.'

Foundation-stone Ceremony

———◆———

I loitered in Uncle Chen's shop. I was stalling. I knew it and didn't like myself for doing it, but that didn't make any difference.

Right now the back room was very appealing.

My small, ridiculous but immediate problem was the invitation from Mrs Viola Jane McPherson.

The governor of the Straits Settlements, Sir Gregory McPherson, was going to lay the foundation stone of the Supreme Court Building. A time capsule beneath would be retrieved in the year 3000. Presumably the stone would be smashed with equal ceremony for that to happen. Today's ceremony and party doubled as an occasion to introduce new arrivals to Singapore and each other. Recently appointed officials and their families traditionally came out at the start of the school holidays to get to know the area.

I had been to such events before. Previously I had been one of the 'safe' locals provided to answer questions such as whether local servants would mind sleeping outside with the family dogs and what it would cost them to get local herbal concoctions to increase male ability and decrease female fertility. Usually I ended up helping with food in the kitchen or keeping the children occupied and out of trouble.

Western-style formal parties are not fun. People stand about in uncomfortable clothes instead of sitting around platters of food with their shoes off. The *ang mohs* would be well behaved during the ceremony, but later the men would go out to get more drinks and create trouble on the streets and the women would go home and be nasty to their servants.

On those occasions, I had been summoned with strict instructions: show your identification papers at the back door; only English speakers allowed. And for such occasions, I wore my *samfoo*. The short-sleeved loose-fitting top and loose elastic-waisted trousers made of coarse cotton were much more comfortable in the heat than the starched, formal clothes the white people wore on special occasions. Also, there was no risk that a gust of wind from a passing car or a drunken soldier would flick up my skirt revealing my underwear. And it rendered me invisible.

But where did an invitation from the governor's wife place me? I looked at the clothes on my narrow plank bed: two cotton dresses, one floral, one checked, and a *samfoo* much like the one I was wearing now, but less worn and therefore less faded.

If I were a guest, as Mrs McPherson's invitation suggested, I should wear a frock. I decided on the brown-and-yellow check. As I got changed I reminded myself Mrs McPherson was being nice, and I really wanted to find out more about Bernie Hemsworth's murder. Or at least find proof that Dr Shankar couldn't have had anything to do with it.

At least I could talk to Prakesh. He was certain to be on duty at the ceremony as the Detective Unit would be responsible for security. If he was in a better mood, I could find out more about Dolly's diamond. And if he was still in a bad mood, I could try to talk him out of it.

———◆———

'You still here, ah?' Uncle Chen, said, through the cigarette in his mouth. He looked so comfortable on his stool in his usual singlet and sarong. 'I thought you were attending some fancy ceremony.'

'I'm going now,' I said flatly. Acting perky and interested took energy that I wasn't willing to waste on Uncle Chen. I would switch it on when I got off the tram.

'Terrible, eh? Some people *kenah* put on fancy clothes and eat fancy foods and talk fancy English to fancy people.' Uncle Chen grinned, his cigarette arm curled around the knee against his chest. '*Kenah*' generally referred to unavoidable duties: 'I *kenah* sit here and smoke cigarette. Have fun. Don't eat too much beef or you will smell like them.'

———◆———

In the sea of *ang moh* faces, far more white men than white women, of course, I saw a few young locals, mostly men from very wealthy families who had been sent away to study in Oxford and Cambridge. But apart from them, and myself, the only locals were the serving staff. It was a grand occasion and the smell of rich food, rich women and rich cigars almost made me dizzy.

I've always liked watching people, and this was my chance to put faces to many of the names I had seen in the newspapers. It is natural to be interested in the people behind big names and celebrities, I think. We are often more amazed to see a famous person doing ordinary things than when someone we know does something extraordinary. Like when the *karang guni* man's son rescued a visiting actress's child who had climbed up the shade trellis of the Sunrise Hotel just before the frame gave way: the papers described how the child's mother cried over her child and was grateful to his 'unknown' rescuer.

I also hoped to see Parshanti outside. She usually came to watch the guests arriving. She would study and sketch outfits that had been brought in from Paris and New York, which would be incorporated into Mrs Shankar's next creations.

But I didn't see Prakesh or Parshanti anywhere.

I shouldn't have been surprised. Maybe they were tracking down the terrorist assassin, Bose, as I stood uselessly at the edge of the gathering, clutching my now limp invitation card that no one had asked to see. Why was I wasting time there?

I saw Governor Gregory McPherson across the courtyard. He was easy to spot, with his height, military bearing and silver-grey hair. There were people around him, and Mrs McPherson, of course. I stayed in my corner by the potted bougainvillaeas, but to my surprise Viola Jane McPherson caught my eye and looked delighted to see me, waving me over to join her, then taking my hand. 'Su Lin, we haven't seen you for ages. The boys told me they met you on a nature hike. They want to visit your uncle's shop. Why haven't you come to see me? How have you been?'

'I am well. Please tell the boys if they let me know when they want to visit my uncle's shop I'll make sure to be there.'

'They will be delighted! But I hope you'll tell them yourself.

They are here somewhere. Some older boys got up a game of rounders and let them play. I hope they're not making a nuisance of themselves.' She looked vaguely around, but there was no sign of trouble. 'And please pass my respects to the dashing chief inspector.'

'I'm no longer working for Inspector Le Froy,' I said.

She looked curious, but I didn't want to go into it in a public place. And not with the wife of the island's highest-ranking public official, no matter how charming.

'Isn't this such a circus?' Mrs McPherson changed the subject. 'The time capsule that's going to be buried underneath the foundations is going to contain today's newspapers and a list of the chief businesses of the Straits Settlements. It is due to be retrieved in the year 3000.'

'Will Singapore still exist by then?'

'Will the world still exist? If it does, you can be sure there will be rich and powerful businessmen, much like there are today. In a very real way it's them and their money that run the Colonial Office and the empire because without money the government can do nothing. Without men like them, we would not need to establish colonial offices out east. We could simply do business with the people already here.'

I could tell she was trying to comfort me for losing my job, and that she had no idea how it had come about.

'I just hope people don't get hurt here,' she went on. 'You hear of such terrible things happening in India these days.'

'People are getting hurt here . . . for not being white people.' I shouldn't have said that, but with my mind on Prakesh and Dr Shankar, it slipped out. 'I'm sorry—'

'Of course.' Mrs McPherson understood immediately. She lowered her voice. 'I heard the sweet doctor who treated my boys was arrested. I'm sorry. If it's any consolation, I don't believe men like Colonel Mosley-Partington know they're prejudiced. They've just never worked with anyone different from themselves until they leave England and are suddenly faced with a world of strange people who don't think them anything special. It must be terrifying.'

It sounded as if she understood them better than I did. But I didn't want to understand men like Bernie Hemsworth and Colonel Mosley-Partington as much as I wanted to go on hating them.

Just then, there was a commotion. Someone came rushing over to say there had been an accident on the other side of the refreshment tent. There had been high jinks going on and someone had climbed up one of the statues in the partially constructed fountain. It had toppled over and landed on a boy. It was thought his leg was broken.

Mrs McPherson hitched her skirts above her knees and ran. When one of her children might be hurt, speed came before decorum. It was one of the reasons I liked her so much. I hurried after her, making good time despite my uneven legs.

It was a broken leg, but not attached to either of the McPherson boys.

The statue's arm had broken under the weight of the young man who had climbed onto it. He was screaming in agony, women were crying and the loudspeaker was calling people to attention for 'God Save The King' to signal the official start of the ceremony.

And I saw Dr Leask give the injured man something to drink that knocked him out in less than a minute.

I pushed my way through the crowd to him, grabbing his arm

when less invasive means didn't work. 'What did you give him? What knocked him out?'

'Chloral hydrate drops. Harmless.'

'But he'll wake up – with no problems?'

'Don't worry. He's just fallen asleep. I give it to children when they can't get to sleep because of toothache. Sometimes to ladies at their time of the month or if they're having trouble sleeping. Never any ill effects. Refreshing, I'm told.'

'Could it be put in orange squash?'

Until now, Dr Leask's attention had been on the makeshift stretcher on which the unconscious man was being manoeuvred into the back seat of the governor's sedan, but now he stopped and looked at me. 'Why would you do that?'

'Those two damp rings on the wooden desk when Mr Hemsworth was found.' I had mentioned them, but they wouldn't mean anything to men who had never had to worry about watermarks on furniture. 'It looked like there had been condensation from two glasses.'

Dr Leask still looked blank. His new patient was in the car and someone was calling to him to join them. Dr Shankar would have understood instantly, I was sure. Right then, I wished Dr Shankar was there so badly I could have screamed. But Dr Shankar was locked up – and I suddenly realised that drawing attention to a drug that he would have had access to might not be doing him any favours. But this was Dr Leask, a friend of Dr Shankar. Dr Leask, whom I suspected of having a secret crush on Parshanti Shankar for years.

'If Bernie Hemsworth had been offered a cold drink by someone he trusted and if chloral hydrate was added to a glass of chilled orange squash . . .'

Of course his immediate responsibility was to the patient now being conveyed to his surgery. But I saw from the dilation of his pupils that he understood.

'Whoever was with Bernard Hemsworth when he died could have given him knockout drops in a drink. He could have been unconscious when he was strangled.'

My mind raced on. If that was the case, a woman could easily have killed him, strangling and stabbing. Neither took too much physical strength if the victim was already unconscious. And if Alan Weston had been killed in India the same way, soon after visiting Dolly ...

Dr Leask nodded. 'Of course. A Mickey Finn Special, as the Americans call it. May not show up in the blood but I'll check. I must go.'

Prakesh might not believe my theory. He might even see it as part of a plan to frame Dr Shankar since he had access to medicines. But I was not thinking of Dr Shankar now. I was thinking of Dolly. I had thought Bernie had a soft spot for her. But what if he had been keeping an eye on her because he suspected her?

Alan Weston had visited Dolly just before he was killed. If she'd asked Bernie to meet her at the Dungeon without telling anyone, he would have done it. I could only swear she had been with me since I'd met her that morning. I had no idea what she might have done during the night.

But despite the facts, it was hard to believe Dolly Darling, who looked so smart and shiny but wasn't the sharpest knife in the drawer, could have killed a man – or two – and then convinced me she was shocked by the body.

Unless, of course, she had fooled us all, including me.

I wanted to find Prakesh and tell him. He wasn't outside with the other men on duty. None of them knew where he was, except that he was supposed to be there and must be around somewhere. The governor's security detail told me they hadn't seen him either.

After our last encounter, I wasn't sure about passing this information to Chief Inspector Le Froy. But I couldn't have, even if I'd wanted to, because he wasn't there either. That was less surprising. He had been known to arrange pirate-tracking raids just to avoid official social functions.

As I was scanning the perimeter for any sign of Prakesh, I saw Mrs Lexington, Rose and Dolly arriving together in a taxi.

'We're late, aren't we? We went to an afternoon film and ordered a taxi to get into the mood for the ceremony. And then our taxi had a puncture. I hope we're in time for the party even if we missed the dreary official speeches.'

Mrs Lexington was trying to be gay and in a party mood. But I could tell she was tense and strained. She hated being late. It went against her love of order.

'You haven't missed anything.' I explained about the broken leg that had delayed the speeches.

Now I was torn between going to find Prakesh and staying to keep an eye on Dolly. I finally decided to go. Even an experienced murderer would have trouble strangling someone in the middle of the crowd at Government House, especially with all the bored security personnel longing for a bit of excitement.

'Keep an eye on Dolly,' I whispered to Rose.

Rose's large dark eyes looked down her (slightly crooked) nose at me. 'What are you talking about?'

'Just watch her,' I said urgently. 'Make sure she doesn't put anything in your drink or anyone else's.'

I doubted Dolly had any reason to poison Rose. But people always pay more attention when they suspect they're under threat.

It worked. Rose's eyes grew larger and she stared at me. 'Dolly? You can't think—'

'I have to go,' I said. 'I'll talk to you later.'

But Prakesh wasn't at the station. He wasn't in his quarters either. I went back to the Detective Shack and left him a note. If I didn't see him soon, I would tell Le Froy about the chloral hydrate.

The Finding of Prakesh

◆

There were no lamps and no windows looking into the alley, so it was a popular spot for courting couples. The old *karang guni*, with his gunny sack, thought of it as his territory. He often found old newspapers, half-smoked cigarettes and even items of clothing there, things that could be sold or put to good use.

There was a sound, a scuffle. A muttered curse.

'Hey! None of that around here,' he called. He was going to back away but heard the sound of feet fleeing. He got the impression it was a woman's feet, though later he couldn't say why. The sound of the footsteps, he said. But, again, he could not say why.

He headed towards the makeshift altar someone had set up next to a collapsed wall. Some people avoided such altars, fearing the spirits of the dead they were set up to appease. But the old *karang guni* saw no reason to fear the dead over the living. No ghosts had ever objected to him helping himself to the sweets and rice cakes people left to propitiate them.

As he moved further from the last streetlamps on the main

road, his eyes gradually adapted. He squinted. It seemed as though tonight a figure was sitting there in the dark. A man.

'Hey, you. What are you doing here?'

The old *karang guni* man moved closer. It was a disappointed lover, he thought, sitting and moping after a fight with his lady-love. Talking him into visiting the bar-brothel on the next street might be worth a tip. More, if the man turned out to be a big spender.

'Hey, why you all alone?'

There was no response from the man.

The *karang guni* man went up to the figure leaning against the wall and tapped him on the shoulder. It was an Indian man, he saw. His face was twisted in pain, and his eyes were wide open and staring.

Part Two

Prakesh Dead

◆

The two men looked down on the body of Sergeant Prakesh
Pillay.

'Do what you can.'

'I'll do whatever I have to.'

◆

I got to the Detective Shack just after eight thirty the next morning,
hoping to catch Prakesh. It was a warm, windy morning and a bright
cloudless sky predicted a really hot day. I reminded myself to give
Shen Shen's plant pots a second watering that evening.

After tossing and turning all night, I had decided that if Prakesh
wasn't at the Detective Shack I would tell Le Froy about the chloral
hydrate. That would explain why there had been rings on the
wooden table top, and why Bernie Hemsworth hadn't put up more
of a fight. He could push Dr Leask to find out if there was some
way of testing for the drug in Bernie's system. The sooner those
tests were run the better.

But as soon as I pushed open the door I saw something was very wrong.

Constable Kwok was the only officer in the main office. He looked miserable and sick, and he was being screamed at. Loudly.

'My husband couldn't have killed Sergeant Pillay. He was locked up by you people. That proves he had nothing to do with all this. But instead of letting him go you put him in solitary confinement? Are you mad? What are you doing to him in there?' It was a furious Mrs Shankar.

'He was killed while my father is in prison so my father can't have done it!' Parshanti was there too, tearful and flaming furious.

'Dr Shankar is in the Naval and Armed Forces Infirmary for his own safety,' Constable Kwok said. He threw me a desperate look, but I couldn't help him.

I had my own screaming to do.

'Prakesh isn't dead!' I heard the high shrill voice coming out of my mouth. 'Of course Prakesh isn't dead. What are you talking about?'

None of them answered. They didn't have to.

'What happened?'

'Sergeant Pillay was found late last night in a back alley near the Jalan Besar entrance to the New World Amusement Park,' Constable Kwok said.

The New World Amusement Park was a huge open-air fairground with rides like Ferris wheels and carousels set among food stalls and amusement stands. There were also barber shops and nightclubs and two cinemas, but those cost extra. Most people stayed outside and watched Malay opera and Chinese theatrical performances for free after you paid the fairground's ten-cent admission fee.

It was a place for family outings with young children, where courting couples went to be terrified together on the ghost train and office workers went to let off steam with arcade games. Even the famous Charlie Chaplin had called it fascinating when he had visited five years ago with his brother Sydney.

It was also a popular meeting spot. But what had Prakesh been doing there when he should have been on duty at the foundation-stone ceremony? Had he followed someone, or had he been lured there and killed?

'I don't believe it. Where is he now?'

'In the mortuary. Or in transit.'

Parshanti turned to attack me. 'The Military Police let my father go when they got the news about Sergeant Pillay, but instead of releasing him, your chief inspector put him in solitary confinement. I tell you, he's gone mad!'

'I don't know,' Constable Kwok said, before I could ask. 'I don't know why. But, yes, Dr Shankar was moved to the isolation ward of the Naval and Armed Forces Infirmary.'

That was the prison quarantine area.

'Why? Is he sick? With something contagious?'

But poor Constable Kwok could only repeat that he didn't know.

Mrs Shankar always said she could smell a lie, the same way she could tell if there was nutmeg in a dish. It was the way her husband Ravi could listen to an excerpt of music and know whether it was by Mozart or Wagner. Now she was shaking her head and saying that everything Le Froy had said was a lie: 'I saw him yesterday evening. If he was coming down with anything I would have known. I'm going to the prison. And I'm not leaving till my husband leaves with me!'

Parshanti left with her mother. I wanted to go with them to find out what was happening to Dr Shankar, but the look she gave me was angry and warned me to stay away. Prakesh had been her friend too, and a good friend of her brother. I wanted to find out what had happened to him.

Constable Kwok looked relieved when the door slammed behind them. He wheezed, tried to clear his throat and spluttered. He had a bad cough and I suspect he would have been at home, sick, if they hadn't been so short-handed.

'They are checking his quarters,' Constable Kwok told me, though I hadn't asked. 'And the chief wanted to go over where he was found. They are talking to his family members.'

I got the feeling he was saying this to reassure himself that everything that could be done was being done. 'Do you know what happened?' Now I really thought Kwok was going to cry. 'Tell me,' I said. 'He wasn't at the ceremony yesterday.'

'He was supposed to go. He went off after getting a message. Several witnesses say they saw him sitting in a booth in the restaurant at the Great Eastern Hotel. Staff thought he was expecting someone. A waiter said there was someone talking with him, but it was dim and he didn't get a good look at them. They were in close conversation, so the waiter thought it best to leave them alone. No one noticed when they left.'

'A man, yes. But the waiter said it was a woman dressed as a man.'

'Why?'

'He didn't say. But he's one of those men who likes dressing as a lady himself so maybe he can tell.'

Prakesh Pillay would not have been on his guard against a woman. Like Bernie Hemsworth, he underrated women even when people were dropping dead around him. I could only guess the person had put something in his drink. Once the drug had taken effect she could have walked him outside and—

'Was Prakesh strangled and stabbed, like Bernie Hemsworth and Alan Weston?'

'I don't know. The autopsy report hasn't come in yet.'

And it would take longer than usual. Dr Leask had always counted on Dr Shankar's help but was working alone now. I had once thought it would be very interesting to study the secrets of the human body by watching a post-mortem. But even the thought of watching Prakesh being cut up made me feel sick. Constable Kwok snorted into a handkerchief. He acted as though it was because of his cold but I knew he was crying.

We both jumped when the door crashed open. But it wasn't Le Froy as I'd hoped.

'Rotten business, this!' Colonel Mosley-Partington said, with relish. 'Still haven't found the poor bugger's gun, have they?'

He looked around the room and his eyes came back to me. 'I thought we'd got rid of you, Miss Chen.' But he didn't tell me to leave and I didn't offer to. 'Did you know Le Froy was once supposed to have a brilliant mind? Perhaps it's deteriorated in this hellish climate.'

Traces

———◆———

Locard Exchange Principle: every contact leaves a trace.

There was no trace of Sergeant Prakesh Pillay's gun. The Webley-Fosbery revolver was the standard weapon in the Straits Settlements police force. According to regulations, local officers were allowed to bear arms only when on duty.

'Sergeant Pillay was in uniform and carrying his Webley,' Le Froy said, 'so he must have been following something up on his own. But there's nothing in his log.'

The pencil between Le Froy's fingers snapped, startling us. He had already broken two, I saw. He was angry with Prakesh for keeping secrets and getting himself killed.

'What does his family say?'

'His sisters thought Prakesh was on duty at the foundation-stone ceremony. But they will come up with a family emergency to explain why he wasn't there if it becomes an issue.'

Of course they would. That was what families did, both to support their dead son and to make sure they did not lose the death-on-duty compensation. And, of course, that would just make the investigation more difficult. It was a good thing they trusted de Souza enough to be honest. They knew he would lie, if he had to, to protect them but also that he wanted to find out what had happened to their brother.

'Kwok?' Le Froy turned to the constable.

Constable Kwok's fingers, still shaking, were clasped around the metal cup of tea I had put in front of him.

Since Dolly had not returned to the Detective Shack since Bernie Hemsworth's death, I had made myself useful. The mail had been sorted, the cups washed, the clocks wound and reset to the correct time. In the shock of Prakesh's death, no one had questioned my presence. Even Colonel Mosley-Partington accepted a cup of tea and a biscuit from me .

'I went out the back for a cigarette and I saw Sergeant Prakesh talking to a woman. He was angry and told me to go away. When he came in he told me he was gathering information that the chief – sorry, Chief – didn't want to see. He asked me as a favour not to mention the woman to you. Not to mention he was going off early. I asked where he was going, and what about later? He said there would be so many people at the event, no one would notice he wasn't there if I signed in for him. And, anyway, the chief probably wouldn't even turn up.' Kwok stopped in a fit of coughing.

'You should go and see Dr Shankar for that cough,' I told him.

I couldn't believe Dr Shankar was still detained. Nobody, no matter how prejudiced, could believe a man in detention was responsible for Prakesh's murder. Could Le Froy have forgotten him with everything that was going on? When Dr Shankar did so much to help the police and Detective Unit?

'I know.' Constable Kwok finished the last mouthful of his

tea and looked at me gratefully. 'Last time, he gave me something that cleared up my throat overnight. It tasted horrible but it worked.'

'You should give him one of the interview rooms and let him see patients,' I told Le Froy. 'Penal servitude.'

Le Froy ignored me. He turned back to de Souza. 'Pillay's family hasn't seen the gun?'

'I searched for it in Sergeant Pillay's parents' house as well as in his quarters and his locker. No sign of it, sir.'

'Not in his kit or the desk either, sir,' Constable Kwok said.

And a thorough search of the area where he was found had turned up nothing. That meant Prakesh must have had it with him last night. And that his killer – or someone else – had taken it.

I knew Prakesh had suspected Dolly, Rose and Mrs Lexington of being involved in Bernie Hemsworth's death but I had seen them all yesterday evening. They had arrived at the party together, having come straight from the cinema. Whatever evidence Prakesh had collected on them, they couldn't have killed him.

'Su Lin?' Le Froy prompted. 'You were helping Prakesh decipher Hemsworth's notebooks. Did he give you any idea what he was working on?'

'We stopped. We quarrelled.' I felt terrible, remembering.

'What about?'

'I thought Bernie Hemsworth and Colonel Mosley-Partington might be right about the terrorist assassin, Bose, being in Singapore. I told him Mr Meganck, the McPherson boys' tutor, said someone had been watching Mrs Lexington's house, two people at least. I thought one of them might be Bose and that made Sergeant Pillay really angry. I think the other was Bernie Hemsworth. But they might not have been there at the same time, so Bose might have been watching Bernie. Or vice versa.'

At that, de Souza and Constable Kwok sat up. Le Froy's expression didn't change. I got the feeling this wasn't news to him. 'Did the tutor describe these someones?'

'He hasn't seen them. He takes the boys bird-watching and tracking, and they found signs that someone had been there. He said one of them was a smoker, and his cigarette stubs were poisoning the birds. He was really angry about that.'

'I want to talk to Meganck,' Le Froy said.

Constable Kwok nodded and left the office. I felt an irrational prick of jealousy. It had been my job to arrange Le Froy's interviews and prepare his background notes.

'Sergeant Pillay wired Calcutta, but he wouldn't say what it was about,' de Souza said.

That raised the worst possibility of all, the one that Colonel Mosley-Partington was sure to seize on: what if Prakesh was really passing information to the Indian Nationalists? What if the Indian Nationalists had killed him for not getting information they wanted, or to tie up loose ends?

I remembered Prakesh ranting, 'If it's not wrong why are they keeping it secret?' when the Home Office gave orders they would not explain, and how angry he had been recently.

'Did Sergeant Pillay mention anyone else, any other place he was investigating? Did he mention anything at all?' de Souza asked.

'Why are you asking me?' I flared up. 'I hardly ever saw him. You were here with him day in, day out. You must know what he was working on better than I.'

I saw his face and felt sorry. Prakesh had been his friend as well as his colleague.

'I keep thinking I must have missed something that got him killed.' De Souza's voice was calm. 'He talked about quitting the force. He said he was fed up and there was no point. I didn't think he was still working on the case. I honestly thought he was looking around for another job because he was going to quit. That was why I didn't say anything about him sending wires and taking time off.'

I wasn't surprised. I, too, had thought Prakesh was on the verge of walking out. 'He made many negative comments about the British system. How even a man like Le Froy, despite his decades of dedicated work, should have no say in the running of Singapore because all his white-man privileges blinded him to real life here. I thought he was just letting off steam.'

But was that true or part of the cover Prakesh had created? Had he been suspicious of someone in the Detective Shack or in Police Headquarters across the road? Or of Colonel Mosley-Partington?

'I talked Prakesh into continuing the investigation,' I said. 'It's my fault he ended up dead.'

De Souza shook his head. 'He might have let you think you did. It doesn't look like he ever stopped working on the Bernard Hemsworth case. He just stopped submitting reports. To us, at least.' He opened a drawer in his own desk and took out a stack of papers. 'These were locked into his desk. Congress Party propaganda. Freedom for India at all costs, even to siding with the Japanese for Indian freedom from colonial rule.'

He must have removed them before Prakesh's desk was officially cleared out.

'A lot of people believe that,' I said, thinking of Parshanti. 'Those opinions wouldn't have got him killed.'

'Might have got him fired. And cost his family compensation.'

'I won't say anything,' I promised.

'Opinions should not get anyone killed.' Le Froy came in fast and silent as he always did. He looked at the papers I had just taken from de Souza, then thumped them onto the table and turned his back on us, staring out of the barred window faced the shabby wall of the Dungeon. Where Bernie had been found.

Oddly, this made me feel like one of the team again, no longer the subject of interrogation.

'Sir?'

'What is it?'

'I have a feeling that Sergeant Pillay didn't really need my help with Hemsworth's notebooks. He wasn't interested in anything I found. He just wanted me to keep them hidden and away from here. He was always asking me about Dolly. Whether she had any visitors. Whether she went out alone.'

'Typical.' De Souza snorted. Prakesh had always been too inter-ested in pretty girls.

'At first I thought he was interested in her, but what if that wasn't it?'

Le Froy turned and waited.

'I think he suspected her of something. I don't know what. He was always asking about her, but he never talked to her. Never flirted with her. He once mentioned something about smugglers using or dressing up as women.'

'He never mentioned that in his reports,' de Souza said.

'Oh, and can you remind Dr Leask to check if Prakesh was

drugged by anything? Like the chloral hydrate he used yesterday? He'll know what I mean.'

Le Froy started to ask why, but was interrupted by Constable Kwok's return.

'Sir, Dr Leask can't do the autopsy.'

'Why not?'

'He just sent word that Colonel Mosley-Partington wants Sergeant Pillay's autopsy results sent straight on to him. But the morgue still hasn't received the body.'

'Impossible.'

'The attending officers said that, for religious reasons, the body had been sent back to Sergeant Pillay's family. Prakesh's family said his body had never arrived.'

Sergeant Prakesh Pillay's gun was not the only thing missing.

No Body

It was publicly announced that Sergeant Prakesh Pillay would be given an honourable burial with an official ceremony once the investigation was over.

The promise of honours and recognition to be heaped on the dead officer might have placated a British family, but it primed Singaporean suspicions. If Sergeant Prakesh Pillay hadn't been worthy of recognition when he was alive, what was the Home Office trying to cover up now he was dead?

Prakesh's family demanded to know when his body would be released to them. They demanded to see it. They gathered en masse at the hospital mortuary, where attendants insisted the dead officer's body was not being hidden. One sympathetic technician took them around the chilly bunkers to prove Prakesh was not there.

In fact, they realised, nobody knew where Prakesh's body was.

Of course administrative hiccups happened now and then. Just not usually with bodies. I thought it was almost fortunate that Dr Shankar was still under detention so he could not be suspected of having spirited the body off to experiment on it, as he had been accused of doing when the corpse of an old woman was found to have the remnants of a conjoined twin attached to her lower body. Fortunately the woman had not left any children to be outraged.

'Why are all you people making such a fuss over a sergeant?' the governor's secretary wanted to know. 'That administrator was a lot more qualified but no one's kicking up a rumpus over his murder!'

'People knew Pillay here. He's connected.'

Prakesh had grown up on the island. But it brought the violence in India frighteningly close when angry mourners accused the police of deliberately concealing his body because of what they had done to him. Sergeant Prakesh Pillay had already been injured in a previous interrogation. What had they done to him now that they were afraid to let his family see?

Prakesh's parents had a police guard around them as though they were criminals, but the officers were all friends of Prakesh and would not arrest them for rioting, though that was the usual British way of dealing with desperate non-white people.

Colonel Mosley-Partington was good at calming a crowd – I have to say that for him. He was the kind of man who looks better at the head of a nation than at the head of your dining table. Standing on the front steps of Police Headquarters, he made clear that, as far as he was concerned, he would get to the bottom of this. Singapore and the safety of its citizens – alive or dead – was the primary concern of himself and his government. And Singapore must remain the safe little gem it was.

But the wailing women in front and the shouting men behind them were not interested in being placated.

'You bring smallpox and slavery,' shouted a sullen-looking teenager, who sounded very like Prakesh. 'Now you won't even tell us what happened to our brother. Did you kill him for disobeying orders? Is that why you won't let his own father and mother see his body?'

I left the group around Police Headquarters because I wanted to think. Le Froy was somewhere inside – I presumed he was still trying to get Dr Shankar released. De Souza hadn't stopped me when I went to Prakesh's desk and looked for Bernie Hemsworth's notebooks. But they weren't there. Neither were any of the notes I had passed him. All that was left were copies of the letters Bernie had sent to the newspaper editor, insisting the diseased trees be cleared: they were shedding bark and killing birds. Why had Prakesh kept copies of them? Or were these letters the only ones he hadn't found worth passing on?

Then I thought I saw Dolly's bright yellow dress further up the road and went after her, hoping to have a private talk with her. I was surprised to see her alone in town, but glad of the opportunity.

She was walking fast. I know some people, like Le Froy, for example, go walking to think. But with my uneven legs and the pain in my hip walking causes, it takes my full attention. I didn't want to stop to get out my Tiger Balm ointment, so the pain in my hip and knee grew as I hurried after her.

So I wasn't thinking as I followed her through the crowd of onlookers. I meant to call out to her once we were away from all the shouting, but as she walked on without slowing down, I found myself drawing closer to the hawker stalls and mats on the roadside, where I would be less noticeable if she turned. Where could she be going? And why was she alone? Dolly always hated doing anything alone. And if she was too upset to go back to work, why was she walking around town? And why was she heading towards the Rent Hope district where the money-lenders and pawnbrokers were located?

I followed her for some time, keeping my distance outside, discreetly looking over trinkets on street stalls as she went into various businesses with heavily barred windows. She didn't spend enough time in any of them to negotiate a loan or a sale. Was she looking for someone or something? I hoped none of my grandmother's people would see me there, or I would have to explain that she hadn't sent me to spy on them. And explain to her what I had been doing there.

I breathed easier when Dolly had to slow down to pick her way past the site where the Cathay Building was being constructed. Other people were stopping to look and comment, blocking the path. This was going to be the first skyscraper in Singapore. The press release said the Cathay Building would be sixteen storeys high and the tallest building in South East Asia. Once it was completed, people would be able to sit in armchairs and watch films indoors. It seemed incredible, but I couldn't imagine it catching on. People were used to watching films and *waying* shows outdoors, where they could bring their own mats and stools. But who knew? Maybe someday even the seventh-month concerts to entertain the dead would be held indoors, in theatres specially built for spirits.

But then the woman turned and I was close enough to see it wasn't Dolly at all but Rose Radley. I felt so stupid. How had I made such a mistake? She was wearing a bright yellow frock, not her usual dark grey or brown. One of Dolly's, it looked like. But, no: I remembered Rose saying it was Dolly who wore *her* dresses. And her hair was done up like Dolly wore hers, and she was carrying Dolly's big yellow bag with feathers. And the sun was bright and I was walking around without my spectacles. But, still, it was such a stupid mistake to make and a great waste of time. I told myself I could never again be angry with the *ang moh*s who said all Asians looked alike.

'Miss Chen!' Rose called. She had seen me and was waving me over. 'What are you doing here? Come back to the house with me. Dolly's in such a terrible state. Maybe you can help to talk some sense into her.'

I joined her gladly. Maybe I hadn't wasted my time after all.

Dolly

———◆———

It was a stroke of luck meeting Rose. If only I could be alone with Dolly, I was sure I could get the full story from her.

I wanted to talk with Mrs Lexington too. I had enjoyed doing secretarial work for her and she paid well. But after what had happened to Prakesh, I really wanted to go back to work at the Detective Shack. I was part of the team there. I wanted to help find Prakesh Pillay's killer.

Dolly's 'terrible state' looked more like a mixture of boredom and excitement. I thought she would feel better if she went out for a walk or did some hard scrubbing. She seemed more frustrated than upset over Prakesh's death.

'I want to see Prakesh's body, to be sure it's really him and he's really dead,' was the first thing Dolly said to me.

Even if his body wasn't missing, this was a strange request. Especially from Dolly.

'Of course it was him,' I said. 'The other police officers know him.'

'Rose says whoever killed Prakesh could have mistaken him

for Bose. So it may have been another policeman who killed him, and they are covering it up. I told her that no one who's seen Chirag Bose could mistake Prakesh Pillay for him.'

'Maybe they've never seen Bose,' I said.

That didn't stop Dolly. It didn't even slow her down. 'Or maybe it's really Chirag Bose who's dead, and Sergeant Pillay killed him. And now he's run away and is hiding because he's afraid that all the other Indian terrorists will kill him. Don't you see how that could have happened? That's why I have to see the body. I'm the only one who can tell them if it's really Bose!'

Rose had seen Chirag Bose too, I thought. But Rose said nothing.

I couldn't say anything about mistaken identities, having followed Rose for an hour thinking she was Dolly.

And I didn't believe his body could really have disappeared. There was definitely something strange going on. Like Prakesh's family, I suspected the Military Police.

'Do the police know what happened to poor Sergeant Pillay?' Mrs Lexington wanted to know. 'Such a nice young man. And with such good manners.'

'They're still investigating.'

'We were all so upset, weren't we, girls? It's a good thing we were together all day yesterday, with a killer on the loose. We went to see a film and then we had such a rush to get ourselves ready for the foundation-stone ceremony. Only, of course, with everything that happened . . .'

'Speaking of dresses, isn't that the dress Dolly was wearing yesterday?' I asked Rose. 'And Dolly's sun-hat – and Dolly's bag?'

'It's my dress. But Dolly said she had nothing to wear yesterday.'

'Nothing new to wear,' Dolly put in. 'Anyway, Rose doesn't like being looked at, so I was just trying out her dress for her. I made all the accessories for it and I wanted to see how they went together.'

Dolly was very clever with her fingers. She tricked out her clothes herself, cleverly making things with bits of chiffon, lace and sequins or ribbon and buttons. Now she was playing with a length of purple silk ribbon. 'I wish I had something to match this. It's silk and so expensive. Su Lin, if only you got some material – say, lavender flowers on pale blue – and made a frock, I could use this to trim a hat for you. You would look so lovely!'

'She doesn't wear hats,' Rose said. 'Anyway, a frock made for Miss Chen would be much too small for you to wear, so it won't work on her.'

Dolly looked petulant. 'I'm only trying to help. She looks so dowdy all the time. Just like you, Rose.'

'You like this purple?' I asked, to distract Dolly from being nasty to Rose.

'Yes, I really do. I couldn't use it in Calcutta because the roll slipped into my purse in the shop. I was afraid if they saw something I made with it, they might think I'd stolen it. But I can use it now. It's very expensive so I'm thinking carefully about what I want to do with it.'

Dolly had an almost amoral enjoyment and gaiety – she was even enjoying the drama and the deaths, I realised. On the surface it looked like a naive simplicity that men found appealing, but something cold and frightening lay beneath it. I had seen it in young white men throwing mud at local girls or stones at stray dogs. Their officers wrote it off as 'high spirits' but underneath it was an inability to imagine pain in others.

Mrs Lexington shook her head, dismissing Dolly's stolen ribbon. 'It's awful, these murders. And to think we left Calcutta to get away from the violence!'

'I thought you'd be glad to get rid of Bernie,' Dolly said. 'Mrs L threatened to charge him rent because he spent so much time here.'

I could understand Mrs Lexington's irritation with Bernie Hemsworth. But, unlike Dolly, I felt she was really upset by what had happened. And she saw I was upset too.

'Do you feel up to taking Mrs Maki's English lesson this afternoon? I can send a message to her to cancel it. I'm sure she'll understand.'

'Oh, no. Please don't. I would like to go. Keeping busy makes it easier. And I like Mrs Maki. But I was needing to know if you'll be wanting me to continue here with you. I mean, if Dolly doesn't feel up to going back to work at the Detective Unit.'

To my surprise Dolly perked up at once. 'I feel quite up to it. I'd like to go back to work. I miss being in town.'

'You must take your time, Dolly. Not too much excitement, remember?' Mrs Lexington said. 'And it's much safer if you stay here with us.'

Dolly pouted. 'But I have things there that I want.'

'You're not ready,' Mrs Lexington said. She sounded kind but firm. 'If you need anything from the office, Rose or I will go and collect it for you.'

Was I smelling lies, like Mrs Shankar? 'Smell' was the wrong word because I wasn't getting the information through my nose. I felt it in the fine hairs inside my ears and the tension in my gut. More like the tone and movement. And 'lies' wasn't the right word either. Mrs Lexington wasn't worried about Dolly's health.

She was afraid of what might happen to her if she went back to work.

I saw how both she and Rose watched Dolly, as though afraid I might say something to upset her. It's nice having friends who care about you, but in Dolly's place I would have felt as though I was surrounded by thick cobwebs. We couldn't even have a word together in private. When I suggested a walk around the house to see if the butterfly pea flowers (so good for making blue tea) were blooming, Mrs Lexington said she would come with us.

'No,' said Dolly. 'It's too hot to walk. I hate how hot it is here. You don't even have highlands where it's cooler and gentlemen can take you for weekends.'

'You must miss England,' I said. 'I suppose you feel much safer there.'

Dolly laughed. 'Oh, all you people in the east think that England is Heaven, but there are poor people too. And it's much worse being poor there. Here everyone complains about how hot it is.' As she had just been doing. 'But the heat doesn't kill you, does it? Not like the cold at home. And there's the dole and them cutting back on benefits—'

'That's enough,' Mrs Lexington said quite sharply.

'I'm only talking to her. Can't I even talk now?' Dolly rolled her eyes.

Had I missed something?

'You know, if it wasn't for having someone else in my heart, I would have married Bald Bernie just to get away from here. I would have got him too, if I'd wanted him. Once I wanted independence but independence isn't all it's made out to be.'

I stared, surprised. I had assumed all educated Western women wanted careers and independence now they had the right to vote.

'He was a pompous ass, but he meant to be nice. And he was always talking about his boss and what a good man he was, and how much he was paying him.'

'Well, you can't marry him now, can you?' Rose said.

'I'd marry any man with four thousand pounds a year who asked me,' Dolly said. 'Now I don't see anyone at all and I can't even go out by myself. And Rose moving into my room to sleep with me. I know you mean well, Rosy-Posy, but I'm really all right. Oh, I never thought I'd say it but I miss Calcutta.'

Dolly Darling, with her bland, amoral cheerfulness, had probably been popular in Calcutta. She would be popular with men anywhere, which might have been what Mrs Lexington and Rose were concerned about. Though it frustrated Dolly to be kept from men, shopping and other diversions, it was good of them to watch out for her.

It was understandable. If I'd had a sister or daughter in such a position I would have been concerned too.

'Dolly's been having nightmares,' Mrs Lexington explained. 'She's fine most of the time, but she has these spells when she thinks someone is following and spying on her.'

But someone had been following and spying on her, I thought. If it had been Bernie Hemsworth, that was over. But what if it was somebody else?

———◆———

Outside, I looked up at the slope behind the house. A few of the old paper bark trees had started to bloom. A few early birds had spotted the new flowers and there were flashes of colour – too far away to make out clearly, but I knew they were hanging upside down to feast on nectar.

Paper bark trees are valuable because their oil treats everything from colic and cholera to burns, cramps and various aches and pains. It was the main ingredient in Tiger Balm, which contains no tiger parts, but is so named because of its warm burn. But, these days, the trees are seldom cultivated because the Bernie Hemsworths of the ruling class couldn't see beneath the 'leprous' peeling bark to the goodness within.

Folk superstition says if you write a problem on a piece of bark, your problem will disappear when it flakes off.

I would have written Prakesh's name on every single tree if I'd thought that would do any good.

Matter of Water

———◆———

'Gain or loss is a matter of chance (勝負は水物だ *shōbu wa mizumono da*), where the literal meaning of the phrase "matter of chance", *mizumono* (水物), is "a matter of water". So, to be strong, find and go with the flow,' said Mrs Maki, sagely.

I nodded. Mrs Maki's sayings were soothing, even when I wasn't sure what she meant.

She was so different from what I'd grown up thinking the Japanese were like. The culture and civilisation in the Maki home was much deeper than any the British had imported. As for Asian culture, most of the people in Singapore were descended from those driven out of their original homelands by poverty or politics. They had not carried culture in their boats, only what they needed for survival. It was years later I realised the drive to survive was at the heart of Singapore culture.

To my surprise I found Hideki Tagawa with Mrs Maki when I arrived for our next session.

Hideki Tagawa was Mrs Maki's cousin, in Singapore as a businessman. From his smooth unmarked hands and precise bespectacled eyes, I could tell he was one of those Le Froy would mark as a spy. Chief Inspector Le Froy considered all Japanese were spies, though his superiors in London dismissed his reports on the Japanese threat.

I apologised for interrupting. 'I can come back another time.'

'No. Please stay, Miss Chen. You must speak to both of us in English today,' Hideki Tagawa said, in beautiful King's English. He clearly had no need of coaching.

'We heard about the dead policeman. You must tell us what is happening. The inside story,' Mrs Maki said.

'I'm sorry. I don't know the inside story. I don't think there is any inside story. They are still investigating.'

Hideki Tagawa smiled at me. 'You are a good girl, my cousin tells me. Please don't worry. I know about the concerns of Chief Inspector Le Froy. But my cousin and I are harmless. I also know about tensions between the chief inspector and Colonel Mosley-Partington. That is how the British are. When they have no enemies, they will fight among themselves. But we are not enemies. We are partners.'

'You are invading China,' I couldn't help saying.

'All we are trying to do is save our people. We want to work with China. Thanks to the Great Depression, millions of Japanese citizens are starving and suffering. Other people in Asia are suffering too, as a result of Western colonial exploitation.'

Prakesh had been saying much the same thing before he was killed.

'Japan only wants to free the rest of Asia from being treated like second-class citizens by the Western colonial powers. We want to free ourselves.'

Mrs Maki hushed him, but didn't seem surprised. I assumed it was a regular topic with him. Uncle Chen also held forth regularly on the Japanese regional expansion, but from a very different viewpoint.

'We heard rumours that an Indian terrorist was in Singapore. Is that true? Have they tracked him down?' Mrs Maki asked. 'Did they mistake Sergeant Pillay for the Indian terrorist? Or was the Indian terrorist pretending to be Sergeant Pillay all along?'

I wasn't surprised. Nothing is ever really secret in Singapore. If anything, people pay more attention to whispers and rumours than to official announcements. The general feeling is that all official news is either propaganda or outdated.

'Oh, no. Sergeant Pillay was definitely Sergeant Pillay.' Prakesh would have enjoyed being mistaken for a terrorist. It was the first time I had thought of the old, joking Prakesh since his death. I was grateful. 'He thought the Indian terrorist is here to meet Japanese arms backers.'

'Japanese arms backers.' Mrs Maki sounded amused. 'Are there any here?'

'They have confirmation Chirag Bose is in Singapore.' There was no urgency in Hideki Tagawa's tone. In fact, I could tell he was making an effort to speak casually. That was what caught my attention and made me more cautious.

'That's what I heard. But it may just be a rumour. And I don't know how dangerous he is.'

'He was a dangerous fast bowler when I knew him.'

'You know Chirag Bose the terrorist?'

'We met at Oxford. He wasn't a terrorist then.'

'Oxford?' I blinked, taking this in. I could picture the slim, conservatively dressed Hideki Tagawa in Oxford among colleges and punts, but Chirag Bose, whom I had imagined to be half wild man, half crazed killer of white men and women?

'He was a year or two behind me but we played on the same team. It was his idea to form an all-Asian team. It was originally an all-South-Asian team, but I was included after two of his teammates were sent down.'

'Sent down?'

'Expelled. They were reported to be practising devil worship in the quad.'

I could imagine the British being upset by that. 'Which devils were they worshipping?'

'They were doing their health exercises to calm themselves for exams. They stretch themselves and stand on their heads. It's called ashtanga yoga. But it frightened some students and their wealthy patron families.'

'What was Chirag Bose like in Oxford?' I wondered if Le Froy was aware of this connection. Could Bose have come to Singapore to get in touch with his old college friend? But no. He could easily have got in touch with Hideki Tagawa in Japan if he'd wanted to. And if they were really in cahoots, Mr Tagawa would hardly mention their connection to me.

'Oxford is full of men who believe in overthrowing their governments. If you need help communicating with him, I offer my services. I would like to be in touch with my old friend again. Asia is our shared past and, I hope, our shared strong future.'

'It is for the best common good that we help moderate the discussion. Bose and the Indian Nationalists have much to contribute to Singapore independence,' Mrs Maki said.

'I don't know how to reach him,' I said.

'You must tell us what the police know of Bose. It will be better for you and for everyone in Singapore.'

He spoke with a smile and such a friendly voice that I couldn't tell if he was making conversation or a threat.

'For instance, some things your relations get up to, you prefer to keep this from the police. Am I right?'

A threat, then. But still with a smile.

'I'm not working with the police any more,' I said. 'I lost my job.'

'Because of that man Hemsworth,' Mrs Maki put in. I wondered if she was defending me from her cousin or warning me. 'The man who died.'

'I hope the Chinese who had the sense to get out of China are more reasonable than the Chinese who stayed there,' Hideki Tagawa said. 'I am telling you this for your own good. Bose is a man with a cause greater than himself. This makes him dangerous to the local police. We spoke with one of your local police. We said, "Sergeant Pillay, we would thank you very much for your help," like we say to you, Miss Chen. And it is safer to help us. Because a man like Bose, if he feels you are betraying him, who knows what he would do?'

'Are you saying Chirag Bose killed Sergeant Pillay?'

'We are not saying anything,' Mrs Maki said.

At the same time, her cousin said, 'We are saying we can help you, Miss Chen. If you help us.'

If I hadn't been shocked and numb from Prakesh's death, I might have reacted very differently. But, as it was, I sat dumbly and nodded. I think they hoped to shock information or agreement out of me, but I was still buffered by that greater shock and my mind was cold, rational and detached.

I had not had a chance yet to sit and process what had happened. Until I did, I was functioning like an automaton.

I still couldn't believe Prakesh was dead. Part of my mind clung to the impossible hope that this was just him playing a prank on us. He had always been a great joker. All these thoughts were going round and round inside my head as I listened and nodded.

But I think I impressed the Japanese cousins.

'Chief Inspector Le Froy cannot be completely trusted,' Mrs Maki said, 'because he obeys Colonel Mosley-Partington.'

'He is his dog,' Hideki Tagawa said. 'Like all the police. The police were given information on the wrongdoings of Colonel Mosley-Partington in India. How he and senior officers in the colonial administration were running schemes and closing their eyes to injustices for their own profit. I wonder how Colonel Mosley-Partington bribed Le Froy to keep him quiet. How did he bribe you, Miss Chen?'

Books and Bookings

———◆———

'Laws are like cobwebs, which may catch small flies, but let wasps and hornets break through.' Jonathan Swift

The quotation, in beautiful copperplate, pinned to the library notice board indicated Miss Shelford's mood for the week.

I loved the tiny library at the Mission Centre. Two standing shelves with books in alphabetical order by author's name, and picture books arranged, spines up, in boxes on the floor, according to age groups. You were allowed to borrow any book you were tall enough to reach without a step stool.

Those were the books that had provided most of my education.

The advantage of having access to few books is that you read and reread the ones you have. If I had been let loose in a huge library, I would likely have spent my days drunk on words and never read a book twice. As it was, I knew the Mission Centre's few books almost by heart.

After leaving Mrs Maki and her cousin, I stopped at the Mission Centre. I heard a group recitation going on in one of the classrooms above and felt a pang for the young girls who still believed that memorising Bible verses and multiplication tables prepared you for life. Or had I been the only one who believed that?

There was no one in the reading corner and I sat on the rug in front of the two bookshelves. I wanted to talk to Le Froy, to tell him what Hideki Tagawa had said about Chirag Bose. But I wasn't comfortable telling him anything while Dr Shankar was still locked away. What if Mrs Maki and her cousin were arrested because of something I said?

And, of course, I wanted to find out what had happened to Prakesh. Knowing wouldn't bring him back, but I had to know before I could move on.

Also, I found I didn't want to go back to Uncle Chen's shophouse where I would be alone. Uncle Chen might already have left for Chen Mansion. As Shen Shen's time drew closer, he was spending less and less time at the shop. It struck me that, despite having so many relatives and friends, I was really very much alone. Unless you have a family unit, or a special friend you need no excuse to spend time with, life can be very lonely.

Maybe that was what had drawn me to the Mission Centre now. Years ago, my first teacher at the school there had told me my polio was a gift from God, since it had brought me to them. I still wasn't sure I believed her, but it was better than being called a curse, as I was in my grandmother's house.

'Su Lin! How nice to see you!' Miss Shelford came in with a big smile for me. The Mission Centre's plump little seventy-year-old childcare supervisor and librarian put her hands on my shoulders and looked anxiously up at me, as she always did. 'Are you well? You look tired, dear girl. But it's lovely to see you. Oh, such terrible things have been happening.'

'Terrible things? Here?'

'Oh, no, not here, thank the Lord. But we heard about the tragic deaths. We are all praying for them, of course, but I wonder if perhaps you could . . .'

'If I could what?'

'If you find a library book among Mr Hemsworth's things perhaps we could have it back.'

'Mr Hemsworth came here to the library?' I hadn't thought he would.

Miss Shelford grew a little pink. 'He had many criticisms. He said we had no right to call ourselves a library when we had fewer books here than he had in his rooms in London. And there were some he said should be banned in a Christian learning environment. The English–Malay dictionary and the English–Chinese dictionary, for example. He said they would encourage young minds to see them as acceptable languages. We had to leave our desk when he was here because we didn't want to say something rude to him. We were feeling most unchristian. May the Lord forgive us but our first thought on hearing of his death was relief that it wasn't someone we would miss,' Miss Shelford whispered piercingly. She was a little deaf.

'The poetry book was on our desk. One of the young ladies put it back on the wrong shelf – behind Wittgenstein's *Tractatus Logico-Philosophicus* – and we wanted to take a look at it. So we knew it was on our desk when Mr Hemsworth walked in. I saw him looking at it. He asked me if we allowed Indian men to come into the library and we said, "Most certainly," and he said Indian men ought not to be allowed in libraries. That was when we left the counter. He must have taken the book and just walked out with it without writing his name in the loans register. There was no one else in here who could have taken it. We would like to have it back, if you find it. It can't have anything to do with what happened to the poor man, God rest his soul.'

'You think Mr Hemsworth took a poetry book?'

'Oh, we know he did!' Miss Shelford looked fiercer than I had ever seen her. 'And we don't have many poetry books. People are always forgetting to return them, unlike volumes of Gibbon or the *Encyclopaedia Britannica*, which always come back to us.'

'Because they're too heavy to ship to England?'

'That may be what people believe. But it's really because we pray for their return,' Miss Shelford said, with the air of one conferring a great secret. 'That's why we feel responsible for Mr Hemsworth's death. We have been praying at him. Yes, dear. *At* him. If he had just returned the book, he would have been safe. But the wretched man would not, so he died.'

For one mad moment I wondered if this sweetest, gentlest of librarians could have killed Bernie over a book. Le Froy believed anyone was capable of murder, given the right incentive.

'So you see why you have to bring it back?' said my temporary murder suspect.

'Colonel Mosley-Partington will have charge of his things,' I said. I remembered seeing a library book among Bernie's things, but wanted to take a closer look at it before bringing it back. And if Miss Shelford was going to put the evil eye on someone else I would rather it wasn't me. 'But I'll see what I can do.'

'Men like Mosley-Partington don't read their Bibles,' Miss Shelford said. 'They hire pastors to preach to them so they don't have to. And they choose pastors who preach what they want to hear.'

'Do you know the colonel?'

'My people know his people. It's one of the things you can't get away from back home. The man is a dreamer of dreams, grandiose dreams of always getting what he wants. That's what makes him so successful, and so dangerous in a world where most people never bother to define what they want, let alone work towards getting it. I would feel sorry for his wife if she wasn't such a goose. Quite different from poor dear Mrs Thomas Le Froy.'

'Did you know Chief Inspector Le Froy's wife too?' I hadn't known that.

'Her life's ambition was to volunteer for an overseas mission. Unfortunately her family was too rich and her health too poor. Yet she knew her own will. She chose to marry a police officer instead of into a family of powerful civil servants. Mrs Le Froy chose the man she thought was trying to do good and make a difference. He had not wanted to leave England, thinking it would be too hard for her to live abroad. Then she died in that traffic accident and straight away he accepted a posting to the Far East. Not even India, where a man can live in relative comfort and civilisation, but Singapore. And he has not returned to England since. But I suppose England's loss is Singapore's gain. God works in mysterious ways.'

Like polio, I thought.

'Oh! Look who's here!' Miss Shelford cried, 'Oh, we are blessed today!'

I saw Parshanti hesitating in the doorway. She looked tired and cross but submitted to being greeted and peered at by Miss Shelford.

'I saw you from outside,' Parshanti said to me, once she had answered Miss Shelford's enquiries about her poor father and dear mother. 'I thought – I mean, I didn't have anywhere else to be so . . .'

'I was just going,' I said, taking her hand. 'Come on. Goodbye, Miss Shelford.'

'Goodbye, Su Lin. Don't forget to bring back the poetry book.'

Parshanti

◆

'My mam's sitting across the road from the prison quarantine area. She says she's going to stay there until she's allowed in to see him or they let him go. She sent me away but I couldn't face going home alone.'

'That's exactly how I was feeling,' I admitted.

It was funny how we had both been drawn to the Mission Centre. But it felt right to come together there where we had first met.

'Anyway, Mam says if Mr Gandhi can do a hunger strike in prison she can do one outside prison. But that's good, I think. If anyone can talk them round, it's Mam.'

'Have you talked to Prakesh's family?'

She nodded. 'I saw his sister. It's bad enough what happened to him. Not having a body just makes it worse. She says her mother thinks he's alive and being tortured somewhere while her father believes he was killed so terribly that they don't want them to see the body.'

I shuddered. All those thoughts had crossed my mind too. The only argument against them was that I didn't think any of the

Military Police or government forces were organised enough to pull it off.

Parshanti and Prakesh had fought and flirted over the years, more out of habit than anything else. But I knew Prakesh had been spending more time with her since the death of Kenneth Mulliner, her fiancé.

'Doesn't it suddenly feel like a lot of people are being killed here?' Parshanti mused.

I remembered what Uncle Chen and Prakesh had said. 'A lot more people are being killed in China and India.'

'People we know,' Parshanti clarified. 'I understand what you mean, but it's like when things are so terrible on such a big scale, my mind can't take it all in and I just want to go home and wash my hair. Because that's one simple thing I can do and get done. I'm not saying what happened to Prakesh is a small thing but it's small enough to take in, and feel how horrible it is, without shutting down.'

That was true. And it was dangerous because the only thing that Singapore had to recommend it was how safe it was. If it turned out that Prakesh had had dealings with the Indian Nationalists, the Home Office in London might ban local men from becoming police officers.

'Coffee?' Parshanti suggested. 'I don't want to go home yet, but we can't just stand out here.'

'I need a *teh tarik*,' I said. I wanted something hot and sweet, frothy and bubbly in my life.

We took an empty table with two stools at the fishball noodle stall next to the *teh tarik* man.

'I'm not hungry,' Parshanti said.

'When did you last eat?'

'How can you think of eating at a time like this?'

'Why do you think not eating will help your father? If you want to go on a hunger strike, like your mam and Mr Gandhi, you should announce it to the newspapers first. Or give me an interview. Miss Parshanti Shankar, why are you going on a hunger strike? What do you hope to achieve?'

'Don't be ridiculous, Su.' But she laughed.

'Then can I order something?'

When she shrugged, I ordered two bowls of noodles. I didn't feel like eating either, but our bodies, like motor-cars, need fuel. I wanted my brain to get all the fuel it needed to work.

'Su, Prakesh lent me books to read about the Indian independ-ence movement.'

'Oh?'

'I was wondering whether that had anything to do with him getting killed.'

'How would it?'

'I don't know. Just white people wanting to keep us down, that's all.'

'So they killed him for reading books? Oh, Shanti, I have to tell you how Miss Shelford brought about Bernie Hemsworth's death.'

'What?'

By the time I got through the story of Bernie Hemsworth and the missing poetry book, our hot, soupy noodles and mugs of frothy tea had arrived. I felt better as my grateful body relaxed to absorb the nourishment. I hadn't known how cold my fingers were till I warmed them against the bowl.

'Maybe Miss Shelford stabbed and strangled Bernie Hemsworth,'

Parshanti suggested. 'You know how she is about her books. And if he just walked out with one and didn't sign it out ...'

For some reason that made me think of the roll of silk ribbon falling into Dolly's bag and her walking off with it. I knew I was missing a connection there, but what was it?

'Mam thinks my father was transferred to solitary because they don't want anybody to see what they've done to him,' Parshanti said. I saw she had needed the courage that hot soup brings to get her mind around the thought. 'What do you think they've done to him? Or, if that's not it, what if he's really sick, with something so infectious he could die of it? Maybe he's already died in there and they're not telling us!'

'It's all so crazy. Pa's not a terrorist or an assassin but they're treating him like dirt just because he has relatives somewhere in India. That's how it's always going to be. What's the point of talking about education and women's rights? We don't even have rights as human beings. When this is over I'm going to ask my parents to arrange a marriage for me back in India. My life is over. At least I won't have to be a burden on them.'

'And have five or six children? Will you let your daughters go to school?'

'Why? What for? So they can find out that white people and their white God decide everything and their only choice is to be stupid or unhappy? I mean, what are you going to do? Take in typing by the sheet for the rest of your life? You were doing so well at the Detective Unit, but as soon as some unqualified white girl came along, you lost your place.'

I had been thinking about that. I still wanted to be a writer. I wanted to write news stories rather than society gossip, but more and more it seemed the official sources didn't want people to know these things. They wanted positive, patriotic stories. I could write those too, of course, but that would be as close to the kind of writing I really wanted to do as typing business advertisements for Mrs Lexington.

Parshanti had stopped talking as the hawker's girl came to collect our bowls and coins and wipe the table. 'Su, do you believe there's one person you are destined to be with?'

Now that wasn't something I'd thought about. But, then, Parshanti wasn't thinking about me.

'If you believe in destiny,' I said, 'a relationship that doesn't last just means you weren't destined to be together after all. Maybe that person came into your life to teach you something or prepare you to recognise the person you're really meant to be with.'

I was taken aback when Parshanti leaned across and hugged me, almost knocking us off our stools into the middle of the street. There were tears in her eyes. 'Thank you, Su. I'm just so angry and scared and confused. I don't know what to think.'

'I'm sure they'll let your father go soon.'

'Yes, but it's not just that. Even if he's all right, even if he comes home safe, things are never going to go back to normal. And Prakesh is still going to be dead. He's going to be dead for ever, Su! I still can't believe it. Do you think it's because they haven't had the funeral yet?'

'Changes take time to sink in,' I said.

Going through the funeral rituals would help, of course. That was why we had them. I had been too young to remember my parents when they died. But the ritual of remembering them with incense sticks at their altars freed me to get on with my life the rest of the time. Besides, as far back as I could remember, I had known what had happened to them.

'Anyway, we still don't know what happened to Prakesh,' I said. 'How can we believe it happened if we don't know what it was?'

Dolly's Dreams

◆

That night I couldn't sleep. The air was heavy, thick with heat and humidity. It would rain soon. I hoped for a good thunderstorm that would clear the atmosphere but until then it was hard to sleep and hard to stay awake during the day. But whether I slept or not, Prakesh would still be dead.

I thought about Parshanti. I suspected that for years she had thought of Prakesh as a back-up plan. Someone she wouldn't mind marrying if no one better came along. Even I could see how much he liked her – from the way he teased but never flirted with her. She had always liked him enough for this to be an option, though Parshanti would never have put it that way.

But instead of feeling sorry for her I felt sorry for myself. I wasn't even a fall-back option for anyone. Of course my grandmother would arrange a marriage for me if that was what I wanted, but I had never felt the mad passion that would drive me to sacrifice my life and independence for someone. Maybe I had never let myself feel it – or maybe I couldn't.

At least I could smack mosquitoes at night without waking anybody else.

———•———

The next morning I decided to tell Le Froy what Mrs Maki and her cousin had said, then leave him to decide what to do. But on my way to the Detective Shack I saw Rose and Mrs Lexington going into Police Headquarters together. That meant Dolly was alone at the house.

I had my key to Mrs Lexington's home and every reason to go to her office to check if she had any new typing assignments for me. In other words, this was my chance to talk to Dolly alone.

———•———

I had not expected to find Dolly locked in her room upstairs.

The key was in the lock. I knocked. Then, on hearing her 'Go away!' I unlocked the door and let myself in.

I found Dolly lying across her bed with her craft work spread out around her. She didn't seem surprised to see me. 'Did Ma Lexington send you to check up on me?'

'No, of course not. I just came to see how you are. There was no one downstairs in the office so I came up. Why are you locked in?'

'Ma Lexington wants to keep me safe. They went to clear out my desk at the Detective Unit. I told them they wouldn't find anything there.'

'You're not going back to work, then?'

'I'm still on medical leave,' Dolly said. 'I can't decide till I get better.'

I thought of the mess the mail and accounts would be in by now, had I not stepped in, and winced. As far as Dolly knew, we still hadn't sorted out the accounts and filing system we had been going to tackle when we found Bernie Hemsworth.

'They can call in temporary help. Why don't you do it? If you get Old Ma Lexy to act as your agent they'll have to pay you more.'

I knew the state of the Detective Unit finances and didn't think they could afford to pay much more.

There was a loud mechanical clanking and straining whine. Dolly jumped and gave a little shriek.

I went to the window. 'It's only the charcoal truck going past below.' The road up Fort Canning ran around the hill slope, so if you were on the higher levels, you heard vehicles two or even three times before you saw them.

'I hate that truck! I hate charcoal. It's all dirty and filthy and evil!'

That seemed excessive even for Dolly. Charcoal was part of life: how could it be 'evil'?

'Why don't you come and look?' Usually when you see something, it is not so frightening as you imagine.

I thought of the enormous charcoal stove back at Chen Mansion. It stood in the open courtyard, the paved but unroofed area between the main house and the servants' quarters. There would always be a pot of stock or laundry and nappies boiling there. In the Western houses they used the gas stove instead.

'Are you hungry?'

'There's nothing to eat in the house. Ma Lexington sent the cook and servant girls away because she said they were spying on us.

She's going shopping after they pick up my things, but they'll be some time.'

'I'll make you some soup, if you like.'

'There's nothing to make soup with.'

I made a light, flavourful soup for Dolly, using salt and dried *ikan bilis*, anchovies, I found in the pantry and rinsing off some bunches of *saan choy* growing in wild profusion in the vegetable plot behind the kitchen. And I added some pearl barley and peanuts, also from the pantry.

It was pretty good, if I say so myself.

Dolly ate hers with gusto. When she announced, 'I'm useless,' I assumed she was referring to cooking soup.

'You're good at a lot of things,' I said. 'And you have a lot of advantages.'

'Like what?'

Like looking helpless, and charming men, and being white with two straight legs, I could have said. But I didn't.

'I'm not as stupid as Rose tells people. I just never had a chance.'

I thought Dolly had been given more chances than most – but I was always irritated when people said, 'How can you complain about your limp when there are people with no feet?' or 'How can you complain about not being allowed to go to university when most girls never even go to school?' so I said nothing.

'I'm not sure I want to go back to the office if Sergeant Pillay won't be there. He used to tease me but, really, you don't know how good he was to me. And now he's dead.'

I was surprised. Prakesh had always seemed to dislike Dolly. Had it just been a cover to hide that, really, he liked her? He had always been attracted by pretty young women of any race, and Dolly was pretty. Or was Dolly imagining things? Again?

'And Bernie. He could be such a nuisance, but he used to try to help me with the work. He didn't believe you were really a secretarial assistant. He said, "Monkeys don't use typewriters"!' Dolly giggled. I didn't.

'He said you were really Le Froy's office wife and all I had to do was look decorative and keep Le Froy's hands off me. But he didn't even try!'

That seemed to sting.

'Bernie guessed something was up. He teased me about my dream man and asked if he sent me poetry. He said that's how they seduce white women.'

Poetry?

'What?'

'Sorry, that's a secret. But it shows Bernie did know about native men.'

'I think he really liked you,' I said, meaning it.

Dolly never gave much of an opinion on anything. But there was something about the way she reacted – or didn't react – that made men project their ideals on her. I had seen it myself in the way Bernie looked at her. Only a truly besotted man would have believed her skills were superior to mine for office work.

But maybe that was me projecting something quite different.

'Prakesh already knew, anyway, that I was getting messages from Bose. He was too.'

'Messages?' I had pretty much decided Bose was a figment of Dolly's imagination.

'He's Indian so he was probably taking him supplies and that kind of thing. I kept bringing it up, trying to get him to let something slip, but he never did. He was too clever.'

I felt cold inside. Had Prakesh known Bose was in touch with Dolly? Had he been in touch himself? If he had known a wanted terrorist was in Singapore and said nothing, he had betrayed us all. I was the one who had been living in a dream. Even Dolly knew more about what was going on than I did.

'Now Sergeant Pillay is gone and the poetry notes have stopped coming, I don't know what I'm going to do.'

'Maybe whoever killed Prakesh killed Bose too,' I said brutally. 'Maybe his body is out there in the jungle somewhere. Even if no one killed him, what's he going to do without Prakesh to bring him supplies? And there are wild pigs out there that can kill a man.'

'Oh, no. He's all right. I was worried about all that, right after he stopped writing. But I know if anything happened to him I would feel it here.' Dolly pressed her tummy. 'We have a bond. A special bond.'

'What kind of bond?' I had spoken too sharply. Dolly frowned at me.

'Are you sure the letters were genuine?' I added quickly. 'It may have been Mrs Lexington trying to make you feel better. How were they delivered?'

Dolly's face cleared. 'Oh, no. Ma Lexington would never do something like that. She would tell me to be glad he's gone. She doesn't like Indians, you see. She used to say that was the only thing wrong with India, that there were so many Indians. Though she doesn't call them Indians, that's who she means. No, they're real notes... Look, if you promise not to tell, I'll show you a photograph of him.'

Dolly took her journal out of a drawer. It was a beautiful book, thick cream paper between pink and yellow marbled boards, bound with purple leather. She had made a privacy tie with her purple silk ribbon.

'May I touch it?' I couldn't resist.

'Just the outside. It's not that I don't trust you,' Dolly said quickly, 'but it's secret. I don't write much, but it's where I keep all my secret and special things.'

The book was bulging with papers and envelopes. Dolly untied the purple bow and took out an envelope tucked into the back cover. I had expected a photograph of the two of them, but it had been cut out of a newspaper. 'Wanted for Murder' the headline said.

Poetry and Love

———◆———

Maybe Dolly found my reaction to her newspaper clipping disappointing because she showed me her big secret. A collection of notes that looked like miniature scrolls – they had been rolled up like cigars.

'Love letters?'

'Better!' Dolly giggled. 'Love poetry!'

I unrolled one piece at random and read,

> *Little White Dolly*
> *Dressed like a bride!*
> *Shining with whiteness,*
> *And crowned beside!*

'Nice,' I said, to be polite.

'You see it, don't you?'

'I don't really understand poetry,' I said awkwardly. Parshanti had gone through a phase of writing romantic poetry and I knew how upset sensitive poets got when you made an innocent comment, like 'That doesn't really rhyme.'

'He's saying he sees me as his bride! When he gets the chance, he'll come for me and marry me!'

Despite Miss Shelford at the Mission Centre library telling us that poetry meant whatever we saw in it, I was pretty sure that was not what it meant.

'Oh, please be careful!' she said, as I picked up and unrolled another piece.

This time I read,

> I breathed a song into the air,
> It fell to earth, I knew not where;
> For who has sight so keen and strong
> That it can follow the flight of song?

Oh dear. If any man ever tried to court me with poetry that confused the senses of sight and sound, the relationship was doomed to failure. But even as I thought it, the deliberate crossover was appealing.

'I would like it better if the last line read, "That it can follow the scent of song",' I said, 'Then it would introduce another of the senses and you would know that he's deliberately mixing things up.'

Dolly shook her head at me. 'This was one of the earliest ones. It was telling me that, even though he didn't know where I'd ended up, he would follow and find me – Ma Lexington said it wasn't safe to let anyone know. That's why she told all her friends we were going back to England when we were coming here. I thought that was silly, because anyone who wanted to could have asked at the steamer office. And, besides, wouldn't they be more put out if they wrote to her in England and didn't hear back from her? Anyway, look at this one . . .'

Then let me to the valley go,
This pretty Dolly to see;
That I may also learn to grow
In sweet humility.

'Did you write these?'

'Oh, no! Of course not!' Dolly lowered her voice to a whisper: 'They're all from Bose!'

'How do you know?' None of the notes was signed.

'It's so obvious! That one you're holding proves it. *Then let me to the valley go,/ This pretty Dolly to see* – that's telling me he's coming to see me. Don't you get it? Poetry isn't that difficult if you know what the things in it mean.'

'Where did they come from?'

'I told you, silly. From him.'

'But how? In the post? Did you keep the envelopes?' The stamp and postmark would tell me where they had been posted. And if there was no stamp, the postal workers could be questioned.

'They just came. Like magic. Like on the porch when I fell asleep out there in the afternoon. That's part of the mystery and romance, don't you see? Oh, you locals are stupid. No wonder you don't understand poetry!'

I understood Dolly was cross with me because she couldn't answer my questions. She snatched back – carefully – her poetry scraps and re-rolled them. It would be so easy, I thought, for someone watching the house from above to sneak in and leave a note on the porch when Dolly was there alone. But if it was Bose, why hadn't he let Dolly see him? My money was still on the late Bernie Hemsworth.

'Rose doesn't like him because he hit her in the face. But, if you ask me, Rose probably asked for it. Rose has a way of saying things that makes me want to slap her sometimes. Do you want to know what Rose says about you?'

'No,' I said firmly. 'Tell me about Bose. How did you two meet?'

'Oh, it was so romantic. We've been in love since we met in Calcutta. At a cinema night. The film was *City Lights* with Charlie Chaplin. I enjoyed it. I was working that night. I mean, I was there with someone else. Not Alan. Podge or Pudge, something like that. One of those rich men who act like babies. But he introduced me to Bose. And the minute I saw him, I knew we were meant to be together.'

'Introduced you?'

'Well, he handed me my umbrella and I dropped it in front of Bose and he picked it up. And he smiled at me and said, "My pleasure." I knew he felt the same way. And there was Podge with his mouth open, going, "Do you know who that was?"'

Fortunately my long experience of Parshanti's romances had prepared me for this. I knew she was not lying to me. At least, not any more than she was lying to herself. And, depending on how Bose felt, she might not even be lying.

'You only met him that one time?'

'Oh, but he was the most amazing gentleman. He wouldn't even let himself look round at me as he walked away. I knew at once we were destined to be together for ever and that he felt it too. I'm that good at sensing these things. I can always tell. I'm never wrong. We just have to wait for the right time to be together. I'm only telling you this because we're best friends. You mustn't tell Ma Lex or Rose!'

I wasn't so sure how good Dolly was at sensing things if she thought we were best friends.

'I'm sure it was the men after Bose who killed Sergeant Pillay. They probably tried to torture him into telling them where Bose was hiding and he wouldn't so he died. That's why Bose never told me where he's hiding, because he doesn't want me to be tortured.'

That wouldn't have saved her, I thought. But maybe Bernie Hemsworth had saved her there, insisting on watching her rather than letting her be questioned. 'Bernie Hemsworth may have helped you.'

'Oh, Bernie Hemsworth helped us a lot. He was reporting back to old Mostly-Fartingham so he knew people here and helped us settle our papers before the colonel arrived from India. He searched all our things, you know. He said he was looking for bugs but Rose said he was checking to make sure we hadn't tried to smuggle anything in. Bose might have killed Alan out of jealousy because he was spending so much time with me. Rose saw that at once. That's why he sent me the notes anonymously and why she and Mrs Lexington made me promise and swear never to tell anyone about them. Bernie knew Bose was coming after me because Rose told him so. She thought he might help protect me from Bose. I don't need protection from him. I know he would never have hit me like he did Rose. She probably screamed and threatened to call the police on him.'

'You told Rose about meeting Bose at the cinema?'

'I had to. She was always cross because the men she liked always liked me better. I wanted her to know I had a beau I liked better than any of them.'

'You didn't tell Sergeant Pillay about this, did you? So you don't know for sure he knew Bose is in Singapore.'

'Look, Sergeant Pillay knew where Bose was because he arranged for me to meet him. The night of that dreary old foundation-stone party. You shouldn't call it a party if you're going to make people stand around for hours and listen to speeches. You should at least have music and dancing and more interesting drinks. Don't you think so? And fans. They should have boys with fans, like back in India. Not that that helped much. Mostly they just moved the warm air around. But at least they were trying.'

'Wait. What did Sergeant Pillay arrange? When exactly was this?'

'The night of the party - not that I consider it a party. I got a note from Sergeant Pillay saying he was arranging a meeting between me and Bose. I was to go to the Alhambra cinema on Beach Road that afternoon. And I was thinking, That's nice, because it's the modern theatre that's air-conditioned. One ticket was included. Mrs Lex and Rose were going out so I told them I wasn't well and sneaked out after they left. But I waited and waited and he never came. When the film was over, I went outside and ran into Ma Lexington and Rose, who had been in the Capitol theatre next door. I was dead scared Ma Lexington was going to make a fuss about me not telling her I was going out, but she didn't because she thought I'd gone to look for them but went to the wrong cinema. And then we were all late coming home to change for the party.'

I thought back to that night. It was the night Prakesh had died. Had he really arranged for Dolly to meet Bose? Had he really been in touch with Bose? Was that why he had been killed?

'Quick, I think they're coming!' A car engine sounded from below. It was Mrs Lexington and Rose returning in a taxi. We hurried up the stairs and Dolly, giggling, let me lock her in again before I slipped downstairs and hid in the pantry. I doubted they would miss the ingredients to which I had helped myself and was glad I had cleared up our meal while listening to Dolly.

I waited there, behind the kitchen, till Mrs Lexington and Rose went upstairs. Then I slipped out of the house and down the slope to the next bend of the road. There was no reason I shouldn't have been there, but I wasn't ready for more conversation. I had so many thoughts in my mind there was no room for more.

The Missing Book

◆

The next morning I found the poetry book, *Poems Every Child Should Know* by Mary E. Burt, in the second box of Prakesh's – not Bernie Hemsworth's – office things I went through. It was in a brown manila envelope and bore the stamp of the Mission Centre Library Service. As I remembered, its loan card was still in the paper pocket glued to its back cover by Miss Shelford's careful fingers.

There were also some scraps of paper and a carbon copy of the numbers I had found in one of the notebooks and passed to Prakesh.

I looked around the Detective Shack. Only de Souza and Constable Kwok were there. Fewer and fewer cases were being sent over from Police Headquarters, and the office felt like a shop about to announce its closing-down 'Everything must go' sale.

I didn't want to discuss my half-formed ideas with the officers. I couldn't even explain them completely to myself. 'I'm going to take this library book and return it,' I said.

'Go ahead,' de Souza said, without looking up. He would already have seen and dismissed it.

'Another thing,' I said. 'Do you know Mrs Maki's cousin, Hideki Tagawa? He's a friend of Chirag Bose and he's looking for him.'

'Can't be too close a friend or he would know where Bose is.'

'Exactly. That shows they aren't working together, doesn't it?'

———◆———

'Miss Shelford notices everything,' Parshanti said, looking at the book. Its dark red cloth cover was worn and its pages yellowing, but Miss Shelford loved every book in her collection. 'She's probably right about Bernie taking it. I don't think Prakesh knew the Mission Centre has a library.'

'Prakesh must have taken it from Bernie Hemsworth's things. Why?'

'Maybe he was going to return it.'

'He didn't, did he?'

I had brought the book with me when I went to see Parshanti. She was alone in the shop, as I'd hoped. She said no one had come in since she opened up that morning just after her mother had left to sit outside the prison. People didn't know what was happening with the Shankars and they didn't want to be marked down as collaborators for picking up a packet of prickly heat powder or a bottle of iodine.

'I don't think it's very good poetry,' Parshanti said, flipping through the book. 'I prefer something more passionate myself. I suppose it does say it's for children.'

'That's not the point. The point is, I think, that some of the poems Dolly showed me came from here! Oh, I wish I had paid more attention! But look here! *Little White Lily/Dressed like a bride*, only in Dolly's note it said *Little White Dolly*. I'm sure of it!'

Parshanti stared at me, then back at the book. 'And if Bernie Hemsworth had the book and didn't want anyone to know he had it . . .'

'Yes! What if Dolly's notes didn't come from Bose at all? She never saw who delivered them. Anyone could have written them. Prakesh even, for whatever reason. It would be so easy to deceive Dolly, who never had a single note from the man till she got to Singapore. But what a stupid thing to do! And look.' I showed her the pieces of dried bark, carefully pressed and cut into rectangles. 'These are exactly like the notes in Dolly's journal.'

'And she hasn't been getting any more letters since Mr Hemsworth died?'

'No. But she was only getting one every fortnight perhaps, so . . .'

'Could Dolly have written them herself? On tree bark so she could imagine Bose was pining for her in the jungle?'

Parshanti was better at working out such things than I was. After all, she had more experience when it came to love. 'Somehow I can't imagine Bernard Hemsworth picking this book to copy poems out of. Why a children's book? It's almost as though he's making fun of her. Or maybe he was making fun of her and that made him fall in love with her.'

'That doesn't make sense.'

'Of course it does, silly!' Parshanti said, 'Most of the time, when you fall in love with someone, a lot of it is pretending to yourself what he's like and how he sees you. Because you don't know enough about him for it to be real. So doing something, like looking up poetry in a book and adapting it to her, that would make him see her that way. And it would make him fall in love too. I'm sure that's what happened!'

I could see how that might happen for someone like Parshanti . . . and maybe Bernie Hemsworth. 'Shanti, you're brilliant. The Detective Unit should hire you as a detective, not a secretarial assistant. Then you wouldn't have to type.'

'There aren't any girl detectives, silly Su. Not unless you're Nancy Drew.'

Nancy Drew was the sixteen-year-old girl detective in the American books that Miss Shelford didn't approve of because she was too bold and outspoken to be a good role model.

'The Pinkerton Detective Agency has been employing women since the Great War,' I told her. 'It's only a matter of time till women are detectives and pilots here too. But have a look at this.'

Parshanti took the slip of paper, 'It's the carbon copy of a pawn ticket, of course. No, wait, not a pawn ticket. It's just an estimate. How much they would pay for your item and what the redemption period will be. But there's no signature and no due date. It looks like Bernie was thinking of pawning something and wanted to get it valued first. But he didn't go through with it. At least, not right away.'

Bernie Hemsworth had never seemed short of money. Le Froy probably knew down to the shilling how much the man had had in the bank, but I had never thought to ask.

'We have to find out where it came from, and who brought it in.'

'How? You mean go round to the pawnshops and say, "I don't know what I'm looking for or who brought it in."?'

I suddenly saw that was what Rose Radley must have been

doing when I'd mistaken her for Dolly. Had she been wearing Dolly's dress and hat to remind them of Dolly? She had fooled me, even though I knew them both.

'How would you find a pawnshop in Singapore if you didn't know anyone here? Or if you didn't want anyone you knew to know?' I asked Parshanti.

'I suppose I would . . . ask a taxi driver.'

Exactly. And, luckily, I knew someone who could deal with taxi drivers.

Dolly Brought In

———◆———

Thanks to my grandmother's connections with the intricate taxi network – Chen Tai had extensive arrangements with official taxi companies and pirate taxi drivers – we found the man who had driven Dolly to and from the pawnbroker's shop.

'She owes me money,' Mr Gan said. 'She cheat me! She asked me to bring her to see a pawnshop uncle. I bring. She ask me to wait. I wait. She ask me bring her to Fort Canning house. I bring. Then she say so expensive, don't want to pay.'

Once I offered to pay him what Dolly had cheated him of, as well as for his time, Mr Gan was happy to drive me to the street and point out the shop to which he had brought her.

And as I had guessed, it was in the area where I had seen Rose in Dolly's dress. Rose either hadn't known which pawnshop Dolly had gone to or had wanted to see if they remembered her.

The pawnbroker was very reluctant to talk at first. He was English-speaking and not one of my grandmother's people. But once Mr Gan told him I was not from the police and had paid him for Dolly's fare, he relaxed enough to admit he had issued the assessment note to Dolly.

'She brought the diamond here and I gave the estimation but she didn't leave the stone with me. She wanted more money. For me it's not worth it, no matter how good the stone, because no papers. If it is stolen property it will just be confiscated.'

Pawnbrokers didn't avoid stolen property. They just paid less for it.

'If I had bought it, it would already have been confiscated when the colonial administration big shot came round asking for it.'

'Colonial administration came round?'

'Fat bald *ang moh*.'

Bernie Hemsworth. He must have traced Dolly there.

'He didn't believe I didn't have it and threatened to have my shop closed down and searched. That is the only reason why I gave him the carbon of the assessment I'd made for the girl.'

So Dolly had tried to hock a diamond, no doubt one of the missing diamonds Alan Weston was carrying. Bernie Hemsworth had found out, and when Prakesh had seen the carbon he had known exactly what the letters and numbers had meant. I had handed it to him myself, without realising what it was.

Prakesh must have followed it up on his own. And it had got him killed.

It was time to tell Chief Inspector Le Froy everything I had found out.

———◆———

Le Froy was not too happy that I had gone round hunting

pawnbrokers on my own. But until I had actually found the man, I had had nothing to go on except a hunch. And they couldn't deny I had come up with something based on the poetry book and scraps of paper bark they had all seen among Prakesh's things.

'We need to talk to Dolly Darling. She's at Mrs Lexington's house?'

'Yes, sir.'

Le Froy sent a messenger to Mrs Lexington's to ask Dolly to come in for an interview at the Detective Shack. 'And wire India. Get me the autopsy report on Alan Weston,' he said. I started towards the wireless machine, then remembered I didn't work there any longer.

'Sir, Colonel Mosley-Partington brought in a copy,' Constable Kwok said. 'It's in the file.'

'Get it from India,' Le Froy said. 'Su Lin, if you don't mind?'

———◆———

It may have been as a reward that I was allowed to sit in on the interview. But maybe Le Froy knew there was no way I was going to be left out when Dolly was questioned. Fortunately Dolly asked me to stay with her.

Mrs Lexington and Rose had wanted to stay for the interview too, but were told they would be questioned separately and were waiting in the main office with de Souza.

'That day in Calcutta? Alan did come to the house the day he died. He showed me the diamonds he was taking to Buenos Aires, though official papers said London. That's how top-secret things are done. Alan knew how much I love diamonds. I just wanted the chance to touch one with my own hands, just once.'

I saw no great love for the dead man. But I didn't see guilt either.

'Why didn't you say so earlier?' It might have helped the authorities pin down the timing of Weston's movements.

'I didn't want to get him into more trouble. Mrs Lexington said he would get court-martialled even after he was dead if they found out he'd brought the diamonds to show me instead of going straight to the airfield. I didn't want that. Alan was a nice man. I wish I'd never met him. Alan Weston wasn't my beau. He just thought he was. He said one day he would give me a diamond like one of those if I was his lady-love.'

'Didn't he give one of them to you anyway?'

Dolly looked awkward. 'Well, I may have dropped it down my dress.'

'May have?'

'Look, I only took one. Only one. Alan never saw. I coughed – like that – and grabbed for my hanky and it must have somehow dropped down the front of my dress, in its tissue wrapper. I couldn't reach in there to get it with a man in the room, could I? I was so afraid he would hear it rustling but he didn't. I didn't think anyone would notice. There were so many and he was in such a rush. So I let him kiss me and hurried upstairs, like I didn't want to let him see I was crying. I didn't even see him out. Rose had to. But that was all right because he thought I was upset that he was leaving. I was hoping he wouldn't notice till after he was out of the country because then no one could pin it on me.

'When I heard Alan was dead, I think I lost my memory from shock. I could have believed I dreamed it all, except I had the diamond. And once he was dead, I didn't think it made a difference. I was sorry I didn't pinch a couple more instead of them all being taken by whoever killed him. I did worry – what if they caught the thief and they knew how many diamonds Alan was supposed to have? But then Rose said it was Chirag Bose so I wasn't worried. It was Rose who said he might have got at Alan because everyone thought Alan was my special beau.'

'But how did you hide it? How did you get the diamond out of the country?' The Calcutta police must have searched them. Especially since Colonel Mosley-Partington clearly suspected them.

'I thought of sewing it into my stays, but that was too much work and Mrs Lexington was getting us out in such a rush. I just put it in my craft basket with my pretty coloured glass beads and no one looked at it twice.'

Surrounded by coloured glass beads, a diamond wouldn't have been noticed . . . 'That was clever,' I said.

'I'm much cleverer than people think, you know,' Dolly said.

Once again I felt chilled by something behind those beautiful blank eyes.

'Did Bernard Hemsworth know about this?' Le Froy asked.

'Bernie was a damned nosy parker. He found out I'd taken the diamond to a pawnbroker and accused me of stealing and selling all the others. I didn't sell it – I just wanted to know how much it was worth in case I had to. And then Bernie came to the house and told Mrs Lexington. I've never seen her so furious. I thought she would understand. Sometimes I may have accidentally pinched things from shops and she was always nice and understanding about it. But that time she told Bernie she would get the truth from me if he'd leave it to her. And then he would have all the diamonds, not just that one. Bernie said she could have forty-eight hours and then he was going to tell the colonel. But he died and we all hoped that would be the end of it. Mrs Lex just said to let that be a lesson to me. I couldn't have told them where the other diamonds are because I didn't know.'

'Where is the diamond now?'

'Rose took it. For safekeeping, she said.'

Rose admitted taking the diamond from Dolly, 'I didn't think it was real. I thought it was just a piece of glass she was making up stories about. So I got rid of it. After all the terrible things that had happened, and people getting killed, I didn't want it in the house. It's like there was a curse on it. So I walked down to Clemenceau Bridge and threw it in the Singapore River.'

It was impossible to prove or disprove without sending divers down to sift through the muddy depths.

'So can we go now?' Dolly wanted to know.

'We need a full statement first, Miss Darling. Miss Chen, would you mind?'

Dolly's Statement

Of course I didn't mind. Dolly's statement meandered on and on, and most of it was irrelevant. But it was work I enjoyed and found interesting, and I think she enjoyed talking about herself too.

My real name is Doris Saunders. Dolly Darling is like my stage name. I could be a good actress, I think. I was the third of ten children. We lived in a small two-up-and-two-down terraced house. The girls slept in one bedroom and boys in the other. My parents slept downstairs in the front room, on a settee that converted into a bed. Makes you wonder how they got so many of us, doesn't it? Two of my brothers died of pneumonia. It cost half a crown to see a doctor, so my parents put it off till it was too late. Anyway, they couldn't come up with the cost of the medicine. It was as cold inside the house as outside when there wasn't a penny for the meter so we wore overcoats indoors and stayed in bed. Food was scarce and my mother would usually go without. She wanted my dad and us children to get enough to eat. She died before she was forty. It made me swear I would never get married and have kids. But now, I don't know, if I could settle down somewhere warm with someone rich, I would.

I left home as soon as I could.

But lodging-house life is miserable. You think town life is going to be the best thing but everyone is too busy trying to make their wages. And it's all grey and cold. Though I wouldn't mind it being a little cooler here, I don't think I ever want to go back to scrambling for the price of coal.

One of my sisters got a job as a telephonist. She didn't have to make up to customers till she was dead on her feet like I did. No, from six to six she got to sit down listening to conversations all day. Now that was a good job. I could have done that, though our Daisy complained non-stop.

At least the countryside in England is not like the jungles here, full of snakes and spiders and slime.

I thought of the jungles here as being full of good things to eat. I would take Dolly out to hunt for fruit and roots one day when this was all over. But now I gave her a gentle nudge towards something I wanted to learn more about: 'That morning we found Bernie? Who did you tell we were going there?'

It was Rose who suggested I leave the door to the storage room unlocked so that anyone coming in early wouldn't see the key wasn't on the hook. She's smart that way. I had to tell her, of course. I needed to ask her to set the alarm and wake me. I can sleep through any alarm. I'm a good sleeper, not like Rose.

Rose's real name is Rita Cooper. Of course Mrs Lexington knows my real name. It was Mrs Lexington who helped me get papers under my new name. It's a much nicer name. And Mrs Lexington isn't really 'Mrs', but it sounds more respectable for work.

Back in Calcutta we kept men company. We weren't prostitutes, don't say it like that. We were escorts, like the Japanese geishas in tea rooms. Just being friendly to lonely men far away from home. The men all liked me best, of course. Rose said it was because of my boobies. But I think it's because I'm nicer to them. Rose is always cold and uppity and men don't like that.

Anyway, after Rose got hit in the face, Mrs Lexington decided it wasn't safe to stay in Calcutta and we came to Singapore. We haven't been working at all here. Except this awful typing business that pays next to nothing. So we can't be arrested for anything here.

All in all I'd say I have no family back in England, at least nobody who gives a fig for me, and I never want to go back. If I could just get word to Bose I'd marry him and help him fight whatever he's fighting about.

When we had finished, I told Dolly I would type it out and send her a copy.

She seemed relieved she had told her story. But when she started to leave, with Mrs Lexington and Rose, who had waited for us, Le Froy stopped her. 'I'm afraid you have to stay, Miss Darling.'

Dolly looked at me, sudden panic in her eyes. 'Su Lin, you said I only had to tell the truth and then I could go!'

'That's what I said,' I said. 'Sir, there's no reason Miss Darling has to stay here.'

'Miss Darling is detained until further notice,' Chief Inspector Le Froy said.

Colonel Mosley-Partington had come in while I was taking down Dolly's story, but he sat and stared at us in silence. And why not? He had Le Froy doing his dirty work for him now.

Dolly Released

———◆———

I was furious, and I was determined to get Dolly released, especially after what had happened to Dr Shankar, who was still in prison in what amounted to solitary confinement in the quarantine area. I wasn't going to let that happen to someone else.

Chief Inspector Le Froy told me not to interfere, but I wasn't working for him any more. I was working to right an injustice in the system he was part of. How could people be detained without trial, without even being charged, on the whim of one man, however important he might be?

This time I didn't depend only on Parshanti for help. I spoke with Mrs Lexington and Mrs McPherson. Mrs McPherson agreed to write a letter stating that if Dolly were released she would stay at Government House until she was formally charged or charges against her were officially dropped.

To my surprise, Mrs Shankar wouldn't commit to helping us. I could understand that, with her husband still detained, she didn't want to think about anything else. But surely that should have made this case even more important to her. Dolly was being detained just like her husband. If we didn't do something, Singapore could get the reputation for locking people up for no reason, just because they displeased the people in power.

But no.

'I've been very lucky,' Mrs Shankar said. 'I was pretty and gay as a girl too, though you young ones won't believe it now. And I married the man I loved, against everyone's advice. And he never stopped loving me. I can only hope that poor girl is as lucky.'

Which had nothing to do with what was going on. I wondered whether her mind was a bit touched.

Le Froy was angry with me, but other people were rallying round.

It was Mrs Maki's idea, for example, to speak to the newspaper reporters – better yet to let Dolly tell her story to them. How she was being detained because she'd fallen in love with the wrong man. I spoke to a few reporters I knew, but it was Mrs Lexington who arranged a press conference.

If Mrs Lexington had been a man, she could have been a success at anything she turned her hand to. With her acute business sense, her genius for organisation, the way she assessed people and put them to work, she could made a success of running a huge company or a small country. Instead she had run a high-priced escort service and small-time typing bureau. And seeing how callously women were treated, even by the man I'd once respected, I thought she had made the right decision.

I told her so. She seemed surprised, then smiled.

'You understand because it's a very eastern thing. Like geishas in Japan. Men like the colonel think it's all about sex. The more religious they claim to be, the more they obsess about all the sex they think the sinners are having. But sometimes all a man needs is quietness and someone interested in him, in how he is feeling. That's what most need.'

'I'm sure it was a successful business,' I said.

'Too successful for its own good.'

———◆———

Even Miss Thompson and little Miss Shelford got on board, starting a petition at the Mission Centre calling for the release of the 'innocent young woman'. I had told Miss Shelford about Dolly's detention when I went to ask her if I could borrow the poetry book on behalf of the Detective Unit until the case was over. She agreed – as long as I filled in the library card.

'At least Mr Hemsworth won't have to pay months of overdue charges!' I joked.

'Oh, no. He took it less than two weeks ago. If he had filled in the card and got it chopped, it wouldn't even be due yet.'

———◆———

I felt like a suffragette working for a cause bigger than myself.

I think the turning point came when news sheets carrying Dolly's story were released. Dolly had talked to reporters about her poetic love affair with Chirag Bose. The reporters had also talked to Rose. Reading between the lines, it was clear Rose believed that Dolly had imagined the relationship between her and Bose and faked the poems. And that the incompetent police, desperate for a target, had detained an innocent little girl, with a big imagination and a crush on someone she had never spoken to.

Finally, Colonel Mosley-Partington added his help and influence, wiring back to the Home Office that the natives were upset and protesting against this case of detention without cause.

The Home Office in London instructed that Dolly should be released. She had been held for twenty-four hours.

———◆———

'You know those two *ang moh zha bo* are planning to sail for Australia?' Uncle Chen said. 'The old one and the other young one.'

Since the taxi driver who had provided me with information on Dolly's pawnbroker had been rewarded and not arrested, others came forward to volunteer information that might be worth something.

Were Mrs Lexington and Rose planning to leave without Dolly? More likely, I thought, Mrs Lexington was making 'just in case' plans, lest Dolly ended up in prison.

———◆———

Le Froy called Rose and Mrs Lexington into the Detective Shack after Dolly was released. Just to spoil the celebrations, I thought. I went in, too, to sit in on the interview if the ladies wished for a female chaperone. I was pretty certain my former colleagues at the Detective Shack wouldn't welcome more interference, but I was still in a Joan of Arc mood.

Rose came in alone, saying Mrs Lexington had gone to bring Dolly home.

'I thought she was going to stay with Mrs McPherson at Government House.'

'She wanted to go home for a wash first. She wants to make herself pretty in case any other reporters turn up. And she needs to pack her things to meet the governor.' That sounded like Dolly, I thought.

'Yes, if you want,' Rose said, when I asked if she'd like me to sit in on her interview.

I brought in my shorthand notepad and pencil, though Le Froy didn't ask me to. Constable Kwok looked relieved because otherwise he would have had to take notes.

'Can you tell us about your earlier encounter with Bose, when Alan Weston was murdered?'

'I told your chums in Calcutta a hundred times. I surprised Bose when he was leaving. And to stop me screaming he picked up a rock and hit me in the face with it. I still have photos of the bruise it left, if you want to see them. And I hope he'll be charged with assault if you ever catch him.'

'What kind of rock was it?'

Rose exhaled noisy impatience, 'A rock is a rock. What can I say about it? It was hard. It hurt.'

'From the marks in the photograph, it looks like a lot of small rocks in a net bag so they would leave surface marks but not do deep damage.'

So Le Froy had already sent for the photographs taken in Calcutta after the attack. I had gone in determined not to let Rose be hounded, but I was getting interested.

'Most of the city was originally marshy wetlands, predominantly alluvial in origin, with clay, silt, several grades of sand and gravel. It wouldn't be that easy to find a rock to hit someone with. Where do you think he found it?'

'How would I know? If I ever see him again, I'll ask him and let you know.'

'Are you sure it was Bose who attacked you?' I asked. They both looked surprised, but Rose answered.

'It was him. He was going after our Dolly, who had been stupid enough to entertain him.'

'So you'd seen him before? And you got a good look at him before he hit you?'

'Can't be sure because one Indian looks the same as another. It could have been Bose or it could have been that dead Indian sergeant. But, given Bose just killed Alan, it was most likely Bose, wasn't it? Stands to reason. Anyway, the knock on the head gave me a concussion and I can't remember.'

———◆———

After Rose had left, I could see Le Froy was worried and preoccupied.

But I wasn't going to let him avoid talking to me. I wanted to strike while the iron was hot.

'You have to release Dr Shankar too. Why are you keeping him locked up? You know he didn't do anything.'

'Dr Shankar knows why he is in detention. And he accepts it.'

———◆———

Colonel Mosley-Partington latched on to me when I left the Detective Shack. He must have been waiting for me. 'I'm not prejudiced, dear girl. I respect winners. Whatever colour they come in. You did well today. You could be a winner if you trust me.'

'Thank you.' I started on my way back to Uncle Chen's shop but the colonel tucked my hand into his arm and clamped down, walking with me.

'You must tell the authorities – hmm, tell me all you know, to save your own life. These people are dangerous. If you know where the blackguard Bose is, if you know where he's hiding, you must tell me at once.'

I sensed he was really trying to find out how much I knew. But he seemed to believe me after I said several times that I knew nothing. Now I was clear on how things stood with him, he wasn't nearly so intimidating.

I thought he might have had too much to drink, but I wasn't going to say so in case he remembered when he sobered up. I wondered what his wife, safely back in England, would think of him on his return.

Dolly Dead

———◆———

'**Y**our friend. That *ang moh* girl. She is dead!'

I heard the news when Uncle Chen arrived in the morning. He had heard it coming into town from East Coast. The newspapers had not got the story before press time so they had printed five-cent news sheets to sell at traffic lights and Uncle Chen bought me a copy.

Dolly's body had been found by some children looking for ripe rambutans in the primary forest off the lane beyond Mrs Lexington's house. She had been lying in the tangle of undergrowth growing just beyond and above the clump of paper bark trees. She had not been strangled or stabbed. A scribbled note, 'Meet me at our spot. CB', had been found on her.

I remembered Dolly saying she would go anywhere with Chirag Bose, not only because she trusted him but because she had nothing to lose. And she had believed those poetry notes were from him. So when this note came, she had gone. But if I was right about Bernie Hemsworth faking those notes, who had sent this one?

Could it have been Chirag Bose all along? Furious that Dolly had gone public about their secret love affair?

If only she had gone straight to Mrs McPherson at Government House as she was supposed to. She would have been safe there. But she had wanted to fetch her clothes first. She had insisted she would have friends with her at all times and would be quite safe.

'Dolly must have slipped out when I was upstairs,' Mrs Lexington said. 'I didn't see anyone bring a note. She was excited but wouldn't say why. I've seen enough of the way young girls get excited to know she had a special young man on her mind. But I thought it was someone she was meeting at Government House. One of the officers in town, or one of the reporters she knew. I thought that was why she wanted to get her clothes and make-up before going over there. I wouldn't have allowed her to meet anyone if I'd known. I wanted to keep her safe. But she slipped out while I was occupied in the powder room. Those shellfish will be the death of me. Then she disappeared, and I assumed her young man had come with a car to take her driving. Dolly loved cars. Poor Dolly.'

The authorities kept close tabs on Dolly's body. I couldn't get in to see her, but de Souza showed me some photographs of her, taken where she was found. She was wearing the same dress she'd had on when she was being interviewed, the dress she had spent the night in. That felt wrong. No matter whom she kept waiting, Dolly would have changed her dress if she was going to meet a young man.

When it was revealed she had been poisoned, the official view was that Dolly had been involved in the previous murders. Seeing the game was up, as soon as she'd got the chance she had run away and swallowed something to kill herself.

It wasn't right. I was sure Dolly was too silly and selfish to commit suicide. And I saw how stupid I had been.

———•———

Le Froy didn't look up when I went into his office.

'I know,' I said. 'It's my fault Dolly's dead. If she had stayed in prison she would still be alive.'

Le Froy swivelled his chair and looked out of the window.

'You knew she was in danger, didn't you?' I said to his back. 'You didn't take her in because you suspected her. You were trying to keep her safe. You should have told me. Why didn't you tell me?'

And I had helped get her out of prison. I had released Dolly to her death.

'Who are you keeping Dr Shankar safe from?' I asked him.

Part Three

The Paper Bark Tree

———◆———

It was Colonel Mosley-Partington who ordered the search of Mrs Lexington's house.

Nobody objected. The sheer number of deaths shouted down any talk of rights and privacy.

I hitched a ride in Le Froy's car. I had my notebook and camera with me. Dolly would never be going back to work. I might be of help.

If Bose was really in Singapore, had he known how Dolly felt about him? He would have, if he read any of the papers. Had her stories been enough for him or his supporters to kill her? Or had she been killed because someone believed her and was jealous? But anyone with any sense must have seen Dolly didn't have the sense of a grasshopper and was about as dangerous as one.

Rose and Mrs Lexington steadfastly denied knowing Dolly's diamond was real. Dolly was always making up stories. Or perhaps some admirer had given her a piece of glass and told her it was a diamond. Rose had got rid of it because she thought Dolly was too obsessed with it. Since they were white women, they were given the benefit of the doubt. But now that Dolly, also a white woman, was dead, things changed.

I watched Colonel Mosley-Partington order the Military Police to search not only Dolly's things but the whole house and the area around it. Mrs Lexington was flustered, of course, but she didn't object to the disruption and invasion. In fact, she invited them in to search. 'We have nothing to hide here. The sooner we convince you all of that, the sooner you'll go after whoever killed poor Dolly.'

I thought she looked at Rose with some apprehension, probably because she was worried this would bring back memories of her previous attack.

'Do you want us to show you what's under our petticoats?' Rose asked Le Froy, though he was only observing Colonel Mosley-Partington run the search. 'I'm very particular about the men who get to look under my skirts.'

The colonel ordered Mrs Lexington and Rose watched – 'Even in the WC. Especially in the WC. Get a white woman. A nurse from the hospital.'

I was certain they wouldn't find Dolly's diamond anywhere in the house. Rose was too confidently contemptuous. If she had any regrets about throwing a real diamond into the river, she didn't show it.

But why the Singapore River? If you wanted to get rid of something that size you could throw it into any nearby storm drain.

While the men searched I walked up the slope to the grove of paper bark trees where Dolly's body had been found. The footpath from the house had been widened by the feet of searchers but the wilderness beyond seemed much the same. I could hear the forest insects and birds. It was business as usual for them, detached from human deaths as humans were from theirs. Each in our own cycles of 'eat or be eaten'.

Dolly had not imagined she was being watched. I had dismissed her stories as fancies, assuming she was making things up to attract attention. I reminded myself to take silly people more seriously in future.

Now I imagined being Bernard Hemsworth, standing up here and spying on Dolly down in the house. He had been a man of habit. He would have followed her back from the Detective Shack after work. Then, after making sure she went into the house, he would have walked up here and watched it. With his cigarettes.

The cigarette stubs had been taken away, but I could still see the spots of blackened grass where he had dropped and left them to smoulder, like little physical echoes of his presence. To the plants and trees, we humans must seem like mosquitoes, moving fast and dying fast, but sucking their blood and sometimes killing them.

This had been Bernie Hemsworth's spot. But why? Once he had learned about Dolly and Chirag Bose, why hadn't he informed the colonel and spared himself the discomfort? But what was there to tell? Even if Dolly had once met Bose, there was no sign to suggest they were still in touch.

And once Bernie Hemsworth had tracked Dolly to the pawnbroker and discovered she had tried to sell one of the stolen diamonds, why hadn't he had her brought in straight away?

Standing there in his place, I thought I could answer that. He had wanted to bring in a diamond as confirmation of his success, rather than just a slip of paper. Once the pawnbroker's carbon had gone into the system, Colonel Mosley-Partington would take over and Bernie Hemsworth would be pushed aside again. But if he brought in a diamond – or diamonds – no one would ever be able to push him aside again.

Things would finally come together for him if he found the diamonds, thereby solving the murder and the theft that had stumped police in India and Malaya. Colonel Mosley-Partington would be impressed by him and he would be promoted . . .

Diamond or diamonds?

Leaning against a tree trunk for balance, I lowered myself carefully to sit on a large root. I wanted to grab on to a thought that had drifted by: diamond or diamonds?

I had accepted Dolly's story that she had stolen one of the diamonds from Alan Weston. But what if she had stolen them all? What if Dolly was the diamond thief? Did that mean she was also a murderer? Could she have been involved in Alan Weston's murder? And Bernie Hemsworth's? And poor Prakesh's?

I found that hard to imagine. Dolly Darling – or Doris Saunders – might have been a habitual liar and skilled pickpocket, but not a killer. I believed her when she said her only regret was not stealing more diamonds when she'd had the chance, given Weston was murdered straight afterwards.

Dolly hadn't had the brains or the nerve to keep quiet about a murder. She hadn't even been able to keep that one diamond to herself.

Leaning against the trunk, I felt the rough bark through my thin cotton top but its thick sponginess made a comfortable back rest. If Bose had killed Alan Weston and stolen the rest of the diamonds, would he bother to come after the single stone Dolly had taken?

A flake of greyish white bark came off under my fingers and I played with it as I thought. Its faint medicinal smell was comforting and familiar, reminding me of the sampans set upside down to dry on the breakwater behind my grandmother's house. Since the papery bark swells and sets in water, it is used to seal and caulk wooden boats. Sometimes the stories we tell ourselves swell and block us from seeing truths in the world beyond.

Being up there gave me some idea why Bernie Hemsworth had been so obsessed with the paper bark trees. The paper bark is a tough, generous tree that tolerates poor soil, wind, heat and even fires. But its flaky bark doesn't look like the well-behaved English trees he was used to. Just as we skinny brown and beige locals didn't look like the soft white people he was used to.

I saw signs on several of the trees that someone, probably Bernie Hemsworth, had cut and peeled away slabs of bark sheets in straight lines to reveal the pinkish-grey wood beneath. He must have taken them home to dry, those he had copied poems onto for Dolly. It didn't make sense to me. If he saw the bark as diseased and rotten, why would he present pieces of it to Dolly as love tokens?

I remembered Mr Meganck saying he had found two different kinds of cigarette stub. Could Dolly have been the second smoker? Had she cut out the bark sheets? In the note that had been found on her, 'CB' had called this 'our spot'. Which didn't make any sense if Bernie Hemsworth had been spying on the house from here.

Poor Dolly, whose only dream was to marry a rich man and live happily ever after. More than ever I thought the Western custom of tossing young women into the marriage market instead of arranging good unions for them was barbaric.

The rainbow lorikeets and other birds were coming back to life above me, now that I was sitting down quietly. At least, with no more cigarette stubs, there would be no more dead birds.

Someone came out of the house and whistled, then waved to me to come down. I suspected I was wanted to help search Rose and Mrs Lexington. It had been one of my routine duties at the Detective Shack. I would do a thorough job. But I already knew I wouldn't find anything.

There are trees that are far more dangerous than the paper bark tree. The banyan, for instance. The colonials love it for its shade and for its aerial roots, so perfect for hanging Christmas decorations from. According to Mr Meganck, banyans grow from fig seeds that establish themselves on the treetops before launching roots that compete with the host tree for nutrients and eventually strangle it to death from the top down, even as they admire its size and enjoy its shade.

Rather like our colonial rulers were doing to us.

Sweet Potato Porridge

———◆———

'Do you think Le Froy's keeping my pa in prison for his own safety too?'

Parshanti had come to Uncle Chen's shop that evening to keep me company. We were eating the sweet potato porridge he had left to cook slowly in the earthenware pot while I was still at Fort Canning. He had left by the time I got back so we hadn't talked since he'd told me of Dolly's death that morning. But he'd known I would be upset. Rice porridge is the ultimate comfort food. He used the expensive fragrant white rice and the *satsuma-imo*, Japanese sweet potatoes, he stocked for the Japanese population. Local people would not pay for them when it was so easy to grow tapioca. It was Uncle Chen's way of showing me he cared. I was very touched that he'd taken the trouble.

There was enough porridge for at least two more people, so I knew he wouldn't mind Parshanti joining me. It made a simple meal, with vegetable pickles, fermented bean curd and salted duck eggs. Along with Parshanti's company, it was just what I needed.

'I don't know. Your mother's been allowed to see him, hasn't she? What does she say?'

'She won't say anything!' Parshanti's exasperation launched her spoon onto the floor and she had to lean over to pick it up. 'All she'll say is that he's all right, not hurt, not sick, and I'm not to worry. How can I not worry if I don't know what's happening? But if you think Le Froy arrested Dolly to keep her safe, couldn't he be doing that to my pa too?'

'But keeping him safe from whom?'

'Whoever killed Dolly – and the others.'

'If it's the same person.'

Dolly hadn't been killed in the same way as Bernie Hemsworth and Alan Weston. Dr Leask said she had clearly been poisoned, though he had not been able to identify the substance. And he said he could not rule out suicide.

'Dolly wouldn't have killed herself,' I said.

'No,' Parshanti agreed. 'And even if she did, she wouldn't kill herself in that old frock. She would have dressed herself up.'

I thought so too. 'How do you know what she was wearing when she died?'

'Mam sometimes helps the undertaker with clothes, so she went along to see if anything was needed. They said no, the family would be taking care of everything, but since she was there, she took a quick look. I know, that sounds more like you than my mam. But when I said so, she told me she'd just wanted to see for herself that the girl was really dead.'

'What?'

'That's what she said. She's hiding something from me, I know. She's a lousy liar. And nothing she tells me they've done to Dad can be worse than what I'm imagining, but she still won't say. It doesn't make sense.'

'Anything your mam does makes more sense than your pa being locked up in prison for no reason.'

'She's very strange about that too. She's not as angry or worried as before. Just really closed up. Keeping secrets. Why won't she tell me?'

Parshanti had never been very good at guarding secrets. But I kept that to myself.

'Who would want to kill Dolly?' I went back to the big question.

'I was thinking about that. What if the Indian terrorists found out she stole one of the diamonds and wanted to make an example of her?'

'Why? They still have all the rest. Anyway, she didn't steal it from them. You said she got it from Alan Weston.'

'Then maybe Colonel Mosley-Partington had her killed for taking it,' I said. The more I saw of the man, the less I liked him, though I couldn't say why. 'That makes it my fault too. If I hadn't told them about the pawnshop receipt no one would have known.'

'Until she tried to pawn it again,' Parshanti said, 'or wear it. And you know she would have. What use is a diamond if you can't show it off or get thousands for it? But wait – first Alan Weston, then Bernie, now Dolly. It's like there's a curse on that diamond. Like Marie Antoinette owning the Hope Diamond and getting guillotined.'

Parshanti was always one for a romantic story. But I didn't have a better explanation.

'The Japanese may have wanted her to help them make contact with the Indian Nationalists,' I said. 'She was always talking about

Chirag Bose. They asked Prakesh as well.' I remembered the hard edge to Hideki Tagawa.

'You too,' Parshanti pointed out. 'They haven't killed you. Yet.'

I'd told Le Froy about that, even though I felt I was betraying Mrs Maki's confidence. 'I'm sure we're missing something. I just don't know what.'

'Maybe Mr Meganck killed Mr Hemsworth because he was threatening the trees his precious lorikeets love so much,' Parshanti suggested. 'Then Prakesh found out and was going to arrest him, so he killed Prakesh. And he found out Dolly had all those lorikeet feathers, so he killed Dolly.'

I had to laugh at the thought of serious, gentle Mr Meganck killing anyone. Mr Meganck blew bugs off his arms rather than squash them. 'It had to be someone who was in India when Alan Weston was killed, and who is here now.'

'That's simple enough, isn't it? Hundreds of travellers make the trip!'

'Including Colonel Mosley-Partington and Chirag Bose. But it must have been someone who was in touch with Dolly since she came out here. I have to go through Bernie Hemsworth's notebooks again. He was watching and recording everything Dolly did. There must be something in them.' I pushed back my stool and stood up.

'You're not going to the office now?'

'No. Of course not.' I would have if I could, but I no longer had the key to the Detective Shack.

'Are you going back to work there now Dolly's gone?'

'I don't know. I'm going in to help out at the moment, but I haven't been officially re-employed.'

I thought I probably would be. Bernie Hemsworth's reasons

why I shouldn't be allowed in the Detective Shack still held, of course, but with him and Dolly gone, it was unlikely anyone would fuss about it. That gave me a motive, I suppose, if anyone thought an administrative post worth killing over.

Maybe it was to make up for how slowly I walked but I tended to do everything else as quickly as I could. Staying still while trying to decide the right thing to do doesn't get you anywhere. But taking steps in any direction can help you to see why it's wrong. And that is a step forward. But now all I could do was pace round and round Uncle Chen's tiny walled courtyard and it was hugely frustrating.

'You know, Su, Bernie Hemsworth's death was a shock. But it was almost like reading about an air accident in the newspapers. It had nothing really to do with us, until Pa was taken in for questioning. Then Prakesh. I still can't believe Prakesh is dead. I'm almost glad they haven't found his body yet because it makes it not quite real. And now Dolly is dead too.'

I kept pacing. Parshanti kept talking.

'After Kenneth died I wanted to die too. I didn't want to move on if it meant forgetting him. But this feels like one long nightmare and I just want it to end. But maybe it won't. Maybe this is real life, people dying. There's going to be another war, isn't there? This time we're all going to die.'

I felt my brain start to function again. I didn't have all the answers, but I knew it wasn't over yet. 'Remember the school holidays at my grandmother's house, how we used to go hunting for clams at low tide? We were so bored and we didn't think things would ever change?'

'You wanted to be a news reporter and travel all over the world,' Parshanti said. 'I wanted to marry a man who loved me and have beautiful children. For a while my dream was coming true, but now he's gone and so has everything else.'

Parshanti was crying. I put my arms around her and hugged her tight. 'We're not dead yet.'

'Remember that time I stepped on a horseshoe crab? For days it hurt so much to walk! And my mam told me, "Now you know how it feels for Su, hurting while walking, so you shouldn't keep telling her to hurry up. But I still forget. I'm sorry, Su.'

'I don't mind,' I said. I meant it. After all, I was always wishing people would hurry up in other ways.

'Oh, Su, it hurts so much when I think of Kenneth. Your parents died and I always thought you just got over it, but I don't ever want to forget Kenneth.'

'Do you ever wish you'd never met him?'

'That would be like wishing I'd never been born.'

'It's going to get better,' I said. 'I promise we'll find out what happened to Prakesh. We'll get your father home. Somehow we'll make things get better.'

Detective Shack

———◆———

That night, after Parshanti left, I couldn't get to sleep between the questions tumbling in my head and the sticky sweatiness of the sheets.

It was late enough to be early morning when I went to the window to stretch, hoping for cooler air. My lack of sleep made me think I was imagining things when I saw a white figure walking quickly along the opposite side of the road and slipping down the slope that led to the canal path.

It wasn't Ghost Month. There were no haunted shrines or trees nearby. And I could hear soft, hurried footsteps. It was most likely a real person. Ghosts and spirits don't hurry.

The canal path led down to the sea in one direction. In the other it went towards the Naval and Armed Forces Infirmary, which served as the prison quarantine area.

I leaned out over the window frame to get a better look before the figure disappeared from sight. The shape and gait suggested a woman, an older woman with some stiffness in the knees, carrying something. In fact, it looked like Mrs Shankar, hunched over and hurrying.

Was she taking supplies to her husband? Or breaking him out?

I pulled on a cotton *samfoo* over my singlet and panties and grabbed Uncle Chen's fancy flashlight. He swore flashlights would replace oil lanterns, but so far customers preferred to pay for matches than batteries.

I wasn't sure if I wanted to stop or help Mrs Shankar but I had to find out what was going on.

I knew Dr Shankar was still in solitary confinement. The gossip mill buzzed that the police had evidence he had been working with Chirag Bose or had joined up with the Indian Nationalists. Even that he had killed Sergeant Prakesh Pillay for flirting with his daughter.

By the time I'd scrambled down the slope to the canal there was no sign of Mrs Shankar – I had convinced myself it was her. But I had a good idea where she was heading.

The Naval and Armed Forces Infirmary quarantine area was located by the cemeteries, for obvious reasons. It was used only during epidemics and would be deserted now. I followed the single train track that ran from Tanjong Pagar. This was the route the coffin train took when large numbers of bodies had to be dealt with quickly. Singapore had been safe for some years now and the tracks were covered with weeds as healthy as the population.

Finally I reached the deserted station, with its blacked-out storage sheds designed to hold eight bodies comfortably, up to fifteen in an emergency.

I had thought I was being discreet. But when I came round the last storage shed, Mrs Shankar was waiting for me. 'Why are you following me? Have you been spying on me?'

She was aggressively defensive but strangely calm. I saw she was carrying a large canvas bag of what looked like clothes or towels. There was a faint smell of carbolic soap and I guessed it contained clean laundry for her husband. Still, I had to ask, 'Do you know where Chirag Bose is hiding?'

'Don't be ridiculous. Go home and mind your own business, girl. Have you nothing better to do? Who told you to spy on me?'

'Nobody. I saw you,' I said. 'It's not safe for you to be out alone at night.'

Mrs Shankar snorted. 'I'm better equipped to look after myself than a skinny, crippled bairn!'

'I couldn't sleep,' I said. 'I'm sorry. It's just that after what happened to Dolly—'

'That girl was a fool. The people in charge here are supposed to be making things safer for the fools. The sheep. But instead they're doing things their way and the sheep are suffering.'

'And Prakesh,' I said. 'I thought Colonel Mosley-Partington had it in for him, but he let him go after he'd questioned him, and he was at the party when Prakesh was killed, so he couldn't have done it.'

'Please go home, Su Lin,' Mrs Shankar said, 'and mind your own business.'

I thought of something that was my business, though she might not agree. 'Please don't shut Parshanti out.'

'What?'

'I talked to her last night. She's feeling shut out of everything. She thinks there's something wrong with her father that you're not telling her because you think it's her fault somehow.'

I sensed Mrs Shankar was getting angry with me again. It didn't surprise me. I knew how good it felt to get angry instead of depressed at the unfairness and wrongness of things. But getting angry gave me a headache, and I wanted to save my energy for action. And this was a small action I could take.

'Mrs Shankar, you don't have to talk to me but please talk to Shanti. I know it must be terrible for you, what's happening now. I know what it's like to be the girl everyone makes decisions for but nobody explains anything to. Parshanti would never give away a secret, if only you'll trust her. I promise you, no matter how terrible, she would rather know than not.'

'We have to make choices,' Mrs Shankar said, softening. 'We don't always make the right ones.'

'The chief inspector says being aware of our choices is as important as making them.'

'Le Froy is a good man,' Mrs Shankar said, 'and a total fool. Just like my husband.' She smiled, thinking of them. 'Some people mean well. But you should always trust your instincts. I did. Marrying the man my parents didn't approve of. Sometimes you just have to make the decision. It doesn't matter what you decide, all options end up the same in the end. With us dead in our graves. But after you've chosen, you have to be stubborn enough to make it the right decision.'

'But Prakesh,' I said, 'and Dolly. Prakesh was going to do so many things. You know he really liked Parshanti but he would never have told her because he respected her too much? And because of how good you and Dr Shankar were to him.'

'He said we were good to him?'

'He also said not to tell you. But I suppose none of that matters now.'

'You should talk to Le Froy,' Mrs Shankar said, 'and let Prakesh be. He's in a good place. Sometimes I think the only thing a woman should worry about is how to earn enough to keep her-self going.'

'That's all Dolly wanted,' I remembered.

'The poor girl,' Mrs Shankar said. 'You'll be going to see her off, then?'

'I will. Just so somebody is there.'

'Go home, Su Lin. And thank you. From me and my girl.'

———◆———

Once Uncle Chen arrived from East Coast Road, I made for the Detective Shack. With Dolly gone, they could probably use my help. But there was something I wanted to bring up with Le Froy.

I found him standing on his head in the corner of his office. He had taken to doing that as his yoga practice advanced, believing it increased blood flow to the brain when he was working on something.

'What is it, Su Lin?'

'Sir, I want to talk about money.'

'Money?' A flash of surprise and amusement loosened the tension on his face. He took his time lowering his legs, pausing them at a right angle to the ground, then tilting till his toes touched down. 'You like what Mrs Lexington is paying you?'

'I don't understand it,' I said. 'Yes, there's lots of work coming in. But at the rates she charges, the money just about covers what she pays me. She and Rose aren't doing much, but she's paying rent, house and office supplies. I don't know how the business can be earning enough to make a profit.'

'You haven't been working for her for very long,' he said, but he was paying attention.

'No. And Mrs Lexington hasn't been in Singapore for very long. That's why I want to know how her business was doing in Calcutta. Do you have some way of finding out . . . unofficially?' Without upsetting Colonel Mosley-Partington was what I meant.

'You want to look into her business model.'

'I don't understand how it pays,' I said. 'It must pay. Mrs Lexington's like my grandmother. She wouldn't do it unless she was making a profit. I just want to know how it works. Do you know which bank she uses?'

'Follow the money,' Le Froy murmured, 'backwards and forwards.' He reached for the telephone, then changed his mind. I saw him thinking about Colonel Mosley-Partington posting men at the switchboards. 'I'm going out for lunch,' he said, 'around the Far East Bank. Is there anything else?'

After Le Froy left without waiting for my answer, I asked de Souza, 'Could I go through Bernie Hemsworth's notebooks again? He was watching and recording everything Dolly did. There must be something I missed.'

'His effects are with the Military Police.'

'Colonel Mosley-Partington—'

'Is a pompous old jackass!'

I stopped as Le Froy re-entered and looked round vaguely.

'Sir.' De Souza took a twenty out of petty cash and winked at me as he handed it to Le Froy, along with the chief inspector's sun-hat. I saw he had taken over my housekeeping tasks. When Le Froy departed again, de Souza said, 'Glad you came up with that. The chief's been obsessed with getting Bose. Almost worse than the colonel, I'd say.'

'Why?' I had thought Le Froy more sympathetic to the Indian independence movement. I went over to my old desk and started sorting through the mail. Someone had clearly started opening envelopes but given up. De Souza got up and added a stack of letters to the mess. Clearly, he wouldn't mind passing back the administration tasks.

'One of the local Indian Nationalist supporters approached Sergeant Pillay four months ago. The chief agreed he should keep the channel open.'

'It's possible Bose found out Prakesh was passing information back to us and had him killed.'

'Why? Why would he bother? Why not just cut him off?'

'Maybe that's how he does things. As a lesson or something.' A shiver twisted my gut at the thought of the deadly, ruthless terrorist. But if he had accepted Prakesh as one of them—

'If Prakesh was meeting with him, could the colonel or one of his men have killed Prakesh, thinking he was Bose?'

I saw the idea wasn't new to de Souza.

'Le Froy won't do anything till he gets more information.'

'That's stupid. If it had been a white officer who'd died you'd be pulling men off the street for questioning!' I wanted to be angry with somebody other than myself, and Le Froy was a convenient target. 'Look at poor Dr Shankar still in detention because Bernie Hemsworth made some stupid comments about him. And he's sick, did you know?'

'Always difficult finding out your role model has feet of clay, isn't it?'

'Don't know what you're talking about.' I tapped a stack of bills together. 'These need to be paid.'

De Souza leaned forward, as though to share a secret. 'It's not just his feet, you know. Le Froy will tell you himself. He's clay right through.'

I had to laugh. "'All are of the dust, and all turn to dust again.'" A Straits-born raised in Hokkien and Malay, and a Dutch- and Portuguese-speaking Kristang Eurasian finding common ground in the English of the King James Bible. 'I don't know what's right any more, Ferdie. Not only what to do, I don't know what to think.'

'Dead bodies, terrorists, another war looming on the horizon, and they've got us running after stolen diamonds but won't tell us who they were stolen from.'

'Colonel Mosley-Partington. They were stolen from him. From his courier.' I thought it was obvious.

De Souza shook his head. 'Diamonds are strictly controlled by His Majesty and the East India Department. Each stone is marked by its cutters. It'll be interesting to see the marks on this lot. Which mines they came from especially.'

'Makes you wonder if the colonel's more worried about someone else finding them. He doesn't trust Le Froy, does he?'

'He thinks Le Froy consorting with the natives and learning local languages is a disgrace to his position.'

'The colonel sees white people like the Japanese see themselves – as superior to all other Asians. That's the impression I get from Mrs Maki and her cousin.'

'We all use different things to put other people down,' de Souza said. 'You should hear my mother talking about her sisters' husbands' families! Or the things they say about the colonel.'

'What things?' De Souza's Eurasian family had better access to *ang moh* gossip than maids and cleaners.

'Apparently Mosley-Partington has a heroin habit. He started with morphine after an accident, then moved up during convalescence in mainland Europe. That's why he requested the posting to India. It's where they get their supply of drugs.'

It was only well-to-do foreigners who could afford a drug habit. Locals might get a bit of heroin in medicine, but never enough to form a dependency. Dr Shankar had described heroin as a painkilling drug that could produce intense euphoria. It was banned in America, but the English supported the drug as a fast, cheap analgesic.

'The colonel doesn't seem like an addict,' I said, thinking of drunks and opium smokers.

'Apparently as long as he has his supply he's fine. He sends money to his family and reports to the Crown, but it might be difficult for him to fit back into London life.'

'He must hate those like Le Froy who don't seem to want to go back.' I longed to travel, but couldn't imagine never being able to return home.

I had stacked all the mail that needed to be handled and put the rest in labelled manila envelopes for filing.

'We could use you back here,' de Souza said. 'We have to find out what happened to Prakesh.'

That was what I wanted too. 'I'll tell Mrs Lexington. And Mrs Maki.'

'You're going now?'

'I'm going to pay my respects at Dolly's wake. Do you want to come?'

'I didn't really know her. Besides, I have to stay here. Kwok went to take lunch with a girlfriend at the biscuit factory.' De Souza had been sitting in the office with Dolly for two weeks. But it was well known that he didn't like funerals unless they came with full Catholic rites and guarantees of Heaven. But he was right. Nobody here had really known Dolly – or Doris.

Japanese Empire

◆

'Once your opponent has his head down, never give him a chance to look up again' – an old Japanese martial adage.

The funeral houses were on the outskirts of town. They had to balance between convenience for mourners and the bad luck that attended corpses. On the way I called in to tell Mrs Maki I wouldn't be conducting any more English sessions with her. In any case, her English was already so good I didn't feel she needed me. 'I hope to go back to my old job at the Detective Shack. I can work there as a temporary assistant until they get the paperwork sorted out.'

'Did you kill Miss Dolly to get your old job back?'

I sat and gaped, like a pregnant toad. Mrs Maki seemed to think it a perfectly normal question. She continued over my silence: 'Or maybe you got Miss Dolly to kill self-kill. That would be the sensible thing to do. I should have given you Miss Nakagawa Koto's dagger. At times like this it is good for a woman to have a *kaiken* in her pocket.

'I respect you, Miss Chen. So many young people these days don't realise that killing others honourably is as much a duty as killing yourself.

'You don't trust me. You trusted me once. What happened, Miss Chen? Is it something I've done? Or something someone told you about me?'

'No – I mean, nothing has changed. There's just so much going on.'

'I will miss your visits, Miss Chen. I trust we will work together in the future, but today before we part I have one more matter to discuss with you. The British are searching for a stolen package. I am correct?'

'Nobody knows where it is.' I was glad she had finally asked a question I could answer. 'I certainly don't.'

'It is not where the missing diamonds are now that is important. It is where they are to go. For now, it is enough that we know they are on Singapore Island, with the man Bose.'

'How do you know that?'

'Because Bose will use the diamonds to bargain with the Japanese for arms and explosives to further his cause against the British. Our help is the only hope of the Indian Nationalist movement.'

'Why do you want those diamonds so particularly?'

'Diamonds are not worth anything in themselves. Their price is artificially inflated by the British. They restrict supply in Africa, in India so that they can stay in control.'

'You just said you wanted to buy the stolen diamonds from Bose.'

'I want to make contact with the Indian Nationalists. I want to meet the man Bose.'

Mrs Maki was watching me. 'Why are you telling me this?' I asked.

'I am telling everyone who might know something. But you people here, you are all fools!' Mrs Maki smiled as she said this, as though it was no more than could be expected from stupid children. She poured some roasted green tea for both of us. The ageless, graceful charm with which her hands presented a cup to me made me dizzy for a moment. It was a world away from her words and made me feel I had to be imagining one or the other.

'We fought valiantly for the Allies during the Great War,' she went on. 'Before that, we acted for the British Empire in the Russo-Japanese war, which we easily won. Japan defeated and humiliated the largest country on the globe, leading to the Russian Revolution. But still the British see us as no more than an instrument. They treat us as though we are typical Asians, like the Indonesians, Pinoys, Indians, Malaysians and you Chinese.'

'Don't Japanese see themselves as Asians?'

'Japan is number one in Asia.' Mrs Maki could have been announcing a race result. 'It is a divine destiny. Now we must organise our empire to recognise our emperor. It is time the rest of the world recognises us as one of the colonial masters. It is not about East and West. It is about power and organisation and the quality of our people. Germany has the Luftwaffe. They can shoot anything out of the sky. And we have our Divine Wind. If your British masters go to war with Germany, which seems more and more likely, they will need us. But we will be equals, not servants.'

'Then you should take it up with them – the British. What do you want with us?'

'We need Asian colonies to supply us with raw materials. Once you are part of the Japanese empire, the West will not give you any more trouble.'

'Britain will fight to defend us. They call us their Gibraltar of the East.'

'All the English are good for is talk, tea and dancing tango. Once we have control of the Philippines and their oil, we will sue for peace. And it will be a better peace than you are living under now.'

Suddenly I realised we were not just on the brink of war. What I had taken for peace was the false façade of the strangler fig. The tree within was dying and the deaths were just beginning.

'One last thing, Miss Chen. Remember, the diamond cutter's mark is on each of the stolen diamonds. If he thought Alan Weston gave a diamond to Dolly Darling, Colonel Mosley-Partington might have killed his man Weston himself, then Hemsworth and Pillay, who found out about it. And now the girl, Dolly.'

Dolly's Wake

◆

took the trolleybus the rest of the way to Dolly's wake. I was not in a hurry: I wanted to think over what Mrs Maki had said. I had just decided that, whether her delusions – if that's what they were – of grandeur belonged to her or the entire Japanese nation, she did not know anything about Dolly's death when the conductor shouted my stop.

Most families held wakes in their own homes. The funeral parlours took care of strangers as well as the very rich and very poor. Most of them were found along Jasmine Street, Lavender Street and Tamarind Street, which was where I now went. The businesses catered to different religions according to your preference. I supposed Dolly, being English, would get a Christian funeral, though she had never been to church in Singapore.

The address I had got from the Detective Shack was for one of the Lavender Street houses. I wasn't ready to mourn Dolly but I had to go to her wake. I was surprised they were having one, but part of me was glad Dolly was getting some respect in death.

Walking along in the damp heat, I remembered what she had

told me about the terrible discrimination between classes in England. Being without training or connections, she would never have had a fair chance there. I knew she had been pregnant and lost her baby and there had to be a lot more to that story. I had longed to worm it out of her, but instead had waited until she was ready to talk.

Sometimes you should worm. You never know when a witness is going to die suddenly.

I hadn't believed Dolly's talk about Bose but I was angry with myself for not taking it more seriously: if Dolly had been convinced that those poetry notes came from Bose, she would have gone off to meet him or anyone who claimed to be him.

I was surprised to hear the murmur of low voices as I walked down the cool, dark corridor to the room marked 'Miss Dolly Darling/Christian/No Service'. I hadn't thought Dolly had many friends in Singapore, but there were far more flowers than I had expected.

The first people I recognised were Mrs Maki and her cousin Hideki Tagawa sitting at the back of the room, far from the coffin where the rest of the mourners were gathered. Mrs Maki looked cool and fresh. She must have come by motor-car, I thought. She must have left her house soon after I had. I wondered why she had not mentioned she was coming.

She nodded to me as I made my way past them to pay my respects. Hideki's eyes flicked over and dismissed me. They were moving around the room but always returned to the two entrances: the door through which I had just come in, and the sliding-door screens behind the coffin through which it would be removed.

Mrs Lexington and Rose were sitting in the front row, accepting condolences from acquaintances and curious onlookers. Several men from the local papers stood around the room. I didn't blame them. The death of a white woman crossed all language barriers. I would have covered the story myself. Shared outrage is one of the best ways of uniting a community.

'Did you know the dead girl?' one of the reporters asked me. 'So devoted, her friends. How long have you known Miss Darling? How will you remember her? Who do you think killed her?'

I shook my head and said nothing. No matter what a reporter put together, the publisher would print the version of the truth the people in power wanted.

Maybe it was better, after all, that Prakesh's family wouldn't be able to have a wake for him until after this had died down.

Where had all the flowers come from? I suspected most of the large wreaths had been sent by the newspapers. They would look good in the photographs. And though the cards were addressed to Dolly Darling, they were really a tribute to Doris Saunders. Doris/Dolly would have liked the flowers, I thought. There was a whole row of them around the coffin where Dolly lay all dressed up. She was wearing a pink frock, with a feathered and beaded sash. She looked like a fancy-dress princess ready for a Sleeping Beauty scene.

Poor dead Dolly. It was the opposite of how it had been for the poor dead lorikeets Mr Meganck had found. The birds had been stripped of their bright feathers but Dolly was dressed up in fake finery, including some feathers. I thought there had been more dignity in the birds' death.

'Her family insists on having her shipped home to England for burial,' I heard Mrs Lexington telling a reporter. 'They didn't talk for years, but a tragedy like this makes you think again, doesn't it?

Mr and Mrs Darling sent the money for the passage, a generous amount for the embalmer and coffin. We're packing all her things to send to them. I don't know what they'll make of it, but since it's what they asked for, that's what we're going to do.'

After sympathetic noises, the reporter asked what she would do now.

'Rose and I are going home to England too. We've had enough of being out east. We're not saying exactly where because it's time we had some privacy. But we'll see poor Dolly Darling's things get safely back to her family, don't you worry.'

Nothing wrong there except Mrs Lexington knew Dolly's parents were George and Mary Saunders, not 'Darling'. She had to know because she was the one who'd got Dolly the papers in her new name. I doubted Dolly's parents had the money to ship their girl's remains home.

I guessed Mrs Lexington was trying to keep up appearances. The British can deal with the most horrendous circumstances as long as they are not spoken of. I suspected Mrs Lexington was paying the shipping costs herself, to spare Dolly's parents.

I had not seen her and Rose since the day I helped the police search them. I expected them to resent me for that, so when Mrs Lexington greeted me with her usual gushing friendliness I was grateful.

'Her family will like seeing Dolly's diary,' I said. 'That may help them understand what her life out here was like.' I remembered the bulging book with its purple satin ribbon. 'Perhaps you should take out the poetry notes first, though.'

There was no expression on Mrs Lexington's face. 'Poetry?'

Too late, I remembered Dolly had kept the notes secret. 'She showed them to me once, but her family may not understand. They are in the back of her diary. I can show you, if you like.'

'She didn't have a diary,' Mrs Lexington said. 'The poor girl was never one for writing. Not like you.' There may have been a sting in there. I patted myself on the back for being too generous to notice it.

'She really used it more as a scrapbook,' I said. 'You must remember it. Its cover is mostly purple, with a leather binding. She kept photographs and other things inside it – like feathers and notecards. And she tied a purple satin ribbon around it. It's in her room, in her underwear drawer.' Unless the police had taken it away. 'Dolly said the notes came from Chirag Bose, but I think she may have written them herself.'

Rose had joined us. 'I'm sure it's me he was after. He meant to kill me, to finish me off this time. It's so terrible! I can't take this any more!' She crumpled against Mrs Lexington, who put her arms around her and hushed her.

'She's upset because she was attacked by that terrible man who killed our Dolly,' Mrs Lexington explained to the curious, who immediately drew closer. 'Back in Calcutta.'

Their attention off me, I backed away and hurriedly took my leave. I wanted to find out if the police had taken Dolly's notebook and the pieces of paper bark with children's poetry.

'Excuse me, Miss.' The voice had an upper-class British accent but the speaker was Indian and a stranger.

I had never seen the man before but I knew at once who he was. And I understood why he was nicknamed 'Handsome' Bose.

'You are Chirag Bose,' I said.

I remembered Rose's bashed-up face. If I was going to die anyway, I wouldn't give him the satisfaction of screaming.

Bose

◆

But if I screamed, someone would come. Even if not in time to save me, they might be able to catch this murderer. I took a deep breath and opened my mouth—

'Please. Don't be frightened. I'm not going to hurt you.' The look on his face stopped me. His eyes were beautiful.

Until that instant, I hadn't known what people were talking about when they said someone had beautiful eyes. People have eyes, that's all. Eyes of different shapes. *Ang mohs* like to say that Chinese have slitty eyes. As far as I was concerned, that was just a difference in physiognomy, used for racial discrimination.

But while this man's eyes were truly beautiful (large, hazel, with shades of brown and green, long curling lashes), what caught me was their expression. Bose looked like a man in terrible pain. But at the same time he seemed kind and concerned, like a man who could be trusted. I remembered the romance stories Parshanti loved. Bose was the kind of hero saviour they were talking about.

'I know who you are,' I said, more to remind myself. 'You're Chirag Bose. You killed my friend Prakesh. Sergeant Prakesh Pillay.'

And you killed Dolly.' I nodded back towards the doorway I had just come out of.

'I didn't. I swear to you. Sergeant Pillay was my brother, though I never met him in person. And Dolly was—'

I saw his quick glance back towards the house. It was a look of pain but not guilt. Nor had he been in love with Dolly, despite all the lurid stories the newspapers had been running about their wild, secret romance.

'I know who you are, Miss Chen. I know you know people. I can tell you why Bernard Hemsworth was killed. And Alan Weston. If I knew who killed them, I would tell you that too.'

'And Sergeant Prakesh Pillay?' There was a crack in my voice as I said it. This man was probably going to kill me too, but confronting him with Prakesh's death felt necessary. The other two had been white men I hadn't known or cared for. Prakesh had been my friend. And possibly a traitor, though there was no reason to tarnish his reputation. Especially not to this stranger, who might have been involved in his death.

'Sergeant Pillay found Hemsworth's notes and guessed from them he had tracked down one of the missing diamonds. Sergeant Pillay got in touch with a friend who knew people in the Indian self-government group. They contacted me. Sergeant Pillay wanted to get word to me that he thought he could clear me of the diamond theft and Weston's murder. His only other message to me was to give myself up to him. He swore his boss would see that I got a fair hearing. We had hoped he would help us, but he said that if I didn't want to deal with the authorities here, I would have to leave. Because Singapore is not the place to fight battles. This is the place where people who don't want to fight come to talk.'

'Prakesh was not a traitor.'

'No. He wasn't.'

Chirag Bose sounded sincere and his eyes were pained.

'He was your friend too?'

'As I said, I never met him. But, yes, he was.'

'Then come in and tell your story to the police. Like Sergeant Prakesh Pillay wanted you to.'

'They will never listen to me.'

'Why not?' If we kept talking, sooner or later someone would come out and see us. But now I wasn't sure I wanted him caught. 'You should never give up, especially when the situation looks hopeless,' I said, speaking fast and low, 'because that's when you have nothing to lose. And sometimes your effort can change the situation and make it less hopeless.'

I knew my words lacked conviction. British law tends to distrust South Asian and South East Asian sources. I wouldn't say the British discriminate against us. If you came up with any other kinds of Asian people, they would probably distrust them too.

'You must let your chief inspector know that the Indian Nationalists have been approached by the Japanese. The Japanese underground has been trying to contact me, offering to trade the stolen diamonds for arms. And why shouldn't I, if I had them? After all, they are Indian diamonds. But I don't have them. I didn't kill Alan Weston for them, and I don't want to exchange them for guns and ammunition.

'The chief inspector should also know that the Japanese believe I killed Mr Hemsworth and Miss Darling. That means the Japanese didn't kill them, as Pillay thought your chief inspector believes.'

'Did you meet Dolly outside a cinema in Calcutta? She said you picked up her umbrella for her.'

'If I did, I don't remember.'

'Or her friend Rose?'

'If I had attacked Miss Rose Radley, as the newspapers claim, I'm sure I would remember her. But I don't. I wasn't even in Calcutta the day Weston was killed. I had gone up to Kurseong. I had proof, witnesses, but they didn't care.

'But I have deaths on my conscience. After I was accused of attempted assassination, British soldiers came to my home. I was not there, but my brother, his children and servants were. They were all killed. And one British soldier was killed, probably by their own bullets since there were no guns in my home.

'But I still do not accept the use of violence. We are followers of the Salt Satyagraha – Gandhi's non-violent resistance.'

'Salt Satyagraha?'

'It is illegal for Indians to collect salt from their own land or to pan for salt from the sea. The British claim our salt, just as they claim our diamonds, our lands and our lives.'

'The British mean well.' I thought of the Mission Centre ladies saying that girls should be taught to read and allowed to go to school like boys. 'They try to help us.'

'British colonialism is about aggressive confrontation and domination. India has one of the richest cultural civilisations in the world, but today in India we are considered cultured only when we discard our own cultures. Maybe it's different for you here in Singapore. Maybe you have no culture to be separated from. Your people exist only to make money. That's why it's such a model colony.' He stopped short, awkwardly. 'I'm sorry. I shouldn't – I don't mean to . . .'

I smiled at him. 'It's all right.'

I knew this man would never have sent Dolly love poetry copied out of an English children's book. Someone else, Bernie Hemsworth probably, had copied out those poems, pretending to be him. 'And yet the only way we can speak to each other here is in the English language,' I said.

He had the grace to laugh. 'There's something else you can tell your chief inspector. Amelia Earhart's missing plane was tracked by the Japanese. She is alive. But, if asked, they will deny it. They are holding her and her navigator, Noonan, to bargain with, if need arises. If not, they will never be found.'

'But why?'

'Her aircraft was picking up communication from code machines the Japanese were testing in the area. Why do you think there were so many Japanese trawlers and fishing boats out there? Their signals were blocking the transmissions that Miss Earhart should have received from the US Coast Guard Itasca. The only reason they would be out there is if they are interested in crossing the Pacific. Towards Hawaii.'

'Amelia Earhart? But if she's still alive we must— Wait!'

But he was gone, walking swiftly away. I could still have shouted for help, got someone to stop him. But I didn't.

And, yes, I don't know if it was because of the pain and gentleness in his eyes or his loathing of British culture, declared in that upper-class British accent, but I believed and liked him. And Nationalists were not just from India. Beginning in 1906, Chinese opponents of the Qing Dynasty in China had been moving to Singapore, and men like Uncle Chen were talking of rising against the Japanese as well as the British.

Dolly had been pulled to Bose, like the needle of a compass is pulled north. I understood her now, because I could feel myself being pulled in the same way. If he gave me the least encouragement, I could fall hopelessly, devotedly and mindlessly in love with him, but I was too much a Singaporean to do more than recognise it.

You may feel a desperate craving for durian, but if it is out of season, there is no use thinking about it.

I would have to talk to Le Froy.

I had been convinced Bose was a fanatic and a killer. But now I had met him, he reminded me of Le Froy. Both men were trying to honour positions they had been thrust into against terrible personal losses.

Ways of Mourning

━━━━◆━━━━

'**I** just saw the man everyone's looking for. Bose. He's in Singapore. At Lavender Street. Outside Dolly's wake. I don't believe he killed her.'

I had splurged on a pirate taxi and given the driver an extra twenty cents to get me back into town as fast as possible. As soon as I burst breathless into the Detective Shack, I saw Le Froy had just come in too. De Souza was on his feet, clearly having been summoned into Le Froy's office, leaving Constable Kwok at my (former) desk on phone duty.

I also saw from Le Froy's lack of surprise that he already knew Bose was in Singapore. He didn't seem surprised I hadn't been added to the list of the murdered.

'Are you sure it was Chirag Bose? Where did you see him?'

'I just told you. At Lavender Street. Outside Dolly's wake. He says he didn't kill Dolly or Weston or take the diamonds.'

De Souza snorted softly.

Le Froy glanced at the clock on the wall.

'He left,' I told him, 'before I did.'

'Bring the car round,' Le Froy told de Souza. 'I'll brief you on the way.' De Souza was already halfway out of the back door.

I took it for granted that I was going too.

De Souza drove. I feared for my life and the people, vehicles and animals on the roads, but Le Froy continued the briefing session I had interrupted.

'Wodehouse has no official record of the diamonds. All legal diamonds are registered and marked by their cutter. If Mosley-Partington can't get them back, he'll want them never to be found because they can be traced back to the illegal mines. Unofficially, they've located a diamond cutter who admits working with Mosley-Partington. He is not likely to get into trouble because he can show official receipts. On the other hand, because he is Indian, the cutter is more likely to be thrown under the bus than his colonial masters. They have nothing to pin against the colonel.'

Peveril Wodehouse worked with the Hong Kong police. He was a pale, middle-aged man, nondescript but for his glass eye. I suspected he was really with the Secret Intelligence Service, a section of the Secret Service Bureau specialising in foreign intelligence. I had met him when he happened to drop into the Detective Shack to chat with each of us before a foreign dignitary's visit. Vetting us in person before the event, no doubt. His Chinese butler-cum-driver wore brass buttons with the Wodehouse crest and was much grander than his master.

'That's probably why Mosley-Partington was working with someone like Bernie Hemsworth who would have believed anything he said. He wouldn't have told Hemsworth about the illegal mines and smuggling, but if he found out – and if he told the Colonel he suspected Prakesh or Dolly had found the diamonds–.'

I kicked the back of the driver's seat in frustration, making de Souza protest. 'Why didn't they say something sooner? If Prakesh had known, he would have been on his guard against the colonel.'

'Officially they were also supposed to be reporting to the colonel.'

'Oh.'

'Wodehouse was sitting on the information while working at other investigations. Having Mosley-Partington followed, among other things. Now it's on record that Mosley-Partington has been approached by Hideki Tagawa and failed to report it, they will be returning to the old chain of command.

'They also have evidence that the colonel is working with human smugglers. Rich Europeans running away from Hitler's National Socialists, who can afford to pay for their lives. They all seem to want to go to Australia, South America or South Africa, and Singapore is a good stopping-off point for the first two destinations, so he's been making arrangements.'

That didn't sound so bad to me if people wanted to pay for their passage. 'I thought the Japanese wanted to deal with Bose – I should tell you what Mrs Maki said. She sounded quite mad, like she hates the Western colonial powers.'

'They're keeping their options open.'

I had to lean forward to listen. The noise of the engine, the wind in my ears when we were moving fast, the chatter and calls of street vendors when we weren't, all made it difficult to hear.

'Negotiating with Mosley-Partington isn't quite the same thing as negotiating with England. I wonder why the Japanese unofficial delegation didn't approach me. Makes me feel left out,' Le Froy said.

'Shows they did their research,' I replied.

But how could that have led to Prakesh's murder? I thought about the suspects. Now I had met Bose, I didn't believe the official suspects, the Indian Nationalists fighting for self-government, were responsible for the murders. But could he have charmed and lied to me as he had Dolly? And Mrs Maki and the Japanese movement for regional dominance were clearly as capable of murder as of suspecting me of murder. Which left the jewel smugglers, or government agents under Colonel Mosley-Partington's direction.

But Le Froy was still talking and I leaned forward between the seats again. 'They suspect the girls got information from their men friends in the military and reported back to Mrs Lexington. She was collecting and selling the information in Calcutta. Tried to go back to her dirty tricks in Singapore – she came here to meet up with Hideki Tagawa.'

'Mrs Lexington was running a spy ring?' I'd thought she was saving penniless girls by teaching them secretarial skills. I couldn't see Dolly or Rose as spies.

'Why are the Japanese here?' de Souza asked, after sounding the horn at a group of girls giggling in the middle of the road. 'Don't they have enough to occupy them in China?'

'They want to build an empire,' I said, but my back-seat input went unheard.

'The new Japanese right wing are opportunists. They exploit natural weaknesses,' Le Froy said. 'That terrible earthquake, for example. They used it to get rid of imported labour they no longer needed. Within hours there were rumours that the immorality of Korean immigrants had caused the earthquake. Classic Fascist tactic.

Armed gangs prowled the streets of Yokohama and Tokyo, setting up roadblocks, and massacred over five thousand Koreans.

'Of course not all Japanese are like that.' Le Froy glanced back to me. 'Jimmy Maki is one of those calling for consolidation in Manchuria rather than further expansion into China. He says more war would benefit only the industrial elites and bring suffering to the common people. He is a good man, or I wouldn't have let you work with his wife.'

Well, he had forfeited his right to 'let' me work with anyone when he 'let' Bernie Hemsworth give Dolly my job. And Maki-san might have no more control over his Samurai-born wife than Le Froy had over me. But de Souza was slowing to a stop. We were still two cross junctions from Lavender Street, but traffic all around us had stopped to allow a funeral procession by.

'How long is this going to take?' Le Froy had to shout over the band of musicians at the head of the cortège. The music was to frighten away any malicious spirits that might be lurking, and the men were taking their job seriously.

'Depends how much they were paid.'

The mourners might accompany the coffin on foot all the way to the cemetery or they might only walk a symbolic block to vans provided by the undertaker. Being Chinese doesn't mean you understand all Chinese. All I could tell was that this was some kind of Buddhist or Taoist ritual, or a blend of the two.

A tall burning joss stick went past the car. It was followed by models of buildings, cars, ships and even an aeroplane sculpted out of joss paper. These would be burned for use in the next world. And still the mourners filed by. The deceased must have generated many children, much wealth or both.

'You two get out here and I'll turn around to find somewhere to park,' de Souza said.

'You're not going to be able to turn around.'

We were hemmed in on the narrow street, surrounded by other cars and motorcycles, horns joining the mourning cacophony. The only vehicles moving were the bicycles and motorcycles that had taken to the pedestrian five-foot way. Unusually for Singapore, there was no swearing.

Le Froy opened the door and started to get out. 'Twenty-three Lavender Street, right?'

'Yes, sir.'

I pushed the seat forward and climbed out after him.

'De Souza, with me. The car's not going anywhere.' Most of the vehicles around us were empty, their occupants standing around and smoking or bowing with clasped hands to the passing mourners. 'Miss Chen, bring the car along when this clears.'

I knew Mrs Lexington had arranged for a three-day wake so they would be in plenty of time, but I was frustrated at being left out. The top of the hearse now passing bore an enormous crane, indicating that the deceased was a woman. A powerful woman much like my grandmother, I thought. That made me think of Chen Tai, whom I had not gone to visit since Uncle Chen and his wife had moved into Chen Mansion. I pushed the thought away. I would go back to see her soon, whatever Shen Shen might feel about it. If Ah Ma still wanted to see me, now she had another son's child on the way. When you are feeling frustrated, everything you come across just makes things worse.

'Su Lin!'

I was amazed. 'Shanti, what are you doing here?'

'My mam said you would be at Dolly's wake. She said to go and give them five dollars *bak kum* from us.' *Bak kum*, or white gold, was money given to help the bereaved family pay for funeral expenses. The Shankars might not have a drop of Chinese blood in them, but in Singapore people supported each other when it came to births and deaths.

'Mam said you talked to her. Thank you.'

'Did she tell you how your father is?'

Parshanti switched back to her original subject. 'But when I got there, the doors to the Blue Room were closed and locked and no one's there.'

'You must have gone to the wrong place.'

'No, I was at the right place. The old aunty in charge said the younger *mat salleh* woman closed the mourning and took away the coffin as soon as the reporters and government men left. The older woman left earlier. She said it's not her business because they paid for all three days.'

Closing a mourning period early was not unusual if a physician or fortune-teller recommended cleansing.

'And then Eshan told me they went straight to the port.'

For the first time I noticed Parshanti was not alone. The dark, curly-haired man standing behind her smiled at me. 'This is Eshan.'

'You want to go to Collyer Quay also?' Eshan asked. He was not much taller than I was, with a broad, muscled torso set above short, crooked legs.

'Also?'

'That's where she went. The lady asked for the coffin truck to go to Collyer Quay. I offered to drive her myself. I am the senior driver, very experienced, very careful, so I charge two dollars extra.

If the driver is no good, the coffin can slide left, bang right. Make your ancestors not happy. But she said don't want me.'

I doubted Rose would have balked at an extra two dollars after paying for two extra days' rental. More likely the darkness of his skin and evidence of childhood rickets had put her off. 'She went to Collyer Quay with the coffin?'

Eshan grinned, 'Coffin, luggage, dhobi bags, all stuffed inside. My number-two driver took her. You want to go also?'

'You have another van?'

'Better.' He nodded to a mosquito bike on the pedestrian way. 'Super fast. We can leave now.'

I looked around. The funeral procession continued and traffic remained at a standstill. There was no sign of either Le Froy or de Souza.

So Rose was behind it all, I thought. Once she got to the port, Rose could go anywhere in the world. It would be impossible to track her down. The pieces were still scrambled in my mind, but I was sure the one place she wouldn't be going to was England to take the coffin to Dolly's family. Was Rose running away from Mrs Lexington? Why was she taking the coffin with her?

The wailing professional mourners were still passing us, along with the precious minutes. There was still no sign of Le Froy or de Souza.

'Shanti, stay with the car till Le Froy or de Souza comes back. Here are the keys.'

'Su? What are you going to do? What if they don't come back? I can't drive!'

'They'll be back. Tell Le Froy to find Mrs Lexington. Ask her where Rose would go. Tell him to send men to check ships leaving for – for anywhere, and to get to Collyer Quay as fast as he can!'

I thought Parshanti was going to cry but instead she nodded. 'Please be careful.'

'Let's go,' I told Eshan. 'I'll give you one dollar extra if you get me there in less than twenty minutes!'

Even if I couldn't stop all the things going wrong with the world, I had to try to stop that evil woman. For Prakesh. For Dolly. Even for Bernard Hemsworth and Mrs Lexington whom she had deceived. Because this was personal.

Rose

———◆———

At any other time, being on a mosquito bike – a bicycle with a surprisingly powerful engine attached to its rear wheel – would have been terrifying. Now I wished that we could go faster.

It was only when we reached the warehouses surrounding Collyer Quay that I saw how hopeless it was.

In addition to having the largest naval dock in the world – but a naval dock without a navy, because the British were happy to use our location but didn't trust us with equipment – Singapore was one of the world's busiest shipping ports. How would I find Rose?

Even all the men Le Froy and Mosley-Partington could summon could not check every warehouse before Rose got away.

Eshan slowed beside a cluster of men squatting near the drain. He stopped and tilted the bike to one side so he had a foot on the ground. I started to shift myself off the seat, but he stopped me, hailing the men.

He questioned them in a mix of Malay, which I could follow, Bengali, Punjabi and Urdu, which I could recognise but not understand. One man spat into the drain before answering. He looked at me and said something that made Eshan shout at him. For a moment I thought they were going to fight. We would all be killed and Ah Ma and Uncle Chen would go to war with the dockside gangs without ever knowing what I had been doing there.

'What is it?' I pulled at Eshan's arm.

'He wants five dollars to tell where Gunveer drove the mortuary van. I said I will put him inside the van next.'

I took out two dollars and showed them to the man. He grinned triumphantly and reached out, but I held on to the money until he said something in Punjabi and Eshan said, 'Okay.'

Less than five minutes into the dockyard, Eshan stopped outside what looked like a deserted storage building. 'In there.'

'You sure?'

'One hundred per cent. You cannot put a coffin next to food or halal storage.'

'Wait here,' I told Eshan. 'Watch out for the police and tell them where I am.'

It took my eyes a moment to get used to the dim light inside. Rose was alone, surrounded by piles of clothes. It looked as though she had dumped the contents of Dolly's wardrobe – I recognised the pale blue blouse with its lace cuffs and collar that she was holding – into the laundry sacks she had emptied onto the floor and was searching through.

Of course Dolly had no more use for clothes, but still it seemed wrong.

'What are you looking for?'

'What are you doing here?' Rose looked guarded and hostile.

'I heard,' I said vaguely. Now I had found Rose I didn't have a plan. All I could think was that I shouldn't alarm her and should keep her from boarding any ships until Le Froy found us. 'The woman at the undertaker's thought you might need help with getting Dolly onboard.'

Rose glanced at the massive wooden crate by the back entrance. It was sealed and taped over. I cringed. Even embalmed, even stuffed with insulation, it would make an unpleasant travelling companion.

'I'll manage. After all we've been through together it's the least I can do for Dolly. I had to get her away from that place. I couldn't stand all the people – strangers! – coming and staring at her as if she was a zoo exhibit. This is all her own fault, you know. I warned her so many times about getting involved with native men. You should have seen her back in Calcutta. She treated them like they were regular chaps. You could even say she led him on, the Indian terrorist who murdered Alan Weston. I could see why he thought he could have her if he got rid of Alan. If you ask me, that's why he followed her out here. Then he saw what she was really like and he killed her too.'

Rose spoke in a throaty whisper, as though she was confiding Dolly's deepest secrets to me, but I could tell she meant me to pass it all on to Le Froy.

I suddenly knew that Rose must have eavesdropped on Dolly's meetings with Alan Weston. Rose had followed him when he'd left the Calcutta house, killed him and stolen the diamonds. She might have drugged his drink, and likely Dolly's too, which explained why Dolly could barely remember Weston's visit later.

And Rose must have lied about Bose attacking her. But I already knew that.

She must have been furious when she found out about the

single diamond Dolly had stolen because it linked Weston and the diamonds to Mrs Lexington's house.

My mask of dumb subservience must have slipped because—

'What?' Rose snapped, as suspicious as a snake. 'You don't believe me? Are you calling me a liar?'

'A native man?' Even if I couldn't manipulate my expression, I could work with my words. 'Dolly was involved with an Indian?'

This made Rose smug enough to smile at me. So gullible, I could see her thinking.

'Are you packing this up for her family? Let me help you. You should take it easy,' I said. 'This must all be such a strain for you. You've known Dolly for years, haven't you? Can I get you a cup of tea? Or a cream soda? There are hawkers nearby.'

Once outside I would tell Eshan to call port security and get the police. I should have trusted his informer instead of making sure Rose was inside first.

'Oh, almost seven years. Far too long. It's too hot for tea. Get me a cold bottle of soda. Closed. And the bottle opener.'

Did she think I was going steal a sip from her precious soda?

'Wait. How did you find me here?'

I had nothing to lose now, 'Will you be travelling as Rose Radley or Rita Cooper?'

I saw the expression in her eyes change the instant her old name registered. Surely Rose/Rita would want to know how I knew who she was – and, more importantly, who else knew.

'You didn't run away to Singapore to escape from Bose. You were running away from Colonel Mosley-Partington, who suspected you of killing Alan Weston and stealing the diamonds. What did you do with Mrs Lexington? Did you kill her too?'

I wanted to throw her off balance. Instead, I was the one who was knocked off course. Without taking her eyes off me, Rita/Rose raised her voice and called, 'Mother! Get out here with the gun!'

Mrs Lexington

———◆———

And then Mrs Lexington was in the back of the room, by a door I hadn't noticed till now. She must have been listening. I recognised the service revolver she was holding by the zigzag grooves on its cylinder. Production of the Webley-Fosbery automatic revolver had ceased after the Great War, but it was still the standard weapon in the Straits Settlements police force. That was Sergeant Pillay's missing gun.

Mrs Lexington looked pleased to see me. 'Good. I hate loose ends.'

'You killed Bernie Hemsworth because he found out Dolly had one of the missing diamonds. But why Prakesh?'

'Yes, Bernie found out Dolly had tried to hock a stolen diamond. I was shocked, I can tell you. And furious. Because Dolly shopping a diamond around town linked us to the whole business! Up till then I had no idea the stupid little tart had pinched one.

'Luckily, instead of bringing her in, Bernie asked Rose whether Dolly had been in touch with Bose. He told her to watch Dolly and tell him if Bose turned up.'

'It was ridiculously easy to bend Alan to our will,' Rose said. 'Bernie was harder because the fool had no imagination, but Alan was a pushover. We teased him to show us the diamonds. I accused him of sneaking off to see a secret wife or fiancée in England so he brought them to show us, to prove he was on an official mission. That must have been when greedy little Dolly helped herself to one. That's what she was really upset about, that they would see one was missing and come after her. She was glad when she heard Alan was dead and the diamonds stolen. She never really cared for him, you know. I would have been much better for him, only he wouldn't see it.'

She had killed him for that as much as for the diamonds, I thought.

'Anyway, Bernie wanted to bring Bose in himself. Dolly showed him the messages she was getting from Bose, which made him sure Dolly was in league with Bose over the diamonds.'

'You copied out those poems,' I guessed. 'You left them for Dolly to find.'

'Then Bernie found the poetry book I'd copied them out of at the library. He came and told me he had proof Bose had been to the Mission Centre and the women there were covering up for him. I was frightened because it would come out that Bose had never been there, but I had.'

I had the impression Rose had been dying to tell her story and show off how smart she had been.

'So I told him I'd overheard Dolly planning to meet someone at the Detective Unit. I may have said she was meeting Bose there, to pass him police information.'

'That was how you lured him to the Detective Shack,' I said. 'You drugged his drink, strangled and stabbed him. Just as you did with Alan Weston.'

'When you two found him, it should have been obvious to the police that you were in cahoots with Bose and the three of you killed Hemsworth. But local police are so hopeless.'

What was taking Le Froy so long? Surely Parshanti should have sent him and de Souza over by now.

'But Prakesh? Sergeant Pillay?'

'I went to your Indian sergeant and told him someone was watching us, spying on us, up at the house. I had to find out if the police were watching us or if it was just Bernie. I acted all frightened and scared and couldn't think what anyone would want with us, and now with a killer on the loose . . . Sergeant Pillay thought he was so clever, asking me if there were any glass pieces among Dolly's costume jewellery.

'So, he knew about Dolly's diamond. Worse, he knew Dolly had taken it to a pawnbroker. So I told him I might have found something and asked him to meet me at New World without telling anyone. He agreed like a shot. You should have seen me. I was so torn between betraying my closest friend, almost my sister, and how afraid I was for her, getting mixed up with a terrorist assassin. He swallowed it all!

'I said I would meet him there, show her their special place. He was such a pushover. He didn't have any idea until it was too late.

'When we ran away we were in disguise, wearing scarves covering our heads like the women in India. I wish someone had seen us and blamed Indian women for killing him. But people here, they don't see anything.'

'You drugged Prakesh and killed him.' Oh, why hadn't the silly man reported Rose getting in touch and asked for back-up? Because he had fallen for Rose's helpless frightened-girl act, of course. He had wanted to help her without alarming her.

'Ooh, upset, are we?' Mrs Lexington cut in. 'She's upset. Look at her. You were sweet on him yourself, I can tell. He never gave you a second look, did he? He wouldn't have. The darkest boys all want the whitest women. That's why Dolly was so popular. Besides, you're a cripple. With all your education and accounting skills, you'll never manage to get a man interested in you!' She spoke with relish. Having forced herself to be nice to me for so long had clearly taken a toll on her.

'Then we collected Dolly and we all went on to the party.' Rose returned doggedly to her story. Once I was dead, she would likely never be allowed to discuss it again. 'When we told Dolly to say we'd been together all day before going to the foundation-stone ceremony, she agreed because she thought we were giving her an alibi. She was dead scared of being suspected again.'

'And now it's your turn,' Mrs Lexington said.

'Colonel Mosley-Partington told me what you did in Calcutta,' I said. 'He told me about Elliot Road and you using the girls to get secret information and selling it. You told me you were helping them. Saving them from that life!'

'I *was* saving them. You should have seen Doris when I first laid eyes on her. She was a cheap little tart. That's when I took her in and created Dolly Darling.'

'Expensive dresses and Belgian chocolates. Diamonds and fur coats and beef steaks and ceiling fans and servants to do the cleaning and peel mangoes,' Rose said. 'That's the kind of life for me.'

'You can only eat so much without getting so fat you won't fit into your expensive dresses,' I pointed out.

'Hold her,' Mrs Lexington ordered Rose.

Colonel Mosley-Partington

———◆———

'Come on. Swallow this.' Mrs Lexington tried to force the soft capsule into my mouth. I struggled away from her, but Rose's thick arms held me tight.

'Don't be difficult, girl. The alternative is anal suppositories and this is a lot more pleasant for all of us.'

I managed to tuck the soft capsule under my tongue. Then I sagged and went limp, letting my mouth hang open.

'Better finish her off,' Rose said, dropping me. I tumbled in a heap on the floor, remembering how the boy in the fountain had looked. Now, if only they left me to make their escape.

'What's happening here?' It was Colonel Mosley-Partington's voice.

'The girl fainted,' Mrs Lexington said. 'If you'll help me lift her onto the couch ...'

I thought of warning the colonel. But I trusted him even less than I trusted Mrs Lexington. I stayed slumped where I was and quietly spat out the drug. Breathing in the dust on the floor had never felt so good, and I made a note to warn the warehouse owners their cleaners could do a better job. But no. If I got out of this alive, I would scrub down their cement floors myself. After I'd retrieved the capsule and brought it in to be analysed, of course.

'I suspected you were behind this farce all along, Catherine.'

'Stay where you are, Oswald.'

I opened one eye and saw Mrs Lexington pointing the gun at Colonel Mosley-Partington. He sneered at her. There was something off about him, an over-confidence in his power that made me think he was drunk or drugged.

'It was you that set them on making enquiries to India over my head and behind my back, wasn't it? You who talked about the private mines. I'm not the only one with things to lose, you know,' the colonel said.

'You were squirrelling your little nest egg out of India before all hell broke loose, and Alan Weston was carrying it out of the country for you, bit by bit. Stone by stone. The fool boy thought he was on His Majesty's Service, didn't he?'

'So he was.' Colonel Mosley-Partington sounded vicious. If Alan Weston had been standing in front of him alive, he would have killed him. 'He was also a fool taking them to show his lady-love. And she killed him for them.'

'Oh, no. To be fair to Doris, all she did was take just one. Harmless little thief, she was.'

Colonel Mosley-Partington snorted.

Mrs Lexington said, 'You should have walked away when you had the chance. But it's not only about getting your man's killer, is it? You can't have anyone finding out you're the one shipping those diamonds out. You, preaching about righteousness to all us weak women. Well, the shoe's on the other foot now!'

'What do you want?'

'I want peace on earth and goodwill to all men and women. For that to happen I have to feel safely established in Australia. Or you may find yourself having to explain why you were masterminding the smuggling of diamonds out of illegal mines. You'll probably have to explain the illegal mines too. The Home Office can't afford any more bad press where India is concerned. If they find out about you now, they'll throw you to the wolves!'

This was so exciting I almost forgot my own danger and could barely stay still. Luckily none of them was paying any attention to me. If only I had had a tape-recording machine!

'Nobody will believe the word of a brothel madam over mine. And you won't get much for unregistered stones,' Colonel Mosley-Partington said. 'You have neither the knowledge nor the contacts. Perhaps we can come to an agreement here.'

'I'm only a poor woman doing my duty, doing right by Alan Weston. He believed he was acting for the Crown, didn't he? You know what that is? Treason, Colonel. And you know the penalty for treason? Of course you do. Far greater than the penalty for stealing from the government and cheating poor women.'

'Alan Weston had official papers,' Rose said, 'that you'd signed. He told Dolly you were sending him on a top-secret mission. For the future good of England and the British Empire.'

'He was a fool.'

'All men are fools when it comes to love,' Mrs Lexington said sweetly.

She had said the same thing to me once. At the time, I had thought her so sophisticated and worldly wise. I had seen her as a role model and protector – of myself as well as Dolly and Rose.

'Since you won't be reasonable, we'll do it my way.' Colonel Mosley-Partington took out his own gun. There was a click as he pulled back the hammer. 'I prefer my version of things. I tracked down the vicious female murderers who have already killed two of my men. Unfortunately they resisted arrest and I was forced to kill them.'

Mrs Lexington pointed Prakesh's revolver at him and pulled the trigger. Nothing happened. She swore and shook the gun hard, flinging it around in a way that looked dangerous. Then she pointed it at the colonel again and pulled the trigger, but still nothing happened. The gun didn't fire. I wondered if it was even loaded.

The Home Office sent their outdated revolvers to the colony and ammunition for that model was no longer manufactured. The officers had been issued two cartridges each and told to make them last.

Colonel Mosley-Partington chuckled softly. 'Thank you, Lord Jesus.' He sounded more like a gleeful small boy than an evil man. 'An eye for an eye and all that. I'm genuinely sorry Alan Weston is dead. He was a good man. And I'm genuinely indignant that you killed my man Bernie. He was a fool, but a loyal fool.'

Colonel Mosley-Partington was still laughing when Rose smashed a full bottle of Tiger Beer on the side of his head. He staggered and dropped to his knees. She slashed across his throat with the broken bottle neck.

Despite myself, I gasped.

Mrs Lexington threw down her gun and grabbed the one the colonel had dropped. She pointed it at his head. I knew she would whip around and shoot me next. I would be dead and never have a chance to tell anyone what I'd heard.

'Stop,' said the tall, handsome man standing in the doorway.

Chirag Bose

◆

Chirag 'Handsome' Bose filled the entrance.

I realised Parshanti had not gone for Le Froy after all. She had gone to Chirag Bose instead. I hadn't even known she knew him, but I should have known better than to trust Parshanti with her blind trust in beautiful men. Furious, futile thoughts raced around my mind. I was as good as dead. Not because I thought Bose was a murderer but because it was no use expecting a man who didn't believe in guns and violence to save me now. What was he going to do? Sweet-talk them into letting me go? Le Froy, who didn't approve of force but knew how to use it, had no idea we were there.

'I knew you were around. I could feel you watching us,' Mrs Lexington said.

Rose, still holding her lethal, bloodied bottle neck, stepped over Colonel Mosley-Partington to face the newcomer by Mrs Lexington's side. With blood bubbling out of his nose and mouth, as well as his throat, the moaning colonel was clearly no threat to them.

'Because of silly theft, you committed petty murders.'

'Silly? Petty?'

'You stole only a small amount compared to what the system is stealing from India. And your petty murders? Your empire is thoughtlessly and systematically killing thousands.'

'So what are you going to do?'

'You are Rose Radley. I never hit you.'

'No. That rotter Alan Watson did when he realised what was happening. But he was too groggy to do much damage. My mother added to it to make it look authentic.'

It hadn't fooled Le Froy, I thought. And the women had either forgotten me or didn't consider me a threat either. But what could I do? Their backs were to me, and Mrs Lexington's cast-aside gun was less than a foot from my hand. But I had just seen that gun fail to fire.

'This is very convenient. The Singapore authorities will be impressed by how we managed to shoot you dead with the colonel's gun after you killed him,' Mrs Lexington said.

She didn't say whether she meant to blame my death on Bose or the colonel but I was sure she'd come up with something.

'Are you sure you know how to use that thing?' Though Bose had his eyes fixed on Mrs Lexington, I had the feeling he was talking to me. He laughed. It was an echo of Colonel Mosley-Partington's laugh and I knew then that he was deliberately distracting them.

'Listening, were you? Well, this isn't the same gun, you young fool,' Mrs Lexington said triumphantly. 'That old fool laughed at me and look where he ended up!' She laughed too, and so did Rose, who waved her bottle neck at him. I slid my hand over the gun on the floor.

'You ever fire a revolver before, Mrs Lexington?'

'What difference does that make? I'm going to fire one now.'

But she seemed happy to let him go on talking. Bose had a voice like rich, warm ginger honey. It soothed and stimulated your ears and the inside of your head, just like a warm drink soothes your throat and stomach.

'With the Webley-Fosbery you need a firm hold to properly cycle the cylinder and cock the weapon.'

Bose's eyes never flicked in my direction but now the truth sensor in my gut told me that he was earnestly, urgently talking to me.

Besides, the colonel's gun, which Mrs Lexington was pointing at Bose with both hands, looked like a modern German automatic. I was the one with sweaty fingers clasped firmly around a Webley-Fosbery. I didn't know where this was leading, but anything was better than doing nothing.

'One disadvantage of this gun is it requires manual re-cocking.'

Handsome Bose deserved his nickname. Even now, with my life on the line, I thought he looked like an incarnation of Lord Krishna. His skin was the colour of sweet milk tea, his eyes beautiful and mesmerising, as he said, 'Unlike most revolvers, to cock the Webley-Fosbery you must pull the entire barrel cylinder back across the frame. This is best done with both hands, because the revolver has a safety catch on the left of its frame, on top of the grip.' He spoke quickly but clearly, as though determined to get through the whole recital before he was shot.

'When disengaged, the safety catch lies horizontally along the frame. You must disengage it in order to fire.'

A woman could be happy listening to that voice reading endless amendments to the Straits Settlements Acts on the wireless. I focused my attention and violently trembling fingers on his instructions and silently disengaged the revolver's safety catch.

Fortunately, Rose and Mrs Lexington, confidently armed with bottle neck and gun, were enjoying the show Bose was putting on.

'This is all very interesting, but you can't talk us round.' There was definitely a flirtatious note in Rose's voice. 'We're not as feeble-minded as Doris was, you know. Did you know that was her real name? When she knew she was going to die she cried for you. Will you cry for her?'

Bose flinched. For a moment I thought he would lose control. But he smiled at Rose and his rich creamy voice continued, 'Doris will always be special. Always remember, both hands, straighten your arms, point at the largest mass and pull the trigger. Good timing is vital. One second should do it ...' Bose looked me right in the eye and said, 'Now.'

The safety was already disengaged. I sat up and, holding the revolver with both hands, I straightened my arms and pointed it at Mrs Lexington's massive back. I pulled the trigger just as Bose launched himself sideways at Rose.

Le Froy

◆

My ears were ringing. The tang of metal and hot air felt swollen in my throat.

Mrs Lexington was dead, her last grimace of triumph stretched across her face.

Rose Radley was like a cornered mad dog, twisting with rage, hatred and fear. She spat, tried to bite, screamed vulgarities, shouted that Chirag Bose had broken her arm and assaulted her, but he calmly tied her wrists together behind her back while she screamed at him, 'You black demon! You are dead meat, you and your little Chink whore!'

After Bose had secured her, he turned to examine Colonel Mosley-Partington. I had been keeping pressure on the wound but he was still bleeding.

'He's alive. Pass me something to stem the blood. Something clean. Quick.'

I took a convenient wad of binding cloths off the shelf. Bose unwound a length, which he wadded and pressed over the colonel's neck wound. The makeshift bandage was anchored with additional strips, which he wrapped over the dressing, then crossed several times over opposite shoulders and under armpits. He turned the colonel onto his left side and slid a couple of pillows under the man's hips and legs, raising them slightly above his head.

'Where . . . who . . . you . . .' The colonel struggled to speak.

'It's all right. Don't try to talk. You're going to be all right,' I heard Bose say gently to the man who had been hunting him over the past six months. He gave the colonel's shoulder a comforting squeeze. 'Just keep breathing.'

Rose struggled free and ran off. Bose, focused on trying to save Colonel Mosley-Partington's life, didn't even look round. I thought of going after her, but what good would it do, whether I caught her or not? It would be either on impulse or for show and neither was worth killing my legs for.

'Is he really going to be all right?' I asked Bose, when he straightened up and stretched his lower back with a wince. 'Why did you . . . why didn't you . . .'

There wasn't a good way to ask why he hadn't killed the man. Or let him die.

'He'll have a fighting chance. That's all any of us can ask for.'

If I'd known where those wretched diamonds were, I swear I would have given them to Bose in that instant. And supported whatever cause he was a part of. It didn't have anything to do with how he looked or the fact that he had just saved my life.

'Are you all right, Miss Chen?'

'Me? Yes, thanks to you.' I looked at Mrs Lexington on the floor in a sticky puddle of blood. I knew I had shot her, but it didn't feel quite real.

'Miss Chen – Su Lin – listen to me. She was going to kill us both. You saved our lives,' Bose said. 'Don't feel bad. When the police ask you what happened, just say you can't remember. They'll blame it on me and that's fine. I won't stay around to discuss it with them.'

'You know a lot about guns for someone who doesn't believe in arms and violence.'

'I know this gun.' Bose picked up the revolver I had dropped and slid the safety catch on. 'In Dashiell Hammett's book *The Maltese Falcon*, the hero Sam Spade's partner, Miles Archer, is killed with a Webley-Fosbery automatic revolver. Sam Spade calls it the "thirty-eight eight shot".'

'You read detective novels?'

'I love detective fiction. It's a world where good battles evil and justice always triumphs. When I was a boy, I wanted to be a writer or a film director and tell stories like that. But instead I am trying to save my country in real life. It's much less artistic and inspiring. But much more necessary.'

Quickly and methodically, he was going through the unconscious colonel's pockets.

There was a fat stack of English money in the man's wallet.

Bose hesitated and glanced at me.

'Take it,' I said. 'Thank you for saving his life and mine.'

'You fired into a murderer's back from less than four feet away. You saved your own life. Are you all right?'

'I was a bit angry with Parshanti for going to get you instead of Le Froy, but I'll get over it.'

Handsome Bose smiled, showing straight, strong and very white teeth. He didn't smoke or chew tobacco, I thought, and had been loved as a growing child by someone who could afford to give him good food.

'Please don't blame Parshanti Shankar. I haven't seen her. Some of our people were watching the port and the women. When I saw the colonel come in I followed. I didn't know you were here. It was reckless of you to come alone, especially suspecting what you did.'

'I was only coming to talk to Rose. To try to get her to confess. I didn't think it would be dangerous.' Yes, I had been rash and reckless. But it had worked out, hadn't it?

'The guilty are always dangerous – they see everyone and everything as a threat. If they don't trust themselves, how can they trust anyone else?'

'Do you know where the diamonds are?' I asked him.

'Somewhere on her, I suspect.' Bose jerked his head at Mrs Lexington's massive cooling bulk. 'She would keep them close.'

'I searched her and Rose for the police and didn't find anything. I think they put them in Dolly's – Doris's – coffin.'

Customs officials would not be too stringent about checking a coffin, especially one occupied by a fresh corpse and accompanied by a loudly grieving mother and sister.

'The poor girl,' he said, 'poor silly girl. So she was killed to provide the coffin.'

I felt an irrational spark of jealousy. 'She stole a diamond from Alan Weston,' I reminded him. 'She talked Weston into going to the house to show her the diamonds. If not for her, he might still be alive.'

'And Mosley-Partington's diamond-smuggling scheme would be intact and undetected,' Bose said. He seemed to come to a decision. 'I want you to pass something to Chief Inspector Le Froy. Sergeant Prakesh Pillay seemed to trust him. I can't come in myself. However enlightened your Detective Unit is, they have to follow orders and their orders are to shoot me on sight. Consider this information procured by Sergeant Pillay.

'Japanese spies are already in Singapore. They have plans to move down the Malayan Peninsula and they already have units planted here. Powerful and potentially dangerous agents.'

'I will speak to Le Froy,' I promised. This wouldn't be news to him. Or to my grandmother.

Mrs Maki, with her tea and fans, surely didn't have dangerous contacts. Then I remembered. 'Do you know a man named Hideki Tagawa? He says he knows you.'

'Hideki, like those around him now, believes the Japanese ethnically superior to other Asians. They claim to be descendants of Shinto gods, their emperor a direct descendant of Amaterasu, the sun goddess. Rather like white men claiming to be sons of Adam and Eve. You can work with them but they will only be your allies until they use you to put down your brothers. Then they will turn on you.'

'It's hopeless, isn't it? What can we do?'

'We must stop feeling like outsiders, like undeserving victims. We must build on what is. Claim our position as children and heirs of the empire, even if we decide to walk away from it. And as all healthy children do, we will. It will be better for all concerned if we make that choice rather than wait to be kicked out.'

'Bhaiya, the authorities are at the gate.'

I had forgotten Eshan but now he and a much taller man had come in through the back door Mrs Lexington had used. *Bhaiya* or *paaji* is how you address an elder brother or respected person. More pieces fell into place for me.

'Go first. I'll be with you in five minutes.'

Eshan winked at me before leaving, 'You are very brave, *bhen.*'

'You had me followed?'

'Kept safe.'

We heard shouting outside and police vehicles arriving. Now I regretted Parshanti's action. I went to the door and saw Le Froy.

'Are they gone?'

'Can you come in alone, sir? I want you to see something.'

'Can you give me a minute?'

'Of course.'

It was the code he had taught me when I started working at the Detective Shack. If Bose had been threatening me with the gun I would have answered, 'No, come at once.'

Le Froy came into the storage room alone. He stopped when he saw Chirag Bose and his eyes darted down to Mrs Lexington's body, then to Colonel Mosley-Partington, moaning softly with his eyes closed. For a moment I was afraid Le Froy would shoot Bose. I moved to stand between them.

'Sir, Bose saved Colonel Mosley-Partington's life,' I said, 'He would have died of blood loss otherwise. He didn't attack him. That was Rose and Mrs Lexington. They tried to kill the colonel and me. And he didn't shoot Mrs Lexington either. I did that.'

'Bose?'

'I don't have the diamonds, Chief Inspector,' Bose said. 'I didn't kill Weston. Or Hemsworth. Or your Sergeant Pillay.'

Le Froy waited. He trusted me, but he didn't know what Bose might have told me.

'The diamonds were illegally mined. Just another example of how the *angrezi* are robbing India blind. Diamond mining in India extends back into antiquity. From ancient times, India was the source of all the world's best diamonds. The British limit production to keep the price up. But some, like Mosley-Partington, secretly buy up properties with artisanal mines where they dynamite the rocks and use women and children at slave wages to wash the gravel for diamonds.

'Your colonel here was masterminding jewel-smuggling in India. Alan Weston thought he was working on a secret mission for the Crown. Actually he was supporting the lavish lifestyle of Colonel and Mrs Mosley-Partington back in London. When Alan Weston was murdered and the diamonds he was carrying were stolen, Mosley-Partington was afraid they would be traced back to him. Illegal diamonds out of India and illegal drugs out of China. He was making a fat profit. China is getting difficult now because of the Japanese but he is also hoping to work with them.'

'Are you working with the Japanese for Indian independence?' Le Froy's voice was still formal and cold.

'Britain is like our abusive, exploitative stepmother, but you are still family, you and our half-brothers and -sisters. We will go on fighting you for our independence. But we will not help others fight you.'

'Come in and tell your side of the story,' Le Froy said. 'I'll make sure you get a fair hearing.'

'Can you?'

They both looked at the unconscious and bloody colonel.

'He did save his life, sir,' I put in.

'You think that was of service to the empire?' Le Froy said wryly. I could tell he would let Bose go.

'What about her?' Bose looked at Mrs Lexington's body.

'I'll take care of it,' Le Froy said. 'You'd best leave while I'm seeing to him. I don't suppose I have to tell you to avoid the men out front.'

'Why are you still working for the police if this is how you feel?'

'Some positions are best held by men who don't want them. Because those who do want them for all the wrong reasons.'

Bose smiled and left.

'Not all stepmothers are wicked,' Le Froy observed. 'All's well and all that, I suppose.'

'How can you say so?' The tension that had kept me calm cracked and there were angry tears in my voice. 'What about Prakesh?'

'Prakesh Pillay is doing fine.'

'What?'

'Conscious, recovering and furious at being kept in isolation. But it will be safe for him to go home now.'

I gaped. I tried to cling to my anger in case I needed it for strength, but it was gone.

'Prakesh is alive?'

'It was touch and go. He was unconscious for several days and Dr Shankar kept him alive by implementing a feeding line to give him water and nourishment.'

'Dr Shankar?'

Things were coming together.

I punched Le Froy's arm. 'Why didn't you tell me Prakesh wasn't dead? Why didn't you? I was so—'

I knew the answer even as the questions tumbled out of me. They couldn't know if Prakesh had seen his attacker, couldn't guarantee another attempt wouldn't be made on his life.

'You were hiding him and Dr Shankar in the prison's quarantine area.' It also explained why Dr Shankar had been put in isolation. 'Mrs Shankar was allowed to see her husband and bring the medications he needed from the pharmacy. I thought she was trying to break him out.' Or help him commit suicide. Either way, I was glad I had not voiced my fears. That explained why Mrs Shankar had seemed less rather than more worried after it was announced her husband was dangerously ill and possibly infectious.

'When he regained consciousness, Sergeant Pillay said Mrs Lexington and Rose had arranged a meeting and tried to kill him. We didn't know if Mosley-Partington was in league with them. If he had charged Sergeant Pillay with being in league with the Indian Nationalists, I couldn't have protected him.'

'Why didn't you tell me? How could you have let his parents think— Do they know yet? Who else knows?'

'Only Mrs Shankar and Dr Leask. It wasn't safe.'

'You swear he's alive? He's really all right?'

'Sore in every sense, but nothing that won't heal. He asked me to tell you that he didn't drink the orange fizz. He said you'd understand. And to tell you that's the only reason he's still alive.'

He opened the front door. I saw de Souza outside with men from Headquarters, taking up positions. They stood down at a signal from Le Froy.

Postscript

───◆───

As it turned out, Colonel Mosley-Partington took care of most things himself. He claimed Jesus Christ had appeared to him in a vision, taking the form of a heavenly Indian, saying, 'Oswald, Oswald, why persecutest thou me?'

They didn't quite know what to do with him. For our colonial masters, the only thing worse than not going to church on Sundays was mentioning God outside church. He was shipped home for medical leave and an honourable retirement was arranged.

We heard that his wife Daphne, who had been a de Havilland before her marriage, tried to have him placed in an institution because he wanted to give ten per cent of her dress allowance to the poor.

More seriously, after his conversion Colonel Mosley-Partington admitted knowing that an over-eager subordinate had killed Le Froy's wife. 'Lawson was only meant to push her over and give her a scare. That would teach her what living among common people does to a lady. He never meant for that damned motorbus to kill her. Those blasted things shouldn't be allowed on the roads with people. Anyway, I dismissed the man. Damned incompetent bugger. I would have married that woman myself, if only she'd had the sense to accept me.'

There was no point in dragging out the old affair again, Le Froy said. And it wouldn't bring his wife back.

Colonel Mosley-Partington became highly successful as a preacher. He would always run others' lives, but at least he meant to do good, or he would have been a very successful criminal mastermind. Almost as good as my grandmother, probably.

The diamonds and Rose were never (officially) found. But there were rumours of a madwoman living on one of the offshore islands. Rose had always struck me as a little mad.

Jimmy Maki was called in for questioning and almost immediately recalled to Japan. To the end he insisted the emperor was peace-loving: the war-mongering generals and politicians were deliberately venerating him to divine status for their own reasons. Three months later Jimmy Maki was assassinated. It was said his wife and her cousin were implicated in his death but never charged. Even with all the terrible events that followed, I always wondered what happened to the Makis' young son and daughters.

Shen Shen had a very difficult labour. For a while they were afraid they would lose her and the baby girl. Luckily they both survived, and Shen Shen asked me to come home to see her and her child. 'After what your mother went through for you, she must have wanted you to live so much. You don't have to stay away from my baby,' Shen Shen told me. 'I want her to be modern and to study like you.'

There is a strong and sustaining core of human fellowship even when pieces of our lives seem to be falling apart. Like the paper bark tree that sheds its outer layers, but continues growing within.

And Peveril Wodehouse asked if I would be interested in doing some writing for them, 'No more than passing on messages', if the worst should happen. I said yes.

Acknowledgements

———◆———

Thank you, as always, to my patient agent Priya Doraswamy, who midwifes all my books into existence. I am also massively grateful to the wonderful team at Little, Brown/Constable Crime for their hard work, inspiration and encouragement, especially editor Krystyna Green, desk editor Amanda Keats, Eleanor Russell, Sarah Murphy, Hannah Wann and John Fairweather. Huge thank-yous too, to designer Charlotte Stroomer and artist Andy Bridge (I really love the cover!) and the amazing copy-editor Hazel Orme, who worked magic on my manuscript. Many thanks, too, to Simon McArt and Beth Wright, for getting *The Paper Bark Tree Mystery* out of my head and into your hands.

And, most of all, thank you for picking up this book. I hope you enjoy it!

Please visit my Facebook page if you'd like to share any comments or feedback.

A Q&A
with author Ovidia Yu

◆

As well as being a delightful, twisty crime read, *The Paper Bark Tree Mystery* gives a fascinating insight into Singapore between WWI and WWII. Many readers are unlikely to be familiar with this particularly complex time and place. Why did you choose to set your books there?

Well, the main reason was that so many people – including myself – aren't familiar with that time and place. And the generation that lived through that era (our grandparents and parents) are dying out. But the immediate trigger was Nancy Mitford's *Pursuit of Love* where Linda says future generations will lump the two great wars together and forget the short precious lives they lived between those conflicts. I love that book and I wanted to examine what the interwar years were like here in Singapore. For the first time, perhaps, I saw my mother and her sisters from a romantic point of view.

We see some of the societal effects that British colonialism was having on Singapore in that era – the most obvious example being the overt racism inflicted on Su Lin, when she loses her job because she is a 'local girl'. How much does this reflect the realities of both 1930s and present-day Singapore?

I suspect there's racism – and other forms of discrimination – everywhere all the time. It starts when parents tell toddlers, 'Don't talk to strangers,' which may mean 'Don't talk to anybody who looks different from us.' In the 1930s, as a colony, it was almost accepted that white people were superior in Singapore. By that I mean it was accepted that they ran things. And that was the reality. They were superior in strength and in position. But in a way it was the opposite of the situation in Singapore today: back in the 1930s, the outsiders were the superiors. Today, apart from a very few like Mark Zuckerberg, the outsiders are migrant workers who take on many of the jobs that Singaporeans are no longer willing to do for themselves. So there is still overt, unthinking racism, which is even more wrong now than it was back then. The worst is when you come to believe the people working for you are lesser human beings than those who look like you. I hope that reading about discrimination will make people more aware of it and therefore less likely to practise it.

The work that Su Lin does, as an administrative assistant at the Detective Shack, and her personal life as an inhabitant of the city are so vividly depicted in the book. How much of your personal life did you draw from when writing the series and creating the character of Su Lin?

Not much, I'm afraid. I have led a very sheltered life so far. But I am a busybody and I love listening to stories. When my grandmother was alive, she loved telling stories, not only about herself and her life here but also about other people. I think it was her way of passing things on, making sure they weren't forgotten. And then, of course, there were the old newspapers of the time, the old advertisements and magazines, and a few precious old letters. I've been poring over postcards and comparing them to present-day locations. And that's partly why I focused on the trees that are featured in these books. Sometimes, when I found buildings completely changed and roads built up, expanded and unfamiliar, the same trees would be there. Older, larger, but still recognisable. And that was very special. I'm glad that there are now some heritage trees as well as heritage buildings.

In *The Paper Bark Tree Mystery*, Su Lin has space to write because Mrs Lexington lets her use the typewriter she has at her house. Do you have a favourite way of writing your books and a favourite writing spot?

Oh dear, this is not going to sound good, but my favourite place for writing is in bed. It comfortable, and I have two dogs who like to support my writing process! If I'm at my desk at the computer, there's a fight between them as to who gets to sit on my lap. The winner gets to sniff around and touch my hands as I try to type around it, and the runner-up waffles around on the floor, occasionally making attempts to unseat her sister. In bed they fall asleep around me. As long as there is a point of contact between us, they seem content. I have a little timer, and every twenty-five minutes I get up and walk around or do a few sun salutations. Now, though, when the buzzer goes off, they jump off the bed because they know there's a chance they can persuade me to go outside for five minutes. The bed is also my favourite place for reading and drawing. If I could, I would probably stay in bed all day. That's one of the reasons I feel sorry for Su Lin: while growing up in her grandmother's house, she didn't have a bedroom of her own. She didn't even have a bed – just a roll-up mattress in a corner of her grandmother's room. According to my mother, who was a girl during the pre-war and war years, that was perfectly normal, even in fairly wealthy families like hers, because there wasn't enough space for everyone to have their own room – so many friends, relations and business contacts were constantly coming and going.

Where would you like to take Su Lin and her friends next?

I really want to write about what happened to Su Lin during the war years. To be honest, it's what the series started with. I was watching *Foyle's War*, and thinking about how people tried to go on with their daily lives, holding onto their values and self-respect with that terrible war going on around them. And it must have been much worse here, with the Occupation.

I went to the Singapore War Museum and looked at all the letters and photographs from that time. My parents and grandparents didn't talk much about it: it was just something they lived with. And they were all glad it was over. I had to rely on external sources. But when it came to writing the stories, it felt too invasive to go directly into talking about those people whose lives had been torn apart. So, in a way, in the first three books I was getting to know them so that I would be ready to tell their stories.

THE
Frangipani
TREE MYSTERY
≫≫≫ Ovidia Yu ≪≪≪

First in a delightfully charming crime series set in 1930s Singapore, introducing amateur sleuth Su Lin, a local girl stepping in as governess for the Acting Governor of Singapore.

1936 in the Crown Colony of Singapore, and the British abdication crisis and rising Japanese threat seem very far away. When the Irish nanny looking after Acting Governor Palin's daughter dies suddenly – and in mysterious circumstances – mission school-educated local girl Su Lin – an aspiring journalist trying to escape an arranged marriage – is invited to take her place.

But then another murder at the residence occurs and it seems very likely that a killer is stalking the corridors of Government House. It now takes all Su Lin's traditional skills and intelligence to help British-born Chief Inspector Thomas LeFroy solve the murders – and escape with her own life.

Available now

The second novel in Ovidia Yu's delightfully charming crime series set in 1930s Singapore, featuring amateur sleuth Su Lin.

What we came to think of as the betel nut affair began in the middle of a tropical thunderstorm in December 1937 . . .

Singapore is agog with the news of King Edward VIII's abdication to marry American heiress Wallis Simpson. Chen Su Lin, now Chief Inspector Le Froy's secretarial assistant in Singapore's newly formed detective unit, still dreams of becoming a journalist and hopes to cover the story when the Hon Victor Glossop announces he is marrying an American widow of his own, Mrs Nicole Covington, in the Colony. But things go horribly wrong when Victor Glossop is found dead, his body covered in bizarre symbols and soaked in betel nut juice.

The beautiful, highly-strung Nicole claims it's her fault he's dead . . . just like the others. And when investigations into her past reveal a dead lover, as well as a husband, the case against her appears to be stacking up. Begrudgingly on Le Froy's part, Su Lin agrees to chaperon Nicole at the Farquhar Hotel, intending to get the truth out of her somehow. But as she uncovers secrets and further deaths occur, Su Lin realises she may not be able to save Nicole's life – or even her own.

Available now